MOONLIGHT KISSES

Spencer's arms tightened around Kendall—as he rubbed the bare skin of her arms—leaving a warm tingly feeling in its wake. "I just want you to know that you really do look lovely," he said softly.

"Thank you." Kendall lifted her face to his. He looked so handsome, she thought. The moonlight softened his sharp, distinct features. "I'm glad we came to the party together, Spencer," she said, her words for his ears alone.

He nodded, not taking his eyes off her beautifully expressive face. At that instant Kendall felt something sweep through her, a nameless premonition that told her she belonged right here, in Spencer's embrace.

But Spencer felt it, also. Suddenly he knew that Kendall Lucas was the woman he had been waiting for, the special person destined to be his life's partner. But unlike Kendall, he was able to identify the feeling.

He was falling in love with her.

<u>BOOK YOUR PLACE ON OUR WEBSITE AND MAKE THE ARABESQUE ROMANCE CONNECTION!</u>

We've created a customized website just for our very special Arabesque readers, where you can get the inside scoop on everything that's going on with Arabesque romance novels.

When you come online, you'll have the exciting opportunity to:

- View covers of upcoming books
- Read sample chapters
- Learn about our future publishing schedule (listed by publication month *and author*)
- Find out when your favorite authors will be visiting a city near you
- Search for and order backlist books from our online catalog
- Check out author bios and background information
- Send e-mail to your favorite authors
- Meet the Kensington staff online
- Join us in weekly chats with authors, readers and other guests
- Get writing guidelines
- AND MUCH MORE!

**Visit our website at
http://www.arabesquebooks.com**

AT LONG LAST LOVE

BETTYE GRIFFIN

Pinnacle Books
Kensington Publishing Corp.

http://www.arabesquebooks.com

DEDICATION

For this, my first novel, I want to go back to the people I
knew first, my parents, James Gordon Griffin and
Eva Mae Smith Griffin (AKA "Brown Betty"), who from
early childhood have always told me "You can. . . ."

PINNACLE BOOKS are published by

Kensington Publishing Corp.
850 Third Avenue
New York, NY 10022

First Printing: January, 1999
10 9 8 7 6 5 4 3 2 1

Printed in the United States of America

CHAPTER ONE

"Looks nice," one of the delivery men remarked.

"It does, doesn't it?" Kendall replied, nodding in agreement. The new look of her living room was just what the apartment needed to spruce it up, to say nothing of her own spirits. The soft peach color of the sofa, love seat, and chair couldn't have defined Florida better. The contemporary design with big roll arms, extra pillows, and a skirted bottom would never look dated, even if she kept it for years. The terra-cotta floor lamps, one by the sofa and the other in a corner, had gentle swirls of mint green and peach on an egg-shell-colored background, and the accent tables were made of sturdy pecan wood.

"Enjoy it, ma'am," he said in parting. His helper, who looked barely old enough to vote and had hardly uttered a word, gave her a shy smile.

Kendall locked the door behind them, then walked out onto her patio. It was another beautiful Saturday afternoon in Palmdale, Florida. Much of the northern part of the country was dealing with late season snowstorms and frigid temperatures, as winter went out with a bang. She was glad March was finding her in her shirtsleeves.

Kendall had lived in Florida for nearly twenty years, since her mother remarried. The weather was just part of what she didn't miss about Philadelphia. Small town living had city life beat out from every angle. When they left she hadn't looked back, nor had she been back to visit, not once in all those years.

She stood before the thick brick railing of the patio. The more loquacious of the deliverymen looked up and waved. She waved back, suppressing a chuckle. "Ma'am," he had called her. It was ludicrous. You'd think she was a hundred and two ... but at thirty-four, she was easily a dozen years his senior.

It really was lovely out, a great day to go bike riding or rollerblading. But first she needed to go by her restaurants and see how things were going.

She turned and went inside. The sight of her new furniture automatically made her smile. The nubby Haitian cotton fabric was a perfect complement for the apartment's gleaming hardwood floors. It was like stepping into the perfect summer day without leaving the house.

Impulsively she sat on the sofa and, grasping the coffee table at its edge, pulled it into an upright position. The table top was now close enough to where she sat that it could serve as a desk or a table. If she wasn't careful, she'd find herself turning into a couch potato.

She lowered the table top, and the corners of her mouth turned upward with the sense of satisfaction she always experienced when she accomplished something. Between expanding her business and replacing a living room that had been dismally barren in the three months since her roommate moved out, she was on a roll. She felt like she was putting down roots, not merely sticking around for the time being. It was a good feeling.

But it wasn't enough. There was something missing, all right, and she knew exactly what it was. And it didn't look like she was ever going to get it.

She shrugged. In that case, *I might as well go to work.*

* * *

Kendall paused at the back door to enter the code for the security alarm, then skipped down the steep stairs, the pattern of which she had long since memorized.

There was a strange car parked next to her Altima, a forest green Saab with a black convertible roof. Kendall looked at it curiously. She wondered if someone had moved into the apartment downstairs, which had been vacant for several months after the Robinson family moved out.

She quickly got settled behind the wheel. As she turned on the ignition, a man came out of the back door of the downstairs apartment and walked toward the Saab with long, purposeful strides. His fluid movements corresponded with his lean frame that Kendall estimated at maybe a shade under six feet. She depressed a button on the door panel, lowering the window. "Hi," she called before he could get into the car.

He grinned, and now that he was closer, she was immediately struck by how good-looking he was; almost pretty, but in a masculine way. He had a clean-shaven complexion in a chocolate shade of brown with no signs of the razor bumps that prompted so many black men to grow beards. His eyes—deep brown pools accented by flecks of gold— and mouth were expressive and sensual; and his nose, more aquiline than broad, could easily be used as a model by plastic surgeons. What appeared to be the aftermath of a lacerated right eyebrow was his only facial flaw.

"Hi," he replied in a husky voice that sounded almost hoarse. "You must be Kendall, my neighbor."

"That's right," she said as she gracefully got out of the car and leaned against it. Absently she wondered if he was recovering from a cold. "Kendall Lucas. You must have been talking to Naomi. Most people would expect someone named Kendall to be a he."

He nodded, and the slight upturn of the corners of his mouth told her that was precisely what he had thought before the landlord informed him of her gender. "I asked her about who lived upstairs before I signed the lease. I've never lived in a duplex before, and even though it's only temporary, I wanted to make sure it wasn't anyone who throws loud parties. I was told you're a hard-working, serious woman." He held out his hand. "I'm Spencer Barnes."

Kendall was less than enthused about the landlord's description of her. Some nerve, she thought. All Naomi knows about me is that I pay my rent on time and I own two restaurants, and for that she pegs me as a librarian type. Still, even though she was casually dressed in jeans and a plaid collared short-sleeved shirt, she knew she did look the part, with her tall, thin frame, her black hair pinned into a neat French roll, and no makeup. At least her eyesight was holding out, and she didn't yet have to wear glasses.

She resisted the urge to wrinkle her nose at the portrayal. Instead she responded by extending her own right hand, which was immediately swallowed up in his firm grasp. His hand, she noticed, felt like sandpaper. Spencer Barnes was a man who obviously worked with his hands. It was certainly not a turnoff, though; if anything, it was the perfect masculine complement to his nearly flawless pretty-boy looks . . . and it matched the rough-hewn speaking voice, which she was beginning to think might be normal for him. While they shook hands, she stole a glance at his left hand. He wore no wedding ring, she noticed immediately. Interesting. "When did you move in?" she asked.

"Yesterday afternoon. The truck was right behind us, so our furniture got in right when we did. They had us unloaded in about an hour."

"That was certainly convenient," she replied, immediately disinterested. Spencer's references to "us," "our," and "we" all in one sentence did not escape her. He probably was married after all. Too bad, she thought with more than a touch of wistfulness. He was a fine specimen of a man, that was for sure. Aloud she said, "At least you were spared having to spend your first night sleeping on the floor. Are you from this area?"

"Not directly. I've been in suburban Atlanta the last fifteen years."

That disclosure piqued Kendall's curiosity. Palmdale, a sleepy community of thirty thousand or so just three miles inland from the Atlantic Ocean, was certainly light-years away from the major city dubbed "Hot-Lanta." Definitely married, she thought, and no doubt with kids. He probably wanted a small town, picket fence type of environment for them. "Well, I hope our town isn't too sleepy for you," she said with a smile. "I must have been at work when you guys were moving in." Nor had she seen the Saab when she got home; maybe he'd taken the family out to dinner. "I can't tell you how glad I am to have neighbors at last. It can get a little spooky being the only one in the building."

"You live here alone?"

"For the past three months, since my roommate moved. The people who used to live in your apartment moved a month before that." She smiled, then welcomed him to the neighborhood.

"Thanks, Kendall. It was nice meeting you, and I know I'll see you again."

Fine by me, she thought as she slipped back behind the wheel. Spencer Barnes might be married, but she appreciated the sight of a good-looking man as much as any woman.

The car's engine was still running, and as she smoothly backed up and made a U-turn she noticed Spencer getting into his car. The narrow alley behind the duplex was used as a parking area by residents who lived in the pre-Depression-era structures, none of which were equipped with garages. By the time she reached the stop sign at the corner, the Saab was right behind her.

She turned right, and so did he. That was no surprise; this was the way to the downtown business district.

Kendall found herself wondering about Spencer Barnes as she drove through the historic area of Victorian and

Queen Anne homes. She was curious about his family, especially his wife. Whomever she was, Kendall hoped her looks were on a par with his. She hated to see a really good-looking man paired with a dumpy woman. In her opinion, Spencer Barnes's ideal woman was someone tall and slim . . . someone not unlike herself, she noted wryly.

Her eyes automatically glanced at the rearview mirror at each stop sign. The Saab was still right behind her.

The neighborhood children were out enjoying the sunshine on roller skates, in-line skates, and bicycles, usually on the newly paved sidewalks but occasionally in the streets. Kendall drove slowly.

She sped up when she got to Main Street. She had planned to first go to her newer, larger restaurant in the neighboring oceanside community of Nile Beach, but when the light turned green she impulsively turned onto the main boulevard. The Saab behind her shot straight ahead. Kendall felt a little pang of disappointment, although she didn't know why. Spencer was probably headed for someplace in Nile Beach, the community that bordered Palmdale on the Atlantic Ocean. Wherever he was going, it certainly wasn't any of her business.

Then why was she so curious? she asked herself.

Pushing the thoughts of Spencer Barnes aside, Kendall steered the Nissan into the small parking lot of the little drive-up stand that had been her first restaurant, Soul Food to Go. Before she got out of the car she removed the pins that held her roll in place and shook out her shoulder-length tresses in a pageboy. She grabbed a comb out of the glove compartment and neatened the look, including her bangs. Now she looked less like the serious, hard-working type her landlord had described and more like a regular person.

She pulled down the visor to get a better look in the mirror there. The mild acne that had plagued her teenage years was long gone, but the memory of the embarrassment of those red zits, which against her fair complexion had stood out like the mark of measles, left her uninterested in wearing makeup except for special occasions. She did wear lipstick when she remembered to apply it. She probably needed to do something about that. She was getting too old to go around barefaced. And after all this time, she doubted that makeup would cause her skin to break out.

As she alighted from the car she felt her stomach do a little contortion that she recognized as guilt. She was so busy running her new place that she really hadn't been spending as much time here as she should.

"Hey," she said in greeting after walking through the door marked EMPLOYEES ONLY.

"Hi, Kendall," a chorus of voices greeted her.

"Hi. How's business?"

The five people present all shrugged.

"That good, huh?" Kendall said with a laugh. She approached the manager, her younger brother David. "Everything under control here?" she asked, her hand resting comfortably on his shoulder.

"Oh, sure. Getting ready for the lunch rush, whenever that will be." During the week, the traffic in the drive-through lanes and walk-up window heightened between eleven forty-five and two fifteen, but daytime business on the weekends was unpredictable. There was usually a steady stream of customers, but often not a real rush until the evening hours, which tended to be busier on Saturdays. "We've had a few orders, mostly for salads and a few fish sandwiches."

Soul Food to Go featured a soulful but reasonably healthy menu. The only fried items on the menu were the popular country fried steaks and the whiting sandwiches . . . and they were fried in lower fat canola oil. Kendall felt there was plenty of room for good food that would not clog arteries and raise cholesterol levels among a people who were already often in the danger zone for the onset of hypertension and heart disease.

"Have you been getting your deliveries?" she asked.

"Yeah. Even the bread. That little talk I had with the

bakery's traffic manager did a world of good," David replied with a smile.

"Good for you, kid." At twenty-seven, David had proven to be a capable and effective manager. Kendall felt herself relax. No wonder she hadn't stopped in too often; with David in control she really didn't have to. He shared her love of the business, and he had a firm handle on it. There was no goofing off or pilfering going on here. She thought of the secured tables, benches, and umbrellas on the side of the restaurant. The entire area had been spotless to her sharp eye. "So no problems, ay?"

"Relax, Ken. Everything's under control."

"Okay." She helped herself to a large paper cup and poured ice and a pink lemonade from the dispenser. "I'm going outside. Send me out a fish sandwich, will you?"

"Sure thing. And for you, it'll be on the house," David joked.

Kendall wandered outside while she was waiting for her food and took a seat on one of the cement benches that lined the side of the building. The tops of the benches and of the accompanying tables were covered with tile to deflect the heat of the sun. Grounded umbrellas helped keep each table shaded.

This place would always hold a special place in her heart. Kendall had dreamed of having her own restaurant ever since her first waitressing job as a teenager. When a small drive-through hamburger-and-fry establishment on Main Street bowed to the abundant competition and closed its doors, she saw her chance. She inspected it and knew it could accommodate space for preparation of the soul food menu she envisioned—fried whiting sandwiches, broiled chicken sandwiches, smothered pork chops, crunchy salads with strips of grilled chicken or pork.

Getting a loan was not as difficult as it might have been had Palmdale not been in the process of rebuilding its historic district. The city was anxious for the pawn shops and liquor stores that lined Main Street to be replaced with chic cafes and tony boutiques. Not that Soul Food to Go fit either of those categories, but at least it was something new and different. It caught on immediately from the day it opened. Main Street was full of fast-food restaurants, but Kendall's was the only one that didn't sell burgers, pizza, or fried chicken. In her opinion Soul Food to Go wasn't fast food, but rather good food served fast.

She sat and watched the traffic pass on the four-lane-wide boulevard. Main Street lived up to its name. This had once been the heart of town, but after the Second World War, the focus had shifted farther west. Now the town was dotted with modern residential communities, schools, and a shopping mall, while the area surrounding Main Street had fallen into disrepair.

The transformation of this older part of town was progressing slowly, but in full force. The four- and five-story previously abandoned apartment buildings of Main Street were being restored one by one to their former glory, with original features intact. A number of smart shops, cafes, and even doctor's offices had already moved into the area. Most of the Victorian-style homes on the boulevard had been converted into commercial space; their locations on a busy street made them unappealing for consumers to invest in as residences. Instead, it was the homes on the quieter side streets that had been purchased by enterprising individuals, many of whom acted at the first signs that a renaissance was about to begin, buying the structures for a song immediately after the neighborhood had been declared a historic district. Now entire blocks were dotted with newly restored turn-of-the-century gingerbread houses, painted in colorful hues like yellow, blue, peach, and dusty rose. The once run-down neighborhood was coming back nearly a hundred years after its peak, with one notable change—the area once reserved for the well-to-do residents of Palmdale, during the shameful days of Jim Crow, was now fully integrated.

Kendall caught sight of the unmistakable shape of a

Saab pass by and drew in her breath for an instant before realizing it was black, not dark green. Good grief, she was letting a brief encounter with her handsome new neighbor drive her to distraction. Spencer Barnes was just that kind of man, with his devastating smile and sexy voice. She had a feeling she was going to be reacting this way every time she glimpsed him; a sure sign she needed to get out more and meet men . . . eligible men. Spencer Barnes's marital status automatically disqualified him, but she couldn't seem to control her reactions to him. Her response puzzled her; it was out of character for her to entertain such improper thoughts about another woman's husband.

"Miss Kendall?"

Startled by both the soft voice and the odd form of address, Kendall looked up to see a young girl hesitantly holding out a white paper bag. Recognizing the employee, she broke out into a smile. "You're Eddie's daughter, aren't you?" she asked. Eddie Samuels was the night manager of her Nile Beach bistro.

"Yes."

"He told me you were working here; that it's your first job. I hope you like it."

"Yes, ma'am," the girl said shyly. "I do. David's real nice to work for. He doesn't take any stuff, but he's fair."

Kendall suppressed a smile at the youthful assessment of her brother. "What's your name, dear?"

"Tina."

"Well, Tina, you can call me just plain Kendall. There's no need for any fancy titles at Soul Food to Go." She'd already been ma'am-ed once today, she thought, remembering the deliveryman, and that was quite enough.

Tina nodded happily. "Okay, Kendall. Oh . . . here's your sandwich." She held out the white bag.

Kendall automatically made a mental count of the number of cars in the parking lot of her second, larger restaurant as she pulled in. The oceanside hamlet of Nile Beach, where it was located, had also undergone a resurgence and had become a mecca for vacationing African-Americans from all over the East Coast, South and Midwest, like it had been back in the forties, fifties and sixties. Kendall had managed to convince the bank that a second Soul Food to Go would do well in this historic town that hosted numerous family reunions, singles' jamborees, and the spring break crowd from traditionally black colleges. To her surprise they agreed.

The financing required to construct a restaurant from the ground up staggered Kendall, but Soul Food to Go . . . or to Eat In, as she had added in smaller letters on the sign out front to dispel potential confusion about the restaurant's status, had been profitable from the first day she opened the doors, with nearly every seat filled two to three times over for lunch and once to twice over at dinner.

This was where she devoted most of her attention. In the building plans, Kendall had allotted space for a roomy private office for herself, complete with tinted windows so she could keep an eye on both her staff behind the counter and the goings-on in the dining room as she worked. Another smaller cubicle right behind her office was the work area of her part-time bookkeeper.

After determining that everything behind the counter was going smoothly, Kendall retired to her office, where she approved several bills for payment and went over the previous evening's register receipts, as well as a preliminary payroll report. Although she employed a bookkeeper, Kendall believed in keeping a firm hand on both her receivables and payables. She went over all the entries the bookkeeper made on the computerized accounting system and signed every check that went out, and the bookkeeper was instructed to work with David on the off chance Kendall was unavailable.

She determined all was well before calling it a day. She spent ten to twelve hours a day at the restaurant from Monday through Friday, and she felt she was entitled to take the weekends off. Still, she usually popped in for an hour or so on Saturdays and Sundays unless there was a special event in town, when she often worked at least half a day to make sure her customers were satisfied.

As she approached her car she thought she saw a green Saab go by on Ocean Avenue, half a block away. Snap out of it, she told herself. Lots of people drive green Saabs with convertible tops.

Once again she asked herself why her thoughts kept going to Spencer Barnes, a man who by her account had a wife and family. And once again she had no answer.

Kendall spent the afternoon completing two loads of laundry. She noted with irony that now that she had a washer and dryer at home, the wash took longer to do than when she went to the laundromat, since now she could only do one load at a time. She folded the dry garments to the sound of a classic James Brown collection. Kendall had always loved the music of the Godfather of Soul, and the finger-snapping arrangements of musicians Fred Wesley and Maceo Parker always made housework go much faster. As she folded the last towel she had an idea, one that would be good business as well as neighborly . . . and at the same time ease her burning curiosity about her new neighbors as well.

She drove down Main Street and turned into the drive-through lane of Soul Food to Go. "It's Kendall," she said into the microphone when it was her turn to pull up to it. "Get me an order of smothered chops, a pork salad—ranch dressing—two whiting sandwiches, and for sides"—she paused to consider—"macaroni and cheese and potato salad. Make that a large macaroni and cheese."

David's voice radiated back at her. "What's going on, you throwing a party and didn't invite me?"

"Don't I wish," she answered with a chuckle. "No, believe it or not, this is business." The smile remained on her face, even after it occurred to her that just about everything she did was related to business in one way or another.

She parked on the street in front of the brick duplex rather than in the back alley. She was bringing a pretty fair amount of food with her, but she figured the "we" Spencer Barnes referred to probably included at least two other people. The apartment, with its two large bedrooms and sunroom, formal dining room, and eat-in kitchen, was really too large for one person. Sometimes it felt positively palatial to her since Ava left.

Kendall missed Ava. It wasn't the matter of the extra rent; that she could handle easily. The house Ava had purchased was only five minutes away, but it was the close camaraderie of apartment-sharing Kendall missed; those impromptu late-night gab sessions at the kitchen table with wine and cheese; even the good-natured hollering that went on as one of them would demand that the other get out of the one full bathroom—the half bathroom was of no use if one of them wanted to take a shower or bath.

While Kendall had never even considered getting another roommate, it did seem strange coming home to an empty apartment day after day. She compensated by moving her things into Ava's old room, which had an attached sunroom, and going on a redecorating binge. In addition to the living room furniture, she had already bought a few new pieces for the sunroom, an overstuffed sofa on a wicker base with a matching chair and ottoman, as well as a bistro table with two sweetheart chairs. That room had quickly become her favorite. She ate most of her meals there rather than in the dining room, where the large table for four only drove home the point that she should not be eating her meals alone.

Kendall gathered the bags and went to knock on the Barnes's door. She was not surprised when a woman answered, but what was unexpected was the woman's apparent youth. Spencer Barnes had appeared to be in the upper end of his thirties, and this petite, attractive, brown-skinned woman was easily a dozen years younger.

Somehow Spencer hadn't struck her as the type to have a wife so much younger. A Jennifer complex, psychologists called it, although at least Spencer wasn't twice this woman's age.

"Hi," Kendall said. "I'm Kendall Lucas. I live upstairs."

"Hi!" the young woman replied, managing to inject a world of friendliness into the monosyllable . . . actually, she pronounced it so that it made two syllables. "I'm Michelle Barnes."

Kendall smiled at the woman's infectious warmth. "I met Spencer earlier. He mentioned you guys had just moved in yesterday, and"—she held out the thin plastic tote bags—"I thought I'd play welcome wagon and bring you guys some dinner."

Michelle drew in her breath. "How sweet!" she exclaimed. "But you shouldn't have gone through all the trouble . . . to say nothing of the expense."

"It's no trouble at all, and little expense. I just went by my restaurant and picked out some items I thought you might like."

"Oh, you have a restaurant?"

"Yes, it's called Soul Food to Go. It's right on Main Street, and in January I opened a second place on King Street in Nile Beach, near Ocean Avenue."

"Oh!"

There was something strange about the exclamation, and Kendall inadvertently raised an eyebrow. "Do you know it?"

"Yes, actually I do. I saw it yesterday when we were out at the beach . . . um . . . I didn't know there were two of them. That's great. I mean . . . Main Street is so close to here."

Kendall nodded politely. For some reason Michelle Barnes had become flustered. She wondered why.

Michelle quickly accepted the numerous bags. "This was really sweet, Kendall," she repeated. "I'd ask you in, but the place is a mess. I've been working on getting it in order. And Spencer's not even here. He and the boys went out for a minute."

As long as they didn't go out for pizza, Kendall thought with a touch of amusement. Then she silently repeated, the boys. No doubt two cute-as-a-button tykes with their father's good looks, only on a less mature note. Who knows, maybe they were even twins. Good heavens, this was ridiculous. All signals pointed to the fact that she needed to stop thinking about Spencer Barnes. He was spoken for, and now she knew precisely by whom. She waved Michelle off. "It's all right, I know how it is when you move. Just enjoy your food; that's all I ask."

"Thanks again," Michelle called out as Kendall retreated. "This is a real treat."

Upstairs in her apartment, Kendall decided to relax with the new *Essence* magazine that came in the day's mail. As was her habit, she got settled in the plump lounge recliner she kept on the small covered front patio. Here there was almost always a breeze. Kendall had the entire surface covered in ocean blue outdoor carpet to accommodate bare feet. She loved lounging here in privacy, concealed from view by those on the street while she reclined behind the brick balcony wall and enjoyed the Florida breezes.

She was engrossed in an article about successful African-American women in corporate America when she heard car doors slamming below. There wasn't any way she could simply stand up and look over the balcony without giving the appearance of a truly nosy neighbor-lady, but Kendall was nonetheless overcome by curiosity to see the rest of Spencer Barnes's family, "the boys," as Michelle had said.

Kendall recognized Spencer's distinctive voice as he said something to his children. She waited until she was sure they were practically inside before peering over the ledge. Just as quickly, she retreated, surprised for the second time that day. Spencer's children were older than she expected, maybe ten and twelve. One thing was certain—Michelle Barnes was not the mother of these children. She was too young. This was apparently Spencer's second marriage.

* * *

"Yoo hoo, Kendall! You up there?"

Kendall cringed. It was Zena, her sister-in-law. Zena knew that Kendall often sat on her terrace, so if she happened to be driving past she simply stopped and shouted. Kendall wished she wouldn't do that—it reminded her of her childhood in a Philadelphia housing project, where raucous behavior was the norm. She could still hear her brother Barry's Tarzan yell, which he would express in the playground as a way of telling her it was time to eat dinner. He sounded just like Johnny Weissmuller in all those old movies.

She got up and stood by the railing. Zena was coming down the walkway. "Hey!" she said in a voice only slightly louder than normal, since Zena was so close. "Are you coming up?"

Zena stopped a few yards away, her head back and looking up. "No. Why don't you come take a ride with me?"

Why not, Kendall decided. It wasn't like she had anything else to do. "Okay. Be right down."

Inside, she grabbed her purse and keys and took a moment to put on lipstick.

Spencer Barnes was waiting in his own doorway when she got downstairs. "I was just about to come up and thank you," he said. "I, uh, heard your friend calling you and thought you might be coming down."

Kendall recalled his concern about loud neighbors and felt her face growing warm. "I'm sorry. I've asked my sister-in-law not to shout like that. I know it's distracting."

"Hey, no problem. I mean, it's not like it's the middle of the night. I just wanted to thank you for bringing us dinner. Poor Michelle was tearing her hair out with all the unpacking."

"I hope you enjoyed it."

"We're still eating, actually. And it's delicious. We had driven past the restaurant when we first got in town and I was curious about it. We'll be back for more, believe me." Spencer glanced over at Zena waiting in the car. "Well, I won't keep you. I just wanted you to know how much we appreciated what you did for us."

"I'm glad I could help." Kendall glanced at Zena waiting in her car. "Well, good night, Spencer."

"Good night."

Spencer stood and watched as she walked away. There was warmth in his smile, but in actuality he had felt unnerved ever since his niece Michelle told him Kendall was, of all things, the proprietor of Soul Food to Go. Kendall Lucas was a nice woman, and good-looking, too. The good neighbor relations they had already developed were bound to be strained when she learned what had brought him to this area, and of course eventually she would. Just as well, he thought. He had felt drawn to Kendall Lucas from the start—she was one of the prettiest women he'd ever seen—but her being his upstairs neighbor was definitely a drawback. Spencer always liked some distance between himself and the woman he was involved with; it kept his life from being an open book. The potential for tension when the truth came out was just what he needed to prevent him from making a disastrous exception in Kendall's case. Under the circumstances, it wasn't at all unreasonable that the situation could become so uncomfortable that he, Michelle, and the boys would have to move even before their six-month lease was up. He decided it was best to keep his objective—at least the major one—from Kendall for as long as possible, he decided, and thus preserve the peace. And he needed to forget about any ideas of pursuing a relationship with her, regardless of how attractive he found her. It wouldn't—no, it *couldn't*, work.

Regardless, he found himself rooted to the spot as she walked toward a champagne-colored Escort and got in on the passenger side. Her round hips swayed with a life of their own in her mid-thigh cutoffs, making the view from the rear every bit as appealing as that from the front. As he watched her, he entertained thoughts of her dark eyes and their ever so slightly upward tilt at the outer corners, as well as the wispy black bangs that framed her flawless face like a halo. He thought of how soft her hand had felt in his when she offered it to him. Even as he insisted that he needed to stay away from her, Spencer found he could think of nothing else.

Kendall hurried to the curb and got in the passenger seat beside Zena. "Sorry about that."

"Who was that?"

"My new neighbor. Spencer Barnes."

"And a fine neighbor he is," Zena commented as she put the car in gear. "Does he look as good close up as he does from a distance?"

"Don't get excited, Zena. He's married."

"Married!"

"Yeah, you know, like you and Barry. You remember him—my brother, your husband . . ."

Zena shook her head in wonder. "I can't believe it. The way he was looking at you . . ."

Kendall giggled. "He's married, Zena. He's not dead. It's okay to appreciate the other sex. Besides, the last time I looked I wasn't too unpleasant a sight." She glanced out at the passing cityscape. "Where are we going, anyway?"

"The mall. There's a sale on towels."

"Well, that's an exciting way to spend a Saturday night," Kendall remarked.

"Humph," Zena replied. "You need to go out and do something. Meet people."

Kendall loudly blew out her breath. "Now you sound like Mom."

"Hey, your mom knew what she was talking about. She got herself another husband, didn't she?"

At that Kendall felt a familiar tightness develop in her jaw. It was true that her mother had found happiness in her second marriage, but Kendall felt it shouldn't have been necessary for her mother to have to look. Kenneth

Lucas's abandonment of his family was a sore spot that had plagued her for years.

Zena went on. "The First Coast might not be the most populated area, but there's plenty of prospects around. Look at Ava. She never has a problem when it comes to dating, even if she dumps them before dating can turn into relationships. If she can do it so can you, but you've got to stop staying home Saturday nights."

"I like to think that's all it will take," Kendall said with a touch of wistfulness. But more and more often she found herself thinking she would never find someone with whom she could build a lifetime relationship, someone who truly understood why she felt so driven, someone who didn't try to discourage her ambition and her plans for Soul Food to Go and steer her instead in a direction she simply wasn't interested in. It hadn't happened yet, and she was just six years away from being forty. Besides, she simply wasn't *like* other women. If she was, she wouldn't object to a more conventional life, the kind most women would jump at if given the chance.

"You might start by looking right downstairs," Zena continued. "I don't care what you say. The more I think about how Spencer Barnes was just standing there looking at you . . . Kendall, if that man is married, I swear I'll eat a plate full of liver and onions. And you know I hate liver and onions."

CHAPTER TWO

Kendall beamed. Sundays usually weren't particularly busy at Soul Food to Go, but this one was filled with the ringing sound of cash drawers constantly opening and closing as money changed hands. It was Memorial Day weekend, and the summer season already seemed to be in full swing. It looked like it was going to be a profitable summer indeed for her new location.

She glanced over at a family who had three children in tow, two elementary-school-aged girls and a boy toddler. They appeared to be vacationers. She went to the frozen yogurt machine and filled three two-ounce sample cups with vanilla, chocolate, and strawberry flavors.

"Hi," she said as she approached their table. "My name is Kendall Lucas, and I'm the owner. I hope you're enjoying your meal."

"Ooh, ice cream!" the two older children cried out.

Kendall handed the sample cups around to the children with a smile. "It's actually frozen yogurt, but it tastes just like ice cream," she said. "I hope you like it." The parents were obviously pleased by her action, and Kendall was sure they would be back. Sometimes a little goodwill went a long way.

She chatted with the parents briefly—they were about her own age and were visiting from Ocala in central Florida—before excusing herself to return to her office. The Barnes family filed in as she approached the hall leading to the entrance to the employees' area.

She stopped, and Spencer and Michelle greeted her warmly. "I'm so glad you came in," Kendall said, "When I brought you our food, I hoped you would." Although she had seen Michelle a few times and exchanged small talk, this was the first time she had seen Spencer in the two months since they'd moved in. Nor had she seen his car in the back alley; only a blue Sentra that apparently belonged to Michelle.

Spencer patted his stomach, which Kendall couldn't help noticing was washboard flat. "Are you kidding?" he said. "I've been thinking about your pork chops for two months. We would have come before this, but I've been spending a lot of time in Atlanta these last few weeks."

"I'm just glad you're here now. And these handsome young men are no doubt your sons," Kendall said, nodding at the preteens.

"Yes. Brian and Carlton, this is Ms. Lucas, our neighbor who was kind enough to bring us dinner our first night in town."

The boys uttered shy hellos.

Kendall smiled, then she realized there really wasn't anything else to say. "Enjoy your meal," she said in parting, then hurried around the corner.

"I had no idea the menu was so extensive," she heard Michelle saying as she moved on. She smiled in satisfaction. Somehow she had known they would be in.

She went into her office and closed the door, then watched behind the cloak of tinted glass as the Barneses took seats at a window table. The boys sat on one side, and Spencer and Michelle were on the other, he on the outside and she next to the wall. They made quite an attractive family, Spencer in jeans and Michelle and the boys wearing shorts. It was the kind of family unit Kendall had longed for as a child, but she and Barry had seen little of their father, who apparently had more important things to do than spend time with his children, like seeking out Johnnie Walker, Jack Daniels, Jim Beam, and others in that crowd. The traditional two-parent household did not become a reality for Kendall until her mother remarried, and by then, she and Barry were nearing adulthood. Even now, after all this time, she occasionally found herself wishing she had known the kind of lifestyle that she'd seen on all the television shows from her childhood. If she had, perhaps her outlook as an adult would have been different. But Kendall knew that disadvantages and advantages usually went hand-in-hand; and she tried to take comfort in the knowledge that unlike most childless women her age, she had no cause to experience anxiety about her biological clock. The truth was she simply had no interest in motherhood. She knew her perspective might be considered atypical at best and an anomaly at worst, and it usually caused her a good deal of anguish, but for once she felt defiant rather than agitated about it.

Kendall had not been able to see for herself the look Spencer gave her when she went to join Zena in the car that day, but there certainly was nothing improper in his behavior this afternoon, with Michelle present. Men, she thought in exasperation as she returned to her work, resolving not to let herself get distracted.

But regardless of her vow, she found her gaze lifting every time an order number was announced as being ready. When Spencer rose from his seat, she caught her breath at the sight of his lean form, the defined waistline and well-developed thighs the denim of his jeans intimately hugged. Then she sighed again, this time in annoyance. For the life of her she didn't understand why she was so preoccupied with Spencer Barnes. Zena's opinion and his lack of a wedding band aside, the man was married. She'd had the opportunity during his long absence to get him out of her mind, and here it was starting all over again.

Regardless, she watched as he distributed everyone's order from two trays. He had a nice butt, she thought absently.

Stop it! her mind cried out.

Kendall took a deep breath and slowly exhaled. "That's it. I've got work to do, and I'm going to do it," she said aloud.

"Mmm. This is fabulous," Michelle exclaimed as she ingested a forkful of pork salad.

"Looks good," Spencer agreed. He took in the attractive arrangement of iceberg lettuce, tomato chunks, green pepper strips, shredded carrots, and sliced cucumber, topped with a generous helping of pork strips and oversize croutons. The thousand island salad dressing Michelle requested was served in a prepackaged plastic packet.

"You know, you really ought to tell Kendall what you plan to do here. I mean, she's been real nice," Michelle remarked.

Spencer took a large bit of his smothered pork chop. It was served atop a generous slice of French bread and topped with thick brown gravy with sauteed green pepper and onion rings. He looked at his brother Vincent's daughter thoughtfully. "Kendall doesn't have to know everything, Michelle. I'll get around to telling her eventually. In the meantime, I suggest you enjoy her congeniality. I'm sure it's not going to last."

Michelle sighed. "I hope you're wrong. I'd really like to keep things friendly, like they are. And I'm not convinced you're as cool about this as you try to make out." She rested her elbow on his shoulder and leaned in conspiratorially. "I've seen the way you look at her."

"I always look at attractive women, Michelle. I've been doing it for years, even before you were born." But Spencer was unable to conceal a smile at his niece's words. No doubt that he found Kendall Lucas quite appealing, and she was certainly ambitious, a trait he admired in women. He was impressed with the looks of Soul Food to Go. It was immaculate, it had good service, and it featured food that actually resembled the photographs on the menu boards up front, unlike most restaurants that featured photographs on their menu boards. The numerous hamburger houses could certainly take a cue from her example, he thought.

Soul Food to Go had still been under construction when he first began to pursue business interests in Nile Beach, and his first concern was that its location would perhaps interfere with his own plans. Now he wasn't worried about that, not really. His attitude was that if anything, *they* were the ones in trouble.

That was precisely what concerned him, now that the impersonal *they* had a name. How would Kendall react when she learned how closely his interests paralleled her own? It wasn't feasible that she'd be happy about it—if anything she'd probably give him a piece of her mind— so he'd better do his admiring from afar rather than up close and personal.

"Earth to Spencer, earth to Spencer."

He blinked, and Michelle and the boys laughed at his inattentiveness.

"Thinking about anything, or anyone, in particular?" Michelle inquired sweetly, a look of false innocence on her face.

"Oh, you." He impulsively reached over and pinched her cheek. She was quite perceptive, Michelle was. But he was glad she was here. She was a real lifesaver, running the household and keeping watch over Brian and Carlton while he made his frequent trips to Atlanta. If it wasn't for her presence Arjorie, his ex-wife, never would have agreed to let the boys move to Florida with him. He didn't know what he'd do without her.

* * *

Kendall looked up just in time to see the intimate exchange between Spencer and Michelle. Her arm was resting comfortably on his shoulder, and he was flashing her a knowing look. Just one look at the scene between two people obviously familiar with each other was all Kendall needed to be convinced that Zena had been desperately wrong about Spencer's eyes lingering on her. *The girl must need glasses,* she thought with good-natured amusement, but it quickly turned to a dull ache in the region of her heart.

Kendall did a double take as she drove past the duplex. There was an unusually high number of cars parked on the street. Someone on the street was obviously entertaining this holiday weekend, even though the actual holiday wasn't until tomorrow.

The thought had no sooner occurred to her when she noticed people milling about the Barnes apartment downstairs. She glimpsed children, adults . . . even a gray head or two. Spencer Barnes certainly knew a lot of people for someone who hadn't been in town long, Kendall thought. Then she wondered if he or Michelle had family in the area. That might have been a factor in their decision to relocate.

He caught sight of her car and waved, then indicated he would meet her in the alley when she parked.

"Oh, great," Kendall said aloud, although she was alone in the car. The last thing she needed was a few minutes alone with a ladies' man. There was something unsettling about Spencer Barnes, something she couldn't quite identify. Just two minutes of contact had had him etched in her mind the first time they met, and she feared nothing had changed, in spite of her resolve not to think about him.

He approached as she brought her car to a halt. "I meant to tell you before . . . nice car."

"Thanks." The light green, late model Altima had been her one splurge until she redecorated her apartment. "What's going on?"

"Just celebrating our move with some family members," he replied jovially. "We're grilling chicken and burgers. I hope you can spend some time with us."

Kendall had her excuse ready. "I'd love to, Spencer, but we're really busy at the restaurant. I just came home to catch a quick nap before I go back in time for the dinner crowd."

Spencer bodily blocked the car door and leaned in intimately, the window framing his upper body to Kendall's view. "Don't you ever relax, Kendall?"

It was an innocent enough query, but his tone held a sexy resonance that Kendall found uncomfortable . . . and highly inappropriate. She removed her keys from the ignition and reached for the inside door handle. As she anticipated he would, Spencer stepped back to let her alight. "I'll try to stop by for at least a few minutes," she said, slamming the car door with more force than was needed. It was a lie and she knew it, but if she didn't say something quick she risked making a fool of herself. Spencer Barnes was just too good-looking. His brown eyes bore into hers, their golden flecks like searchlights to her soul. She hurried on before he saw something in her expression that she would rather keep to herself . . . namely the untamed attraction for him she was struggling so valiantly—and with little success—to control.

He walked the few steps beside her silently. "Get some rest, Kendall," he said gently as she unlocked the door. Every spoken word was a caress, and she knew it was meant just for her. "I promise we'll keep the noise down." Then he walked off to where his guests were waiting.

It was all Kendall could do not to scream at him to leave her alone. Her reaction troubled her. He wasn't really bothering her; he was only being nice. She must be imagining the combustible atmosphere whenever he was near her. It wasn't Spencer's fault that he affected her the way he did.

She closed her downstairs door normally, but she did run up the inside stairs to the sanctuary of her empty apartment like her legs were on fire.

Kendall hadn't been fibbing when she told Spencer she wanted to rest; she really was tired. It hadn't been this busy at the Nile Beach restaurant since spring break, which began just a few weeks after their grand opening. David, too, had reported an upsurge in business at the Main Street site. With the increasing hot weather, people seemed more apt to eat out than cook at home.

She usually kept her apartment windows open. Most of her rooms had two or three windows, and the large, stately oak trees by the duplex made for both shade and a nice breeze. She had ceiling fans installed in every room and consequently hardly ever ran her central air conditioning.

Spencer and his guests were not rowdy by any means, but laughter and voices nonetheless drifted up to Kendall's bedroom. She also heard a Chuck Mangione jazz classic playing in the background at a comfortable volume. She got up and made her way to the window, careful to stand at an angle where she could not be seen from below.

Spencer was talking to Jim Mullins, who owned the brick cottage next door, probably extending an invitation for Jim to join them, while Michelle was talking with one of the older women present a few yards away. Spencer waved off Jim and joined them, and Kendall heard the woman exclaim, "You'd better hold on to this girl, Spencer, she's a prize!"

Kendall shrank away as Spencer put an arm around Michelle and hugged her. Only then was she ready to admit that she was jealous of Michelle Barnes for her status as Spencer's wife. She was jealous of the familiar and affectionate glances they shared. Looking at them reminded her of precisely what was missing from her own life.

She drew in her breath deeply. Some people simply weren't meant to have domestic bliss, and she was one of them. Domestic bliss was supposed to include family life with children, and her lack of enthusiasm for little ones didn't fit in with the picture. Besides, even if she found someone who felt the same way she did, no one she had ever dated could accept her devotion to her restaurants and the long hours she put in. No, love and marriage simply wasn't a possibility for her. Kendall had been telling herself that for years—and each passing year without the promise of a lasting romance only confirmed her belief.

But that was no reason for her to hole away like a hermit. Kendall went to wash her face. She'd join the others, even if only for a little while. It was the neighborly thing to do.

She took a moment to splash some cold water on her face—Kendall seldom wore makeup except for a dusky-rose-colored lipstick—and to adjust the wispy strands that framed her forehead and face and added height all along the back of her crown. Those shorter hairs in front kept her shoulder-length bob, usually worn pinned up in a bun or a French roll, from being flat and uninteresting.

Michelle approached her the moment she saw her coming. "Oh, Kendall, I'm so glad you decided to stop by," she said sincerely, taking Kendall's hand. Kendall immediately felt guilty for her jealousy. How could she possibly resent this warm and friendly young woman? "Spencer wanted to have the family over."

Kendall murmured an acknowledgment. "Are you two from Palmdale?" She'd already asked Spencer as much, but obviously there was something he hadn't mentioned.

"Actually, no. I'm from Atlanta and Spencer is from New Jersey, but we've got a bunch of aunts, uncles, and cousins here. It's a big family," Michelle said with a smile, "and this was their original hometown. It's just that some of them branched out to other places."

Kendall presumed she was referring to her in-laws, Spencer's side of the family. "It was nice of you to invite me," she said, directing her acknowledgment to Michelle as well as Spencer.

"Of course, we would invite you! Oh, I made some spice cake I want you to try—" Michelle's head turned sharply in the direction of a crying toddler who had apparently tripped. "Time for the rescue squad. I swear, that Justine never watches her baby." She dashed off without completing her sentence.

Kendall caught sight of the shiny stainless steel chafing dishes set up on a long table covered with a vinyl tablecloth and curiously went over to see what was inside them. Apparently the Barneses had called a caterer. She knew most of the locals and wondered which one had gotten the job.

She was helping herself to a grilled chicken leg quarter, potato salad, and baked beans when she felt someone's presence just behind her. She stiffened, thinking it was Spencer coming to unnerve her again. But the man who at that moment moved to stand beside her was not Spencer. "You must let me know how you enjoy the chicken. I cooked it, you know," he said.

She smiled at him. "As long as you're not one of those people who ask for opinions and then don't want to hear them." There was a vacant folding chair nearby, and she moved the few steps and sat down, balancing her plate on her lap so she could cut the meat.

It was tender, juicy, and seasoned with just the right touch of flavoring and barbecue sauce. "Mmm . . . my compliments to the, um, grillmaster," Kendall said in approval.

"Can I get you another piece?"

She laughed. "No, this will do nicely. But if you would be nice enough to get me something to drink?"

"Sure," he replied amiably. He left and returned moments later with a cup of a fruity concoction with a hint of ginger ale, as well as an introduction. His name was Todd Barnes.

"You must be Spencer's cousin," Kendall remarked, after she gave him her own name.

He shook his head. "Actually, I'm his nephew, even though I'm only a few years younger than he is. I'm actually the oldest of my generation; my father is the oldest of his." His gaze swept over her appreciatively. "So you live upstairs, huh?"

Kendall decided he must have seen her come home and unlock the door to the back stairs. "Yes. And it was a pleasure to have such nice people like Spencer and Michelle move in."

"You were expecting some loud partygivers?" It was Spencer, and as Kendall looked up at him he waved his hand toward the portable cassette player, which was now featuring Grover Washington.

"Oh, it's nice to let loose every now and again," Kendall replied airily. "Besides," she added, reprising his comment about Zena's shouting, "it's not like it's the middle of the night."

"True. I see you met Todd here. Are you two comparing notes about our sleepy little town?"

Todd harumphed. "It won't be sleepy for long, Spence. Not with your plans."

Kendall raised an eyebrow. She had always been curious as to what Spencer planned to do in Palmdale. They had never discussed his profession. "You've got plans to liven up the community, Spencer?"

"If you can call it that," he answered with a touch of evasiveness.

He certainly was closemouthed, Kendall thought. She was wondering what the big secret was when he gave more information.

"I'm going to open a nightclub for teenagers, like I have in Atlanta," he said. "Sixteen to twenty on Saturday nights, and twelve to fifteen in the early evenings on Sundays."

"That's a great idea!" Kendall exclaimed. "But what about Fridays?"

"Well, kids like going to the movies or hanging out at

the mall that night, and the roller rink does a good business, too. I'm not out to interfere with anyone's livelihood;
I think there's plenty of money to be made without
resorting to direct competition."

"Do you have a site?" she asked.

He nodded. "An old supermarket in a strip mall on
Bethune Road, next to the record shop."

"Oh, yes. In Nile Beach." He would be sure to attract
the teenaged children of vacationers, Kendall thought,
leaving their parents free to indulge in quality time
together. Spencer appeared quite the astute businessman.
"That's really a great idea. I remember my brother used
to complain about there being nowhere for him to go if
no one was giving a house party. Of course, that was ten
years ago and he's not seventeen anymore," she added
with a chuckle.

"That's what I do; find a need and fill it," he said. "And
the people of Nile Beach have plenty of needs."

"Yeah, man, tell her—" Todd began.

But Spencer cut him off. "Todd, I need to talk to you
for a minute. Can you excuse us?" he said to Kendall.

"Sure. I'll probably still be here eating," she replied,
smiling.

Kendall didn't stay long at the cookout, but she thoroughly enjoyed herself while she was there. She made
friends with the outgoing, personable Joy, Spencer's four-
year-old niece—or perhaps it was a great-niece, she wasn't
sure. It wasn't until she had returned to her apartment
that she realized Todd did not return to speak with her
again. She wondered what it was Spencer had had to tell
him.

Afterward she went back to the Nile Beach restaurant
and was pleased to learn from preliminary register readings
that it had been a busy afternoon. She talked to the staffers

on duty one at a time to see who was interested in additional hours, and placed calls to the homes of those who had the night off. Then she spent several hours working with the information she collected to put together the work schedule for the next two weeks. The season was in full swing, and Kendall knew an insufficient staff would make for botched orders and sloppy presentation and would lead to an unwanted reputation as a place to avoid among the vacationers, and the locals as well.

Spencer and Michelle's guests were gone when she returned home at eight o'clock. It had been a long day, and, exhausted, Kendall showered and put on a pair of satin-like shortie pajamas after liberally applying scented powder to her chest and back.

She settled down in front of the television—one of the cable stations was running the film noir classic *Double Indemnity,* one of her favorites. She removed the pins that held her French roll in place and brushed her hair vigorously to stimulate her scalp as she watched a blonde Barbara Stanwyck work her wiles on an unwitting but equally devious Fred MacMurray.

When her doorbell rang, she figured it was probably Zena, just about the only person she knew who never called ahead. Kendall grabbed a hip-length print cotton kimono and made her way down the stairs, tying the kimono around her waist as she went. She quickly saw through the peephole that it was actually Spencer who stood outside, not her sister-in-law. She reknotted the kimono's sash around her waist more tightly—though it had been secure to begin with—and opened the door. "Hello," she said carefully, not wanting to sound too enthusiastic to see him.

"Hi." He held out a foil-wrapped triangular package. "Michelle's spice cake. She was so proud of it, and she wanted to make sure you got a piece."

"Oh, that was so sweet of her," Kendall exclaimed. "I'm sure I'll enjoy it."

"It really is good," he said in agreement.

She smiled at him warmly but quickly grew uncomfortable when she realized he was taking in her appearance. The shimmering material of her pajama bottoms protruded ever so slightly from the kimono.

Approval of her attire was obvious by his expression. "I like your hair like that," he said finally.

Kendall inadvertently raised a hand up to touch the dark strands that grazed her shoulders. She had forgotten it was loose. "Thank you." She cleared her throat in what sounded to her own ears like a rather crude attempt to change the mood. "I'll stop by and see Michelle in the morning to thank her," she said pointedly.

"She'll be glad to see you," Spencer replied smoothly. "I won't be around, though. I'm about to leave for Atlanta. I want to be there in the morning, before sunrise."

"That's a long drive. I know, I went to Spelman."

"Long and boring." His gaze met and held hers, and there was no denying the interest in his eyes.

Kendall's discomfort increased. The vestibule, usually cold and impersonal, suddenly seemed like a very intimate setting, a rendezvous for lovers. And it felt warm for a change. Spencer was getting to her again.

"But I try to think of nice things while I'm driving," Spencer concluded.

There was no mistaking the direction of his intent, and Kendall was left speechless by his blatant insinuation. She quickly came to her senses when his upper body began descending toward hers. Good Lord, if she didn't stop him he was actually going to kiss her!

She hastily turned her head and sniffed loudly. "Spencer—I've got something on the stove, and I'd better catch it before it burns up. Thanks for the cake, and you have a safe trip, eh?" With that she was soon halfway up the stairs, safely beyond the reach of his grasp, before he could voice a protest.

"What about this door?" he called after her when she'd gone only a few steps. "Does it automatically lock from the outside?"

"Yes. It's all right; I'll come down and double latch it later." She was so anxious to get away from his sensuous gaze that she barely turned her head as she replied. Instead she literally ran the rest of the way.

CHAPTER THREE

Safe in the haven of her apartment, Kendall's heartbeat accelerated. How dare he, she thought over and over. She was his upstairs neighbor, for heaven's sake. How could he think so little of Michelle . . . and of her? Kendall had never been involved with a married man in her life, and she certainly wasn't going to start now. Apparently Spencer had been told so many times how handsome he was that it had gone to his head and he felt he could break all the rules.

The passage of a quarter hour—usually enough time for any upset to dissipate—did nothing to ease Kendall's anger. She went to the phone and dialed Zena, practically beating up the numbers of the telephone keypad in the process.

"Can Barry and Elgin do without you for an hour or so?" she asked when her sister-in-law answered the phone. "I really need to talk to you."

"Well, Elgin is asleep and we were just about to see if we can make him a baby brother . . ."

"Come on, Zena. This is important."

"Oh, my. Do you want me to come over?"

Kendall thought for a moment before deciding she needed to get out of the house. "No. Meet me at Mr. Robinson's."

"I can be there in half an hour. Just let me tell Barry to put his libido on hold."

"I don't understand it, Zena. Do I have desperate written all over my face?" Talking about Spencer's inappropriate behavior only served to make Kendall angrier.

Zena listened calmly to Kendall's account of what transpired in her vestibule, not uttering a word until Kendall, exasperated, asked, "Why aren't you saying anything?"

Zena sighed. "I've been quiet for two reasons, Kendall. One, the only thing I could possibly do was get in an occasional murmur of support while you vented off all your steam. Two, I know you aren't going to like what I have to say, which naturally makes me reluctant to say it."

"And that is?" Kendall asked suspiciously.

"Spencer Barnes is not married."

Kendall slammed her palm on the table, the force of the hit causing their drinking glasses to slide a half inch or so, the liquid splashing over the sides and forming small puddles. "Why do you keep insisting that?" she demanded, not bothering to conceal her frustration and annoyance.

"Whatever Spencer Barnes is, he's not a fool. You, Kendall, live right upstairs. You say he started to kiss you. You and what's her name are friendly." Zena shook her head. "It just doesn't add up."

Kendall sighed. "So how do you explain old what's her name living there if she's not his wife?"

"That's a toughie," Zena conceded. "But we know that apartment is big enough for them to be sleeping in separate bedrooms. I know there's got to be a perfectly sane reason for her being there . . . I just can't figure out what it is."

"That's because they're married, Zena," Kendall replied confidently, but she felt no triumph. Instead she just felt sadness. She had been so happy to learn that the downstairs half of the duplex finally had tenants, but with all the grief it had brought her, she'd have preferred staying in the building alone and risking her chances of becoming a crime victim.

She took a sip of her beer. The cool liquid soothed her throat. Kendall enjoyed beer—real beer, not the light kind—but she only allowed herself one or two a week, fearful of the effect the fattening beverage would have on her figure. As she lowered the glass, she spotted a familiar figure at the bar. Openmouthed, she slowly replaced her glass on the table.

"What's wrong, you see a ghost?" Zena asked. Getting no response, she hissed across the table, "Kendall! For crying out loud, close your mouth. You look silly."

Her words finally registered, and Kendall complied. "Zena . . . at the bar . . . it's Michelle!"

"Michelle who?"

Kendall glared at her sister-in-law. "What's her name!"

Zena turned to look for a moment before shifting to meet Kendall's gaze. "And from what I've seen of Spencer, that doesn't look like him she's with," she observed dryly.

"I don't get it. What do they have, an open marriage or something?" Kendall asked incredulously.

Zena drained her wine glass. "This, my dear, is a marvelous time for you to get to the bottom of this little enigma."

"How?"

"Kendall, you're a successful businesswoman. Surely you can engineer a subtle change in conversation to Spencer." At Kendall's uncertain look she made a face. "All right, I'll give you a possibility right off the top of my head. You approach her and thank her for the cake. Then you mention how much you enjoyed yourself at the barbecue. Then make some small talk. One thing will lead to another. Just commenting on her being here should be enough. Just find out what the deal is between her and Spencer. And call me in the morning." Zena slid out of the booth, purse in hand. "I'm going home before my husband falls asleep. You know, Kendall, I'll sure be glad when this is all settled. You probably haven't been this worked up over a man since Jermaine married Hazel.''

Kendall giggled. Actually, she couldn't have cared less when the handsome middle brother of the original Jackson Five had married Berry Gordy's daughter—Michael was the one she had a crush on—but she still remembered the disappointment of the older girls in her Philadelphia neighborhood.

Moments later Zena was out the door. Alone at the table, Kendall nursed her beer and kept an eye on Michelle Barnes. She felt perfectly comfortable in her surroundings. Robinson's Bar was a no-frills establishment that had been in business in Nile Beach for years. Affectionately nicknamed "Mr. Robinson's" by its patrons, it was plain but comfortable, and as yet undiscovered by the tourists; and its clientele ranged from newly legal twenty-one-year-olds to retirees who met to catch up with friends or to have one of the bar's locally famous grilled cheese and bacon sandwiches. Kendall recognized many of the three dozen or so people present, most of whom stopped by her table as they passed to chat for a moment.

Michelle was sitting with a female friend on one side of her and a man on the other. Judging by her expression, she was thoroughly enjoying what the man was saying.

Kendall waited until the man excused himself before making her move. "Hey, girl," she said, propping herself up on the recently vacated barstool on Michelle's right.

"Hi, Kendall!" Michelle exclaimed with her usual zest. "Did Spencer bring you the cake?"

"Yes, and it was delicious," Kendall lied. She was sure the cake would be tasty, but the truth was that she had been so upset by Spencer's action in the vestibule she hadn't sampled it yet. "Spencer stopped by before he left for Atlanta," she said pointedly.

"Oh, yes. He always makes that drive at night. He says there's a lot less traffic."

"What about the boys? Are they home alone?"

"Oh, no. Spencer took them with him. They'll miss a few days of school, but the semester will be over next week anyway. This way they'll get to spend some time with their mother before summer vacation." She chuckled. "For the next three days I'm free as a bird. I tell you, what a great setup I have."

"What do you mean?" Kendall asked, sensing she was about to learn the truth about the relationship between Spencer and Michelle. Her body tensed in anticipation.

Michelle shrugged. "Oh, cooking, cleaning, and laundry for Spencer and the boys. Brian and Carlton are big enough where they don't need to be baby-sat, and they really are good kids. But sometimes they get a little carried away and act like we're contemporaries. We might be cousins, but I'm still fifteen years older than they are."

Kendall swallowed hard, and self-consciously she was certain that everyone within five feet heard her Eve's apple reverberate. Even she hadn't realized she was holding her breath. If Michelle was a cousin to Spencer's sons, that meant she was Spencer's niece . . . not his wife. She had a fleeting thought of Todd at the barbecue. He was Spencer's nephew, and he was considerably older than Michelle, probably around her own age. It certainly was plausible.

She wanted to know more, but suddenly she realized she already knew quite a bit. Spencer and Michelle's fathers were brothers, which would account for them carrying the same last name. Michelle's references to "we" and "us" at the barbecue hadn't meant she and Spencer, but the Barnes family in general! Apparently Michelle assumed she knew they were uncle and niece. And so, apparently, had Spencer.

With a shiver of exhilaration Kendall realized there really were no barriers if Spencer wanted to kiss her.

Kendall was awakened the next morning by the shrill sound of her bedside telephone. She opened one eye and looked at the clock. Good grief, it wasn't even 9 A.M. yet. Who on earth would be calling that early?

She closed her eye and groped for the phone. "This better not be a wrong number," she said by way of greeting.

"My, you're charming in the morning."

"Zena, it's eight thirty. What do you want?"

"How did you make out last night?"

"Oh!" Kendall exclaimed. Suddenly more receptive, she recounted the story of her enlightening chat with Michelle. "So that's all there is to it," she concluded triumphantly. Then she waited for the inevitable response, and Zena did not disappoint her.

"I told you he wasn't married."

"Yes, Zena, you were right," Kendall said in a tone both soothing and patronizing.

But Zena was not content to let the matter rest with that alone. "Now don't you feel silly?" she pressed.

"I sure do," Kendall replied, her heartfelt honesty overriding the urge to tell her sister-in-law to take a hike. "Every time I think of my telling Spencer I had something on the stove, I flinch. But when you think about it, Michelle's being his niece is just as trite. I mean, how many middle-aged businessmen have young twentyish girls living or traveling with them that they pass off as their nieces?"

"Hundreds. So when he gets back you two can kiss and make up." Zena laughed heartily at her little joke, but the very idea made Kendall's tongue inadvertently dart out and moisten her lips.

"I meant to ask you, did you know Clyde Simmons is putting in a restaurant?" Zena asked.

"At the hotel? He already has a restaurant."

Zena harumphed. "Yeah, a typical overpriced hotel coffee shop with day-old doughnuts. No, Kendall, he's opening a real restaurant. A soul food restaurant, to boot. They're planning to serve breakfast, lunch, and dinner and have live entertainment on weekends."

Kendall tensed. "Live entertainment?"

"I know what you're thinking," Zena said. "His expansion is likely to have an effect on Soul Food to Go. I mean, the Sunrise Hotel is right next door to you."

"All his guests come to me as it is. No wonder he didn't say anything to me. He probably wants to keep it quiet as long as he can. I haven't even seen him lately; he must be avoiding me." Kendall's mind was racing with the onset of panic. "This is scary, Zena. I mean, competition is okay, but not so close, if you know what I mean. I don't have exact figures, but Sunrise guests account for a pretty fair amount of my business, especially at night. Breakfast doesn't affect me, but if his place starts serving lunch and dinner that might all change."

"Now, don't get frantic over this, Kendall. Nile Beach is growing like crazy. In a couple of years, it'll be chock full of restaurants, all competing for the same hungry people."

"Well, I think this was a very mean thing for Clyde to do," Kendall stated firmly. "It's like I had a McDonald's and he put up a Burger King next door to it."

"It's really not that bad, Ken. Remember, somebody opened a Baskin-Robbins ice cream franchise a few doors down from Sweet Treats, and at last glimpse they were both making money."

"That's because Baskin-Robbins doesn't sell peach cobbler, and Sweet Treats doesn't sell frozen yogurt. They're both specialized. You're telling me that Clyde Simmons is opening a soul food restaurant in his hotel. My restaurant sells soul food."

"Well, Kendall, the fact is that Nile Beach attracts a lot of African-American tourists, most of whom happen to be rather fond of soul food. Different places might be springing up all over town over the next couple of years. But Clyde's menu is bound to be different from yours. More menu choices and almost certainly higher prices ... remember, it's still a hotel restaurant. Clyde will have to pay someone a decent salary to operate it. And he can't get by paying his chef six dollars an hour."

"His cook," Kendall corrected. "Chefs make fancy food, and we're talking about ham and collard greens here."

"All right, cook. Anyway, he'll probably have a lot of fried stuff. You can counter by promoting your menu's nutritional value. There's room for everybody, Ken. It doesn't have to get nasty."

Kendall shrugged. She was deeply disturbed at this news. Her plans for Soul Food to Go did not include falling revenue. "How'd you find out, anyway?"

"I read it in the business section of the paper. You really should make it a point to look that over; there's all kinds of expansion going on in town."

"I don't really need to. After all, I've got a sister-in-law who's a real estate tycoon."

"Don't I wish. Hey, what are you wearing to your father's party?"

"I think the silk cheongsam Mom bought for me in Hong Kong. Why don't you wear yours?"

Zena hedged. "Oh, I don't know. It might be overkill. I know your mom is planning on wearing hers. But then again, it might be cute if we're all dressed Chinese style. Maybe I will. You know, round out the trio."

"Great!" Paul Ridgely, who was married to Kendall's mother and who treated Kendall and her brother Barry like they were his own children, was retiring after twenty years of working for the town of Nile Beach, and her mother was giving a party to mark the occasion. It was going to be quite a grand event, with live music, waiters and bartenders. "All right, Zena, I just wanted to let you know the deal about Spencer," she said conclusively.

"Good. Now you can go full speed ahead. Talk to you later."

Full speed ahead, Kendall repeated to herself.

She could hardly wait for Spencer's return.

Kendall was returning home for an extended break from the restaurant a few days later when a horn tooted behind her. She held her breath at the sight of Spencer's Saab pulling up behind her own parked vehicle. This was the first she'd seen of him since before his trip out of town, and of course much had changed since then.

"Hi, there," she said as she took a few steps toward the curb.

Spencer quickly got out from behind the wheel. "Hey. I thought that was you. Now I'm glad I forgot my keys and had to come back." He looked at her, curiosity in his dark eyes. "Hey, do you have a few minutes to take a ride with me? I could really use your opinion on something."

Kendall shrugged. "I don't see why not. I wasn't planning on going back to the restaurant before five."

"I'll have you back way before then. Here, catch." He tossed a set of keys toward her, which she reflexively caught. "Just give me a minute to grab the keys to my place."

"Sure," Kendall agreed. She felt a twinge of disappointment as she let herself in to the locked passenger side of the Saab. Spencer's demeanor was friendly, but if anything, he was treating her like a buddy. He wasn't glad to see her because he'd missed her or thought about her, he just wanted her input on some professional matter. She fleetingly wondered if he had met someone special while he was in Atlanta. Or maybe the negative signals from her hurried exit last week had really made their impact. She was going to have to reverse it, but how? She didn't want to tell him the truth; he would laugh at her mistake. But neither could she turn around and come on to him. It wasn't her style; and besides, it would make him think she was a tease. She sighed as she opened the back copy of the newspaper she had purchased from the editorial office. She had already thrown out the bulk of it—only the business section interested her.

The article she was looking for was on the inside cover. There was a photograph of the Sunrise Hotel and a header that read, NEW RESTAURANT TO OPEN IN LOCAL HOTEL.

In the text, Clyde Simmons rattled on about how he was renting the space to an Atlanta-based firm called Two Brothers, Inc., who already operated a successful restaurant in that city, The Ruling Class. The Sunrise's current restaurant was being expanded and would have a capacity of one hundred for dining and nearly double that figure in total. "What Nile Beach needs is an intimate environment where patrons can enjoy top-name entertainment, along with good hearty food and drink," he said. "My partners and I plan to fill that need, starting with the first night we open the doors. We'll also be featuring talented locals as well."

Humph, Kendall thought. Any top-name entertainment that came to Nile Beach—which despite its small size was a frequent stop for tour concerts and plays of interest to the African-American community—performed at the Civic Center, which could seat several thousand people. She knew there was considerably more money in that type of setup for the performers because of the number of seats that were filled. Who would want to play for an audience of two hundred if they could play for ten times that many? No one, unless that was the only work they could get. Better change that to fading entertainment, she thought sarcastically as she closed the paper and stuffed it into the large tote bag she always carried back and forth to the office.

In his apartment, Spencer quickly retrieved the keys to the teen club. He welcomed the opportunity to show it off to Kendall. It was silly and he knew it, but somehow it made him feel better to share at least part of his plans with her. He hated this secrecy, but he saw no way around it, at least not at the present time.

Kendall was sitting comfortably in the shade, when, true to his word, he emerged just moments after disappearing inside his apartment. He was dressed in neat but faded jeans and a crisp white shirt that might be worn with a business suit, except it was open at the throat and the cuffs were rolled up to just below the elbow. In spite of his long sleeves and the warmth of the day, he looked cool and refreshed. Kendall got the impression he wasn't much interested in clothes—every time she'd seen him, he was wearing jeans or shorts, usually with the well-worn leather moccasins he had on now. It made sense—as his own boss, Spencer had little cause to put on a suit. He probably saved his dress-to-impress attire for meetings with his banker. That was fine with her, she was partial to jeans and cutoffs herself. Kendall appreciated a well-dressed man as much as anyone, but she found the idea of a man with an entire walk-in closet full of suits, business shoes, and starched shirts distasteful. One of her many aborted romances had been with a high-ranking official at a St. Augustine bank, a man who gave new meaning to the word "meticulous." Kendall felt it was overkill.

Spencer had left the driver's side unlocked, and before she knew it he was sitting at the wheel beside her. Kendall immediately felt a strange euphoria at being in such close quarters with him. She forced herself to breathe normally, afraid he would notice her excitement. "Where are we going, anyway?" she managed to ask calmly as he put the car in gear.

"I want to get your opinion on how the club looks."

"Is it ready to look at?" Kendall's tone reflected her surprise. Somehow she had gotten the impression that Spencer had just begun the job of transforming a former grocery store into a night spot for the under-twenty-one set.

"I should hope so; they've been working on it since March. We're set to open this weekend."

Kendall nodded. Spencer hadn't moved to Palmdale until March; apparently he had spent a considerable amount of time here tending to his interests before actually relocating. "So is that what you do, Spencer? Operate teen clubs?"

He shrugged. "Well, I do have one in the Atlanta area, but it's not an exclusive area of interest for me. I own percentages in all kinds of businesses . . . and I see all kinds of opportunities here."

He certainly sounds sure of himself, Kendall thought with admiration.

The former SaveMart was located on one of Nile Beach's main streets in an older section of town. A massive construction effort of residential subdivisions less than a mile away had prompted some of the major supermarket chains to build stores in the area; and SaveMart, smaller and lacking the modern seafood, gourmet meat, and bakery departments, was unable to compete and eventually closed its doors. The building had been vacant for nearly five years, but the smaller stores in the strip mall thrived. There was a twenty-four-hour drug store, a music shop, a beauty salon, a yogurt shop, and an outlet of Mailboxes USA.

Kendall followed Spencer inside. The first thing she saw when he flipped on the lights was a metal detector. "Do you really think this is necessary, Spencer?" she asked skeptically.

"I know it looks bad, but it's a sign of the times we live in. These are young kids we're dealing with, and you know how they're always having disputes about this or that. No one will ever be injured or killed in one of my clubs if I can help it."

"I suppose they could sue you if anything did happen," she remarked.

"Not me personally, I'm incorporated. But yes, things could get very unpleasant."

Kendall walked through the metal detector, which was not presently connected. "Wow," she said as she took in her surroundings. To the left there was a spacious wood dance floor. An abundance of tables and chairs were arranged around a semicircular bar with empty shelves. "It's almost . . . well, plush. It's sure a whole lot nicer than the teen center in Philadelphia where I used to go, which wasn't much more than a large, dark room. Actually, I don't even remember them having a single chair," she said with a laugh.

"It's not plush, not really," Spencer replied in the raspy voice she was beginning to get accustomed to. "It's actually very low maintenance. No carpeting and no ashtrays—there won't be any smoking in here, even for the older kids. It's a dirty habit, and it's too hard to control, since some kids are old enough while most aren't. Let 'em go outside.''

"But I'm surprised to see a bar. I mean, you'll be serving minors.''

"Ah, you're not looking past the initial purpose. I've put a not-so-small fortune into this little venture, and the bank is looking to be paid back promptly. I wanted a place that would be nice enough that it could be used as a setting for private parties and wedding receptions, that sort of thing. All we have to do is get some tablecloths, some ashtrays, bring out the liquor and put away the metal detector, and we're all set. In the meantime let the kids order their Cokes from a bartender. It'll make them feel more adult.''

She snapped her fingers as if remembering something. "So that's why you're not going to open to the public on Friday nights. You want to reserve that night for private rentals.''

He chuckled, a rich sound that reverberated through the room. "Like I said, I see a lot of prospects in this area. So be sure and mention it to anyone you know who's giving a party.''

"My mother is giving a party next week," Kendall said absently. "Of course, by now it's all planned.'' She took a seat at one of the tables. "Have you ever thought about serving food? I mean, I'm sure you're not licensed for food preparation, but you can have it catered.'' She was thinking about how Soul Food to Go could find a niche in what was sure to be a moneymaking endeavor. She'd have to start thinking about other avenues. Her profits were bound to slide when Clyde Simmons opened his newly refurbished restaurant.

"Actually I was, but something inexpensive and simple, like baloney and cheese sandwiches. But I don't need a caterer for that. I can put Michelle and even the boys to work on slapping them together and cutting them into bite-size pieces. I don't want to serve anything messy. Besides, making that tiny investment helps justify the six bucks I'm going to charge for admission.''

Again Kendall was struck by how shrewd he was. Six dollars was a lot of money to charge for teenagers here in Nile Beach. Then she laughed. "You're really planning on working poor Michelle to death, aren't you?"

"She's a good kid, and she wants to get more involved in the business. This is going to be hers to manage."

"Is it a family-owned business?"

"My brother Vincent and I hold all the shares. He's Michelle's father."

Kendall nodded. "Oh, I get it."

"It'll work out well. Of course," Spencer continued, "the main reason Michelle wanted to come here was so she could meet all the fellows who come down to Nile Beach for vacation. She's only twenty-five, and she's already nervous about not being married." He eyed her curiously. "Speaking of which, Kendall, have you ever been married?"

"No, and I'm a lot older than twenty-five. If Michelle is nervous, I guess I should be downright panicky."

They laughed. "I'm divorced myself," Spencer said. "The boys were living with their mother, who wasn't that far away from where I used to live in Atlanta, but she got married again last year and there's a bit of a clash between the boys and their stepfather's kids, who live with them as well. Besides, they're getting older and need my influence, now more than ever."

"It's not easy being a black man in America," Kendall remarked.

"That's right. We all agreed it would be best if they came here with me right away, even if it meant changing schools with only a little more than two months to go in the semester."

"Do they like it here?"

"Very much. And so do I," he said somewhat pointedly,

resting his palms on the table and leaning in dangerously close to where she sat directly opposite him. Even in the dim lighting Kendall could see the flash of desire in his dark eyes. It was impossible not to get his message. She swallowed hard and began to fidget with the hem of her blouse.

"It really is a nice place to live," she said softly.

"I'm trying to decide if I want to get a place in Palmdale or in Nile Beach. I think Nile Beach is the winner. The boys like the ocean. We didn't have one in Atlanta, you know."

"There wasn't one there last time I checked," Kendall said with a smile.

"Both communities have their advantages."

"So you expect to stick around for a while?"

He nodded. "I lived in the Atlanta area for a dozen years, but it never really felt like home to me. I've been here for six weeks and already I feel like I belong. Of course, knowing this was my parents' hometown and that I still have family here helps. I think it's time I put down some roots, settled down."

A surge she couldn't explain rushed through Kendall's body at his words, and as a result she shivered.

"Are you cold?" Spencer asked.

"No," she said quickly, embarrassed that he had noticed.

He held out his hand. "I guess it's time I got you back."

Kendall put her hand in his rough one. Spencer noted that she had a fresh French manicure. The stark white tips that contrasted so vividly against the pale pink nails weren't very long—they barely extended past her fingertips—but they could nonetheless do a fair amount of damage if she were sufficiently excited. Spencer imagined her long, tapering fingers clutching his naked back and shoulders in bed, and his breathing quickened.

He helped her up but did not release her hand as they walked toward the door. Instead he gently rubbed her skin with the pad of his thumb, creating a warm friction that made Kendall catch her breath.

Spencer flicked off the light switches with his free hand. "Oh, something I forgot," he said.

"What's that?"

Before she knew what was happening she was in his arms. "Last time you said something you were cooking was about to burn up. You can't tell me that now," he said as he lowered his head.

She sucked in her breath, then quickly exhaled just before his lips touched hers. She expected it to be a momentary, lip-to-lip kiss, but to her surprise his arms went around her shoulders—pulling her close, at the same time he slipped his tongue inside her moist mouth. Kendall inadvertently tilted her head backward to maximize both his access and her own enjoyment. She joined in the game he was playing with his tongue and began to playfully run hers over his lips. In what seemed like a perfectly natural movement, her arms wrapped around his lean waist. This, she thought, was heaven.

"Oh," she said softly when he gently broke the kiss.

"That was every bit as good as what I thought it would be," Spencer stated in obvious satisfaction. He pursed his lips inward for a moment. Kendall knew he was running his tongue over them in a reflex action to get the last remnant of her taste. She quickly looked away, knowing that if she didn't, she'd go right back into his embrace and never come out of it. As he reached for the door Kendall hoped no one passing by on the street had been able to see them embrace in the darkened club.

Spencer's hand rested possessively at the small of her back, as he opened the door. They walked the few steps to the car. So much for keeping his distance, he thought, but in his heart he knew he had been fighting a losing battle. He wanted to spend time with Kendall, wanted to pursue that special spark he'd felt toward her from the beginning. He was glad she had been more receptive to him than she had the last time they saw each other, that night in her vestibule. She probably had the same reservations as he did about getting involved with a neighbor.

Catching her off guard to kiss her like that might have been a bit sneaky, but he reasoned this was a spontaneous excursion, so a little impulsive behavior seemed to fit. Besides, that misty look in her eyes didn't lie. She'd enjoyed it as much as he had.

Spencer seated her on the passenger side before walking around and getting behind the wheel.

"I hope you didn't mind," he remarked once the car was out in traffic. "But I've always been the type of man who goes after what he wants."

"Don't worry, Spencer. I've always been the type of woman who objects if I feel I'm being taken advantage of," she countered.

They smiled at each other. "I just want to show you one other thing," he said. "It'll only take a minute."

"Sure." Kendall made her voice sound pleasantly agreeable, but she was actually thrilled that he wanted to extend their brief time together. She found herself wishing the afternoon would never end . . . and she could hardly wait to be held in his arms again.

CHAPTER FOUR

Spencer drove down a side street and then headed in the opposite direction, toward downtown and the beach. Nile Beach's town center was the center of the tourist community. King Street, which like all the other streets in the resort village except Ocean Avenue was named after a prominent person of African descent, and its cross streets were home to most of the restaurants, the town's two movie theaters, and the various shops that catered to tourist needs. Day and night during the season, affluent-looking visitors could be seen strolling or dining in the courtyard of the King Street Cafe or one of the other bistros that featured al fresco dining. King Street was the place to see and be seen, even if it was just to take a walk, window shop, or browse.

Kendall turned to Spencer quizzically when he pulled into one of the diagonal parking spaces. He simply sat and looked at her with an expectant smile that told her she should be able to figure it out on her own. She looked at the street to see if there were any clues.

Immediately she noticed that they were in front of a new store. The overhead sign identified it as IN A FLASH, and in smaller lettering were the words, VIDEO CAMERA RENTAL AND PERSONALIZED POSTCARDS. Kendall turned to Spencer, who was smiling at the shop proudly. "Yours?" she asked.

"Yes. Do you have any idea how difficult it is to rent video cameras?"

"To tell the truth, I really never thought about it."

"Not many places bother, and those that do charge exorbitant rates, like fifty dollars a day."

"So how's business?"

"We just opened two weeks ago, and it's doing very well. But that's not all we do. I mean, you can't really make a living renting video cameras. Lots of people who come here for vacation have their own. I needed a gimmick, something else that would draw people in. So I searched around for some realistic-looking backdrops of beach scenes to use for personalized postcards. Pictures of the family or couple with a printed caption that goes something like, 'Greetings from Bob and Sue' or 'From the Smiths.' "

Kendall drew in her breath. "Spencer, what a great idea!"

"Like I said, it seems to be doing pretty good."

"God, you're a genius."

"Not really. The genius is the one who had the idea to revive this town. I just capitalized on what was a truly great idea."

Kendall chuckled. "Well, in that case, I should thank you. That genius is my father."

"No kidding!"

She nodded. "He accepted a job twenty years ago as their city planner. That's when the whole turnaround started. Back then all the town council knew was that they wanted to get vacationers back down here. You see, once the barriers of segregation broke, black people started going other places on their vacations, like Disney World and cruises, and the town's economy started to dry up. Well, the council did change the name from Freetown to

Nile Beach because it reflected its heritage better. Just about everything else was Dad's idea. The hills of Kiliminjaro and everything," she added, referring to the former county dump located at the northwest section of town. For years the residents of the formerly named community of Freetown, founded just after the Civil War, lived in relative peace, unlike other towns like Rosewood that suffered heavy casualties and property damages in race riots during the 1920s. In spite of the relatively smooth sailing, none of the residents were surprised when, as the only predominantly black town in the county, Nile Beach was chosen as the site for the county dump. The site, located at the town's northwest border, quickly grew into an eyesore, but Paul Ridgely commissioned a specially designed, leak-proof liner and had it installed in a massive cleanup project. The trash itself was mingled with generous portions of soil that served to both kill the stench and to give it a solid shape. As the pile of trash grew to mountainous height, it was nicknamed "Kilimanjaro" after the African continent's tallest and most famous peak. Kilimanjaro was now surrounded by several smaller hills, creating a sight so scenic that developers had actually built housing with views of it. Meanwhile, the monetary advantages of collecting the county's trash over the years had provided the town's residents with numerous fringe benefits, including new schools, a modern senior citizen's center, a youth recreation center, and an extensive public library. Recycling was also a major industry in Nile Beach and had been a requirement long before it became popular in larger cities, to help keep the trash accumulation down.

"Yeah, I heard about that. That was a million-dollar idea if I've ever heard one," Spencer said. "I'd love to meet your father sometime."

Kendall hesitated only for a moment. "You can. He's retiring, and my mom is giving him a party this weekend. You're welcome to join us."

"I'd like that." He reached out for her hand, causing

her senses to reel at the unexpected contact. "May I escort you . . . that is, if you were going alone."

She swallowed hard, hoping he didn't notice the gulping sound that echoed so loudly in her ears. The scratchy sound of his voice sounded so sexy, so intimate, especially after the kiss they had just shared . . .

"I'm going alone," she stated hesitantly, a little embarrassed to admit it, but at the same time anxious to break the feeling that there was no one else in the world at the moment but the two of them. She added brightly, "There's no reason we can't go together. You know, I think you'll like my father. You remind me a lot of him. He was always one to jump on an idea and go full throttle with it."

"Thanks. I consider that a compliment."

"It was meant that way."

They didn't talk much on the drive back, and when they arrived at the duplex they didn't linger over goodbyes. Both of their minds were on business. Kendall was anxious to catch forty winks before returning to Soul Food to Go, and Spencer had another errand to run, an important one he couldn't bring Kendall along on.

He had to check on the construction of his new restaurant in the Sunrise Hotel.

Kendall made it a habit to periodically look up while she was working to look out on the activity in the dining room. The time between lunch and dinner was usually slow. Many of her staffers worked only between eleven and three to help handle the rush.

Business today hadn't been too bad, she thought. A few scattered tables had patrons sitting at them, enjoying frozen yogurt, cheesecake, or beer. Kendall insisted that Soul Food to Go be a place where diners were not rushed out after gulping down food. She knew a lot of people categorized her restaurant along with the typical hamburger and chicken fast-food franchises in the area, an image she tried as hard as she could to discourage. That was her main reason for purchasing the necessary license to enable her to serve beer and wine.

A customer wandered in, hands in pockets and eyes on the menu boards. Kendall watched the middle-aged man approach, and a tightness developed in her jaw. She hadn't expected to see Clyde Simmons here at Soul Food to Go, not after he decided to become a direct competitor.

She immediately became suspicious. He was probably here studying her menu and prices, the creep.

She rose and cleared her throat, although she wasn't hoarse. With determined steps she entered the counter area, waving away the cashier who stood poised to take Clyde's order. "Hello, Clyde," she said, her clipped voice not exactly friendly but yet not belying the animosity she felt.

"Hi, Kendall." Clyde smiled at her, but the smile soon faded when he noticed the cold look in her eyes. "Oh," he said. He toned down his ordinarily booming voice—quite powerful for a man of smaller than average stature—and softly added, "I guess you've heard about my plans for the hotel."

"Yes, the key word being 'heard about it.' I would have liked to have heard it from you instead of reading about it in the paper. I think I deserved as much . . . even if you don't."

"It's not that, Kendall. I was planning on telling you. My partners and I were working on the final details. Apparently someone smelled a news story and wrote an article on it. I certainly wasn't expecting it, and I can't tell you how sorry I am about the whole thing."

"I'm sure," she said.

Clyde took in her unrelenting expression. "Come on, Kendall, you know me better than that."

"Do I? Tell that to my stomach. You see, it starts doing these little flips whenever I think about it, especially when I wonder if you have any other secrets hidden in your little bag of tricks."

"I'm not hiding anything. Like I said, I was going to tell

you when everything was final, when we could talk about what type of place the Sundowner—that's what we're calling it—would be. The only reason I didn't tell you during the negotiations was because I was afraid you'd be upset . . . and obviously I was right.''

Kendall's stubborn nature kicked in. The last thing she wanted to do was to prove him right. ''So why are you here now?'' she asked in a calm, controlled voice.

Clyde shrugged. ''I was hungry. You know I come here to eat all the time.''

''I haven't seen you here lately. Are you sure there's no other reason?'' she asked tonelessly.

Clyde slapped the counter with his palm. ''All right, Kendall, I've had enough of your insinuations. All I wanted was a sandwich. I don't have to submit to a cross-examination. Forget it. I'll go to Subway.'' He turned and left. Kendall watched until he went through the door, then she returned to her office, where she promptly vented her anger by picking up a pencil and breaking it in half.

Throughout her ritual of dressing, which always began with a leisurely soak in a bubble bath in her candlelit bathroom, Kendall wondered if she had made a mistake by inviting Spencer to the party. Her mother was bound to make a big fuss. Chan Ridgely had never accepted Kendall's own belief that the domesticity of marriage was simply not in her stars. Sometimes Kendall thought her mother took each of her failed relationships harder than she did. And she feared that once her mother learned Spencer was a successful entrepreneur, she was likely to embarrass them both in her almost certain efforts to push Kendall into Spencer's arms.

The thought of being in Spencer's arms made Kendall stretch provocatively in the bubble-laden, old-fashioned claw foot tub. She was bound to be wrapped in them for a good night kiss before the night was over, and she couldn't wait.

She raised a silky-smooth leg from the water and rubbed her skin with a thick washcloth. After that she did the other leg. The bubbles began to dissolve with her movements, and so did her reservations about being Spencer's date.

She had the music of her favorite recording artist, James Brown, playing on a portable CD player perched on the covered toilet seat. Usually Kendall preferred mellower music—George Benson or Luther Vandross—when she was "bubbling," but knowing she was going to be dancing tonight put her in a party mood. Now she found herself singing along as she prepared to leave the tub for the stall shower right next to it to rinse off. "I break out—duh-duh-duh-duh—in a coooooold sweat—duh-duh-duh . . . duuuuuh." She hit her crescendo right in step with the horns of James's band, the JBs.

Kendall knew she wasn't a singer, but what the hell, neither was James, not really. Besides, who was to know she was in the privacy of her own bathroom, making an utter fool of herself?

Directly downstairs Spencer was emerging from the shower when he heard Kendall yelling. His eyes narrowed in concern, then he realized she was alternately singing and humming to the catchy music of a classic James Brown number. She certainly didn't have much of a voice, he thought with a smile.

But a lack of musical gifts might well be her only draw-back. No doubt about it, Kendall Lucas had a lot going for her. Each time he saw her he felt more and more drawn to her. She was good-looking and smart, and they had more in common than she knew, being in the same business. Spencer regarded that as a plus. Only a restaurateur could truly understand another restaurateur—the long hours with split shifts, the urge to be the best, and the tireless devotion toward making it all happen. It certainly had been over Arjorie's head, he thought with a touch of amusement, thinking of his ex-wife.

He dried himself off. Kendall was still singing when he opened the bathroom door to return to his bedroom to dress. If she kept it up she would be as hoarse as he was.

"Wow!" Michelle exclaimed when Spencer emerged from his bedroom, clad in a tuxedo with a white jacket. "Going somewhere special?"

Brian and Carlton had similar reactions, jumping up from their spots in front of the television set to pat Spencer's sleeves admiringly. "Hey, watch the hands!" Spencer cautioned good-naturedly. "You guys have probably been eating greasy popcorn."

"So where're you going, Daddy?" Brian asked, as his younger brother echoed the query.

"I'm attending a formal party."

"Isn't it kind of early for that?" Michelle asked.

"It's outdoors, and I think part of the mystique is to be there when the sun sets. Besides, it's after six, so it's late enough to wear a tux."

Michelle glanced at her watch. "Yeah, but it's not much after. And whoever heard of a formal party outside?"

"Stop thinking barbecue, Michelle. Outdoor events can be very elegant in the right setting. We're talking tablecloths, centerpieces, and linen napkins, not wooden picnic tables that put splinters in your butt."

The boys giggled.

"What about the boys? I've got to leave soon for the club," Michelle said.

"It's okay. I'll probably be in by midnight. The boys will be all right for a while by themselves. I'll call and give them the number once I get to the party."

"We can always go to the club with you," Carlton suggested to Michelle, Brian quickly seconding the idea.

"Tomorrow night, when the younger kids come out. You don't have any business hanging out with high school kids," Spencer admonished his eleven-year-old.

The boys quickly returned their attentions to the television, but Michelle walked with Spencer to the front door. "Have a good time—hey, why are you going out this way?"

"What do you mean?"

She sighed. "Your car is parked out back, unc." She only called Spencer "unc" if she was making a valid point on something he had overlooked. Then her eyes widened in realization. "I'll bet I know why you're going out this door. You're taking Kendall, aren't you?"

"As a matter of fact, I am. It's her father's party."

"Oh, Spencer, I'm so happy for you!"

His brows knitted as his handsome features formed a frown. "Michelle, what are you talking about? I'm escorting a lady to a party, and you make it sound like I'm about to get married."

"I know you, Spencer Barnes. You are absolutely enchanted with Kendall."

"Good night, Michelle." Spencer stepped outside and closed the door on his niece's know-it-all smile.

That girl! he thought as he rang Kendall's front doorbell. But he knew Michelle was right. He was indeed mesmerized by his pretty upstairs neighbor. He had kept seeing her face and figure on the drive to Atlanta the night he almost kissed her. The sight of Kendall with her hair down around her shoulders and wearing a short robe that barely covered her hips warmed his blood. What was it that had prompted her to come up with that flimsy excuse about something burning on the stove, he wondered. She'd certainly been agreeable to the idea of him kissing her at the club. Maybe there was some other reason, something that would have been awkward for her to tell him. Another man, perhaps? No, that was unlikely. If Kendall had been entertaining a male guest she would have brought the man to the party with her instead of agreeing to go with him.

One thing for certain. Now that he had tasted her lips, he wanted more, much more. He had given up his inner struggle to maintain a polite but distant persona where she was involved. Professional conflicts and her proximity as his neighbor aside, he simply found himself unable to stay away from Kendall Lucas. All he could do was hope for the best when he told her the truth, which would have to occur before he got in too deep.

Then Spencer considered that it was probably already too late to worry about the depth of his feelings. Already Kendall automatically came to his mind whenever he happened to drive past a house that might be nice for himself and his sons. The whole thing made no sense. He'd just met the woman. He was thirty-eight years old, divorced for the better part of a decade, and had known for some time that he was ready for another try at domesticity with a special woman in his life, but nonetheless his thoughts were moving too quickly. Way too quickly.

Or maybe, he thought, it was because he felt Kendall would be perfect for him. Spencer had made a lot of good moves by listening to his instincts over the years, and now that inner voice was talking to him again, telling him to hold on tightly to Kendall and not to let go.

He heard her footsteps from inside as she tapped down the stairs. To his surprise the woman who opened the door for him was not dressed in some knockout ensemble as he had expected, but instead wore a flowing cotton caftan. Her hair was not pinned up like usual, but flowing and loose, the way it had been the night he brought her the spice cake. It was certainly becoming, but she looked like she was enjoying a quiet evening at home. He wondered if perhaps he had gotten the date of the party mixed up. Lord, how embarrassing that would be.

"Hi," she said. She grinned at his obvious confusion. "Yes, it's the right night," she said. "I'm not quite ready yet. But do come up. It'll only take me ten minutes, I promise."

"Sure," he said, relieved to know he hadn't shown up the wrong night in his formal dress.

"You look very handsome," Kendall said with approval. "I love a man in a white dinner jacket."

"Thanks." He followed her up the stairs, enjoying the view of the movements of Kendall's backside against the caftan. "You know, since we have a few minutes before we leave, I can make a quick run to the florist and get you a wrist corsage . . . once I know what color you're wearing," he suggested.

"Don't worry, I've got everything I need." She gestured toward her sofa. "You have a seat and make yourself comfortable. I'll be out in a sec."

She disappeared toward the bedrooms, and Spencer complied with her request. The fluffy peach sofa and other furnishings looked like they were brand new, he thought. Either that or she didn't use this room much. Funny how furniture could make a room look so different. His apartment had the same layout, but the dark brown sofa and accent tables his living room was furnished with made it difficult to believe it was essentially the same room as this soothing pastel paradise. As a decorator, he definitely got a D.

He leaned forward and helped himself to a piece of cheese Kendall had thoughtfully cut into squares and set out on the coffee table for him. There were sliced apples, too, and a bottle of wine and two stemmed glasses on the table as well. Holding it by its long neck, Spencer turned it around so he could see the label. California Chardonnay, from a vineyard whose name he recognized. He chuckled at his action as he poured himself half a glass. He supposed it was simply the habit of a restaurateur to always look at the label first. He should have known Kendall wouldn't serve him a cheap wine.

His chuckle was still dying down when he heard soft footsteps approaching. He turned—the couch was arranged to face the opposite direction—and the hand holding the wineglass slowly lowered itself to the table as he took in Kendall's appearance.

She was positively stunning in a short-sleeved, authentic Chinese cheongsam of glimmering silk in a print of pale yellow flowers—he'd guess lilies—on an ice blue background. The neckline was high and prim, with a diagonal line of buttons below and to the left of her throat, but the dress's high-cut sides left her legs exposed to midthigh.

Her hair was arranged in its usual French roll with her bangs framing her beautiful face, with a few dramatic differences. She had light blue combs with yellow flowers painted on them on the sides of her hair for added decoration, and her lips were painted a ruby red, as were her fingernails, while her upper and lower eyelids were rimmed with dark blue pencil. The cut of the dress showed off her beautifully rounded hips to fullest advantage.

"You look breathtaking," he said, rising to make his way to where she stood.

"I'm glad you approve." In her sudden shyness, her voice was almost as husky as his. She could see the wonder in his expression. This was the reaction she had dreamed of getting from him, she just hadn't expected to be so overcome by it.

He took her slender hand in his and in a gallant gesture, raised it to his lips. His gaze held hers as he kissed the back of her palm, and Kendall tried not to tremble. Talk about breaking out in a cold sweat!

His lips felt warm against her cool skin. "I can't tell you how lovely you look, Kendall," he said as he lowered her hand. He did not release it, but instead took her other hand in his and took a step back to continue to openly admire her. She wore high-heeled tan mules on her feet, and he noticed that her toes were painted the same luscious shade of red as her lips and fingernails. Everything about this woman pleased him—even her toes were sexy. "You know, I always thought your eyes have a slight tilt to them, but this dress really brings it out. You could almost pass for Asian."

They smiled at each other as their hands naturally fell apart. "Well, there's a reason for that," Kendall replied. "My mother happens to be half Chinese."

"Really?"

"Yes." Kendall walked over to the coffee table and poured herself a glass of wine. She took a sip before seating herself and continuing. "She's had the kind of life you read about in novels. She was literally left on the doorstep of a children's home when she was a baby. Her mother put a note in the basket that explained how she had shamed her family by getting pregnant, and how she had to give her baby up before they learned the child had been fathered by a black man, which apparently would turn her name to sewage rather than mere mud." Kendall paused and shook her head sadly. "Mom's mother wrote that her baby had been born three days before and that her name was Lily Chan. She also warned that her own last name was different, so there was no point in them trying to find her. That may or may not have been the truth, but her identity was never learned.

"Anyway, my mother grew up in that children's home. It's always been difficult for black children to get adopted, and her looks were too exotic for most people's taste. If you think I look Asian, wait till you see Mom."

Spencer sat a respectful distance away from Kendall on the sofa, so engrossed in her story he temporarily forgot his captivation with how lovely she looked. "So she wasn't adopted."

"No. She didn't have a happy childhood, either. The kids used to tease her about her looks. I'm sure they were partially motivated by jealousy, because Mom was so pretty. Anyway, when she was eighteen she got married—"

"To a black man."

"Oh, yes. Mom has always identified with the black community, even though everyone didn't always welcome her. I guess it was the only choice she could make. Her African roots were pretty obvious; no way could she pass for strictly Chinese. But Mom made a poor choice of a husband. He drank and was always out in the street somewhere. Eventually she left him and took a job in the county clerk's office to support her kids." Kendall's eyes grew misty. "She moved into a housing project, because it was the only place she could afford. It was a terrible place, let me tell you.

The elevators smelled like a toilet, all the walls were covered with spray-painted graffiti, and there were fights every single day.''

Spencer watched her intently. He saw the hard set to her jaw and knew she had been one of the children she had referred to in the third person. He knew she was revealing an important part of her emotional makeup to him.

Kendall's expression brightened. ''But then a number of years later she met a wonderful man at work. Actually, he worked in the city planner's office, and she married him just before he accepted a new position to rebuild the glory of Nile Beach.''

''Which he did,'' Spencer said.

''Yes. And I'm happy to say they're living happily ever after.''

''Quite a story. I get the feeling you're absolutely crazy about your stepfather.''

Kendall immediately stiffened. ''Technically Paul Ridgely is my stepfather, but to me he's just Dad. He's the only father I've ever known, or just about.''

''I, um . . . didn't mean to offend you, Kendall,'' he said cautiously. This was obviously a sore spot with her.

She nodded. ''I know. I shouldn't get so testy about it. It's just that my father—my biological father,'' she spat out in contempt, ''hasn't exactly been a major force in my life. I have practically no memories of him. He came to see us before we left Philadelphia and spent something like half an hour with us. Before that Mom said he hadn't been around since I was three years old. I'm thirty-four, Spencer, so you can see how interested he was in my brother and me.'' It occurred to her that she was now the same age her mother was when Paul Ridgely, the man who would become her great love, entered her life. It was just a coincidence that Spencer Barnes was now in *her* life, Kendall quickly told herself. Her neighbor was just so easy to talk to. She rarely discussed Kenneth Lucas with any-one—his abandonment was too painful, and she suspected it always would be. "Good grief, I'm just a blabbering fool tonight." She smiled at him. "Do you always make people talk so much?"

Spencer shrugged. "Not really. And I'll tell you something. I don't always enjoy listening as much as I just did."

Kendall smiled at him. He was sweet, but it was time for a change of pace to something more lighthearted. She really hadn't meant to say as much as she had—it was a private anguish she kept with her secret fears. "Are you about ready to go?" she asked.

"Sure. Can I help you put this away?"

"No, I'll get it. I'll only be a minute." She balanced the wineglasses on the tray with the cheese and fruit and carried it balanced on the palm of one hand, holding the wine bottle in the other. It was a risky move—especially in high heels—but she moved with such perfect symmetry and ease that he was sure she had once been a banquet waitress.

As they descended the steep stairs Kendall, unaccustomed to wearing heels, gripped the banister with one hand while Spencer, on her other side, guided her by the elbow. As she concentrated on keeping her balance—how the women presenters at the Academy Award ceremonies, many of whom were well into middle age, managed to get down those majestic staircases without the support of a banister was beyond her—Kendall took a moment to be glad she made it a practice to rub softening cream into her elbows and knees. Spencer's fingers suddenly stroked the supple skin of her lower arm, and it felt so good that Kendall made a sound that came out halfway between a sigh and a moan.

"Are you all right?" he asked instantly.

She was too embarrassed to look at him. "Yes, fine."

Spencer smiled. She had the smoothest skin of any woman he'd ever known. He could barely keep his hands off its soft, scented warmth. He longed to pull her into his arms and caress her all over while he kissed all that red from her lips.

Later, he told himself.

It was a promise he intended to keep.

CHAPTER FIVE

The Ridgely home was located on Attucks Drive in one of the more affluent sections of Nile Beach. Kendall was surprised to see that her mother had arranged for valet parking. A young man wearing a short-sleeved white shirt, dark slacks, and dark tie approached as Spencer pulled up. "Good evening," he said in greeting.

Spencer returned the salutation. He patted the steering wheel. "You will be careful, won't you? She's not new anymore, but I'm still quite fond of her."

"Of course, sir." The teenager glanced at Kendall and broke into a broad grin. "Hi, Kendall."

She leaned in closer for a better look. "Bobby? Is that you?"

"It's me, all right. Ronnie and I are parking cars for your parents' guests."

Kendall shook her head. "I can't believe it. You're practically grown."

"Seventeen next month. You really look pretty, Kendall."

"Thank you, Bobby," she replied, pleased by the compliment. Then the son of the family next door moved back to allow Spencer to alight.

Spencer walked around to the passenger side and held out a hand for Kendall to grasp. The movement as she turned her body to the side accentuated the high-cut side slits of her dress, exposing a generous portion of light brown thighs. The expanse made her shapely legs look even longer than usual, and he had to close his eyes momentarily to savor a mental picture of those thighs wrapped around his torso, squeezing his back passionately as he made furious love to her.

She grasped his hand, her hand disappearing in his larger one, and he helped her up, holding on tighter than he needed to. With her other hand she uncertainly patted her hair, and he whispered, "Don't worry, you look fine . . . just like Bobby said." Kendall giggled, and Spencer offered her his arm. He knew it was probably a corny thought, but he felt proud to be escorting such a beauty. He noted that in her high-heeled mules, she was nearly as tall as he was. It would make for comfortable kissing, he thought.

Her arm linked in his, they followed the neatly handwritten directional signs for the partygoers, which led to the matching door of a dark wooden privacy fence on the side of the house. Spencer opened the door, and together they entered a setting that was both formal and jovial.

Numerous round tablecloth-covered tables were set up at intervals in the large backyard, on both sides of a moderately sized oval pool. The band and dance floor were on the far side of the pool. Elegantly dressed guests mingled in little pockets, and the air was permeated with the sound of laughter and music. White-jacketed waiters offered the guests a selection of hot and cold hors d'oeuvre trays, and a staff of two took care of all the guests' beverage needs at a well-stocked bar.

Spencer recognized Kendall's mother immediately. Lily Ridgely wore a floor-length gown with the same cut as Kendall's dress, but more dramatic and ornate, with various shades of red, white, and yellow flowers against a black background. Lily's gown also had side splits, but more modest, cut only to just above the knee. She had allowed gray strands to invade what had certainly once been jet-black hair, and she wore it in a very short, flattering cut that projected youth despite the mature color. As Kendall had said, Lily's Chinese background was very obvious even at first glance. Her cheekbones were prominent and her eyes had an unmistakable upward slant at the outer corners, unlike Kendall's, which were more of a subtle accent.

"Kendall, dear!" she exclaimed, embracing her daughter and pressing her cheek against Kendall's. "You look beautiful."

"So do you. And everything is set up so nice. Mom, I want you to meet Spencer Barnes. Spencer, my mother, Chan Ridgely."

"Good evening, Mrs. Ridgely," Spencer said formally, firmly shaking the smooth manicured hand she offered him.

"Nice to meet you, Spencer. And please call me Chan."

"All right, Chan."

Kendall looked on, beaming. She had called ahead and pleaded with her mother not to overdo it, and she was happy to see her wishes were being honored. Her mother was handling the situation very well indeed. Anyone would think she brought dates home every week.

"You two find a seat. Your father is around here somewhere, Kendall. I'll let him know you're here."

"All right."

They took a seat on the side of the pool near the music. "Didn't you say your mother's name was Lily?" Spencer asked.

"Yes, but she hates it. I think it brings back all the unhappy memories of her childhood. Her first husband called her by her maiden name as a nickname, and it just kind of stuck."

The odd phrasing stuck in Spencer's brain. Chan's first husband. That would be Kendall's father. She was so impersonal toward the man who had sired her. Both of his own parents were now deceased, but he had fond memories of growing up surrounded by a large and loving family unit, and their annual vacations south to visit the extended clan in Palmdale. For Kendall it was only she, her mother, and her brother, struggling to eke out a living when it became apparent the traditional head of the household was unwilling to provide for them.

The band swung into a new number, and Spencer chuckled when he recognized the tune. "The Horse" had been a number one instrumental tune back in the late sixties, when he was just a kid. Many of the guests present flocked to the dance floor, and he realized that they, now well into their fifties or even older, had been young at the time the song was released, probably about the age he was now. It was amusing to watch a group of middle-aged people recreate their youth while they did the steps of the dance of the same title.

Zena and Barry showed up at the tail end of the number. Kendall performed introductions, and the Lucases joined them at their table. Spencer would have known Kendall's brother anywhere. Barry was tall and slim, like his sister; but the Asian part of his heritage was quite prominent, more like his mother's than the mere hint Kendall carried. His wife was striking, with flawless golden skin and her wavy hair cut into a sculpted do that tapered at the nape. A white flower was positioned over her left ear. "I've got to ask this," Spencer said, eyeing Zena's white dress, which was cut similarly to Kendall's but had cap sleeves instead of short ones. "Are these dresses the new style?"

Kendall laughed. "No, not really. Mom and Dad went to Hong Kong for their vacation, and Mom bought half the country while she was there. These cheongsams were our souvenirs. We just thought it would be nice if we all wore them tonight. You know, show a little solidarity."

Spencer nodded. "It's a nice look. Very flattering . . . to all of you." His gaze went back to Kendall, who met it with a warm smile.

"You look very handsome in your tux, Spencer," Zena remarked. As Spencer acknowledged the compliment she jabbed Barry in the ribs and added, "I tried to get this fella here to rent one, but he wasn't having any. It's hard enough to get him to put on a business suit."

"Actually, it's not a rental," Spencer explained. "I found myself attending a reasonable number of formal events and decided it was worthwhile to buy my own."

Kendall deliberately avoided looking at Zena, who she knew would be frantically trying to catch her eye to silently convey how impressed she was by this revelation.

Zena had to wait to speak up until Spencer and Barry walked over to the bar to get drinks for all of them. "A man with his own tuxedo," she said with admiration. "Now, that's class. You'd better hold on to him, Ken. I'd say you have a better chance of seeing Quincy Jones date a black woman than meeting another one like him."

Kendall giggled at the brutal honesty of her sister-in-law's observation. "But he's not mine to hold on to, Zee," she pointed out with more than a trace of wistfulness.

"Well, work on it, honey! He certainly seems willing to me. I love his voice. If I were to close my eyes I'd swear it was Harry Belafonte talking. I wonder if he sings."

"I don't know," Kendall replied absently. "But Zena, his living right downstairs from me seems too close for comfort. It can cause all kinds of problems."

"Listen, girl, you find yourself another apartment if you have to. Just don't give up on that man."

The band Kendall's mother hired to entertain her guests put an emphasis on older, classic tunes dating back to the sixties. Kendall studied the group, four men and a woman. They appeared to be in their thirties and forties, certainly not the age of rap specialists.

Lead vocals were alternated between the woman and one of the men. "I know most of you remember this one," the man said into the microphone as the musicians launched into the opening strains. Then he leaned away slightly and began to sing the lyrics to "Never, Never Found Me a Girl Who Loves Me Like You Do."

"Oh, yeah," Spencer said, slapping his thigh in obvious pleasure. "Eddie Floyd. Come on, Kendall, this is for us." He reached for her hand.

The song was a midtempo ballad, and after Spencer led her onto the dance floor he turned and pulled her into his arms, and they fell into the rhythm of a two-step. Their embrace was a close one, so close that Kendall was reminded of the old advertising slogan, "Nothing comes between me and my Calvins." She doubted there was enough space between their bodies to slip as much as a silk scarf through, but she didn't care. She loved being held this close to him, so close she could feel their respective fronts continually graze against each other, so close she could breathe in the unique chemistry of his cologne after it had blended with the warmth of his skin. She closed her eyes and allowed herself to think it was only the two of them, sharing a dance out in the cool breeze of a summer's evening.

Spencer permitted his hand to roam across her slender back. He breathed in the sweet, natural scent of Kendall's skin. Even now she didn't appear to be wearing cologne, which was fine with him. Too many women tended to be heavy-handed with the stuff, much to the distaste of his nose; and they tended to put it in the wrong places, forgetting that while it was pleasantly scented it had an extremely unpleasant, alcohol-laden taste. Still, there was a hint of fragrance about Kendall tonight, perhaps from a special soap, that had not been evident the only previous time he had been this close to her. Spencer liked Kendall's earthiness, the way she was completely feminine without concealing her face under layers of makeup and smothering herself in perfume. Her only regular beauty routine seemed to be getting her nails done.

He closed his eyes for a moment and breathed in her

scent. There was no denying that his thoughts toward Kendall were anything but neighborly.

Spencer's thoughts suddenly became analytical—the businessman was back. Again he told himself it was fruitless to pursue Kendall, for not only one, but two reasons. Besides the fact that he owned a competing business, her living right upstairs would cause all kinds of complications. There was no way he could become involved with her without becoming proprietary. His body tensed at the mere thought of some other man ringing her doorbell. On one hand, he liked the idea of a relationship that was 100 percent voluntary. He wouldn't want her to be feel she had an obligation to see him exclusively, but, on the other hand, he hoped that as the woman in his life she would have no desire for contact with any other man. But somehow Kendall Lucas didn't strike him as the type of woman who wanted strong emotional ties to one special man. For one thing, she was wholly devoted to running her two restaurants. On top of that, he suspected she didn't have a particularly fond view of family life, probably stemming from her own difficult childhood.

Kendall, her left hand resting lightly on Spencer's shoulder, felt his muscles tighten beneath her palm. She opened her eyes and stole a glance at him, wondering if she should ask if anything was wrong. But his expression seemed like he was content, so she relaxed. Perhaps he had just experienced some sort of spasm.

She noticed the grins and nods in their direction from others on the dance floor as well as from people at tables. Apparently she and Spencer made a handsome couple. Kendall happily returned the smiles.

To her delight, Spencer began to sing along softly. His natural huskiness did not prevent him from having a fine singing voice. Kendall unwittingly tightened her grip on his hand when he got to the part about his woman being every poor man's dream and every rich man's prayer. Did Spencer think of her as the answer to a prayer, she wondered. It was certainly a nice thought . . . but then again, it was just a song lyric.

Her dreamy mood continued until the song ended. They applauded the band for a few moments, then Spencer took her elbow and escorted her back to their table, which was empty except for their four drinking glasses. "Oh, that was nice," Kendall said as she lowered her body into the chair Spencer pulled out for her. "Thank you."

"I enjoyed it, too."

The next number was a popular James Brown tune from years gone by. Spencer chuckled as a sixtyish man gyrated to the music, rather jerkily imitating the legendary smooth movements of the Godfather of Soul while the others on the floor cheered him on. "Who's that?" he asked Kendall.

"That's Oscar Signeous. He's a friend of my parents'. Nice enough man, but he drinks like a fish. He's probably already half plastered, but age hasn't done anything to slow down his consumption." Kendall took a moment to study the platter of mini-quiches offered by a black-vested waitress. "I love these. I'm going to take two," she said conspiratorially, her words punctuated with a sunny smile.

"Help yourself," the waitress replied pleasantly. "You, sir?" she said, turning her attentions toward Spencer.

"Sure, why not. I never believed that line about real men and quiche."

"Kendall, why aren't you dancing?" Zena asked as she returned to her seat. "You know your mom had the band play James Brown just for you." Without waiting for an answer she turned to Spencer. "This girl just loves her some James Brown."

Spencer almost said, "I know." He caught himself and instead said, "Who didn't love James in his heyday?"

"That's right," Kendall agreed. "I used to run to the record store every time he came out with a new record."

"You must have done a lot of running," Zena said. "The man didn't go three weeks without putting something out."

"Part one, part two," Spencer shot back.

The three of them laughed uproariously at the memory of youth, when their largest concerns were frivolous matters, like having the latest records.

The evening was progressing perfectly. Spencer and Barry had made another trip to the bar and Zena had gone in to call her baby-sitter when Kendall finally caught sight of her father. She rose to go greet him.

He was talking with Nile Beach's mayor, but stopped to give her a bear hug. "There's my girl. How are you, dear?"

"Just wonderful."

"I guess so," Paul Ridgely said, winking in the direction of the mayor. "I saw you and your young man dancing."

"Oh, Dad." Kendall suddenly felt like a shy seventeen-year-old. She supposed her father would be able to make her feel that way even after she was into her forties.

Paul hugged her again. "Jim, you know my daughter Kendall, don't you?"

"Oh, yes. Soul Food to Go."

Kendall shook the mayor's hand. "I'll bet you know all the business owners in town by corporate name."

"Even if I don't know their real names," the official replied with a smile. "Nice to meet you, Kendall." After a brief chat he excused himself and promptly joined another nearby group.

"So," Paul said to Kendall, "where's your date? I'd like to meet the man who put this smile on your face."

"He and Barry are getting drinks. Oh, here they come." She waved her hand high until she caught their attention.

Kendall tried to keep the pride out of her voice as she introduced Spencer to her father, not entirely succeeding.

"Glad to meet you, Mr. Ridgely," Spencer said sincerely as he shook Paul's hand. "And congratulations on your retirement. You've certainly earned it. Nile Beach is back on the map, better than ever."

"Thanks. I suspect my daughter's been doing some bragging."

"Well, maybe just a little," Spencer admitted.

"You're familiar with this area?"

"I have family in Palmdale. I recently moved here from Atlanta."

"Job transfer?"

Spencer chuckled. He suspected Paul Ridgely was feeling him out. "No, not really. I'm an independent businessman and decided to make the most of the opportunities that exist here. Besides, it's a good place for my boys."

Paul nodded. "I can still recall how excited Kendall and Barry were when they got their first look at Florida. Of course, they were nearly grown when they got here. Barry was just a few months shy of eighteen, and Kendall was fifteen. How old are your children?"

"Two boys, eleven and twelve. They love it already."

Kendall was talking quietly with her brother when she saw a figure in a floral print halter dress approaching. "Hi, Vick!" she exclaimed.

Her friend Vicky Sanders gave her a warm hug, then did the same with Barry. "Hey, I thought you weren't coming," Barry said to his sister's longtime friend, "because you couldn't get anyone to work in your place."

"Unfortunately I couldn't," Vicky replied. "I'll have to leave soon, but I just had to stop by for a little bit. Everything looks so gorgeous, Kendall. Your mom did a fabulous job."

"She did, didn't she?" Kendall agreed. She looked at her friend closely. She seemed jittery, and her eyes had an unusual sparkle. "You look like you're about to bust, Vicky," she commented.

"That's because I've got to tell you something."

"Uh-oh," Barry said good-naturedly. "This is my cue to exit. See y'all."

"So what's up?" Kendall asked when her brother had gone.

"Well, I heard George Graves is sick. I mean, deathly ill."

"Oh, no!" Kendall exclaimed in dismay. George Graves

was an important man in the history of Nile Beach. He had heavy involvement in the town's government, as well as in the handling of racial tensions that occasionally flared, stemming from the resentment of whites in Palmdale and other neighboring communities of the residents' independence and lack of demand for their goods and services. It was sad to hear he might pass away, even though he was very old, she knew, well into his nineties. Then she realized what her friend was getting at. "Oh . . . that means Danny will probably be coming down."

"Uh-huh." Vicky tried to look somber—it was, after all, an unhappy situation—but she was not successful.

Kendall understood. Danny Graves, grandson of George, had been Vicky's first serious romance in their senior year of high school, on past graduation and into classes at the local community college. They eventually broke up and went their separate ways, Danny to Atlanta and Vicky to Miami. Vicky, newly divorced and with a young daughter, had recently returned to the security and familiarity of her hometown, but it was obvious she relished the thought of seeing Danny again after so many years. Kendall felt a desire to protect her friend, who was presently at a vulnerable stage of her life. "Listen," she said, choosing her words carefully, "I know you're looking forward to seeing him, and I know he's not married anymore either. But that doesn't mean he's not engaged, or even seriously involved with someone."

Vicky nodded knowingly. "I know what you're saying. 'Don't get your hopes up.' I know you're concerned and I do appreciate it, believe me. And I'll try to keep my emotions in check." She giggled. "I had no idea it was so obvious."

"It's about as subtle as the proverbial neon sign."

Vicky pointed with her chin toward Spencer, who stood talking with Kendall's father, then spoke in a whisper. "Good Lord, Kendall, is that the neighbor you said you were coming with?"

"That's him."

"Goodness, girl, he's flawless."

Kendall suppressed a smile. "Yes, it would seem so, wouldn't it?"

"You must introduce me before I leave. Oh, there's Ava and her date. C'mon, let's go say hi."

Chan Ridgely approached her husband, and as Spencer watched her get closer he remembered someone once telling him that the best way to see how a woman would age was to look at her mother. Chan surely was closer to sixty than fifty, and she certainly was still quite a lovely woman. "I see you've met Kendall's friend," she said to Paul, beaming at Spencer.

"Yes, we've been talking."

"I hope you're enjoying yourself, Spencer," Chan said.

"Absolutely. It's a lovely party." The strains of a classic Temptations number floated over to Spencer's ears. "Chan, would you like to dance?"

"Why, thank you, Spencer. I'd love to." She turned to her husband. "Excuse us."

"Look, Kendall, there's your fella dancing with your mom."

Kendall was so intrigued by that scenario she didn't bother to remind Vicky that Spencer was not "her fella."

"He's real handsome," said their mutual friend Ava Maxwell. "And I hear he actually has his own tux. Now, how often do you run into somebody like that?"

"About as often as you run into white men named Denzel," Vicky cracked.

Kendall sighed. Apparently Zena had spread the word about Spencer's tuxedo to their friends. Fortunately, their ribbing of her was interrupted by the appearance of David Ridgely, who put an arm around each of his sister's best friends. "Look at me, I'm with the best-looking women in the joint."

"No arguments here," Vicky said with a smile.

"Hi, stranger," Kendall greeted.

"We wouldn't be such strangers if you hadn't been in such a tearing hurry coming out of Robinson's the other week."

"Oh, were you there?"

"I was just parking when you came out. I honked at you, but you didn't even look up."

Kendall averted her gaze. "I . . . must have had something on my mind." And she had, namely Spencer. That was the night she had learned he and Michelle were actually uncle and niece. "You know I would never deliberately snub you." She glanced at the area behind her brother. "Hey, didn't you bring someone?"

David shrugged. "I thought about it, but I knew she had to work so I didn't ask. Besides, I knew you three would be here. Come on, let's dance."

"All of us?" Ava asked, giggling.

"Sure."

"If you think you can handle it," Vicky countered.

The four of them joined the others on the dance floor, with the three women surrounding an obviously exhilarated David. Kendall was caught up in the fun and didn't notice Spencer's presence behind her until he reached for her hand and pulled her to him. "Hey, I'm jealous. Why don't you let me have a little bit of what that guy's got?"

Kendall took a moment to wave to her mother, who was exiting the floor. "Oh, but he's special," she said teasingly. "As a matter of fact, he's got my heart."

She enjoyed the look of disappointment that flashed across Spencer's handsome features. "Is there something you maybe didn't tell me?" he asked. "You know, like you're spoken for?"

She giggled at his use of the outdated phrase. "Spencer, that man over there will always have part of my heart."

"And why is that?" Spencer asked. He was actually panicking. He knew very little about Kendall's private life—

not that he could blame her, for, of course, he was keeping a rather important piece of information about himself from her—and now he found himself wondering if there might be someone special in her life after all, someone who had been at her apartment the night he left for Atlanta. After all, she had been dressed in her nightclothes, and she'd been in an awful hurry to get away from him when he started to kiss her. Perhaps the only reason Kendall agreed to let him escort her was because this preferred companion was away and she hadn't expected him to be able to make it. . . .

She was being maddeningly silent. Spencer made himself sound as casual as he could, but despite his efforts his words rang with anxiety. "Seriously, Kendall, what's the deal here?"

"He's my brother."

Spencer looked at Kendall, not sure if she was teasing or telling the truth. Then he glanced at David. Their complexions weren't too far off, but that was the only thing they had in common. There was absolutely no resemblance. Nor did this stocky man of average height have Kendall's and Barry's tall, slim builds.

She watched his reaction, then companionably took his arm. "Come with me, and I'll tell you all about it."

CHAPTER SIX

"I can tell you don't believe me," she stated as they walked toward the front of the Ridgely home, well away from the other guests.

"I didn't say I didn't believe you, Kendall."

"You don't have to, it shows. Are you jealous?"

"Yes," Spencer replied flatly. It was the truth. But in his heart he knew he had no right to feel that way, none at all.

Kendall felt a tad ashamed of herself for worming Spencer's feelings out of him, but nonetheless she was thrilled to learn how he felt. She released his arm and faced him squarely, her hands clasped in front of her. "Well, this is the story. Dad was married before too, and one day when he, his wife, and their son David were in their car someone who had never had a seizure before had one while he was driving. His car hit theirs head-on, but most of the impact was on the passenger side. Dad's wife was killed, and both he and David were hurt pretty bad. David was just three at the time."

Spencer nodded, now understanding the reason for the lack of resemblance between Kendall and her younger brother. "So he's actually your—" he caught himself just in time, suddenly remembering her vehement response to his observation of Paul Ridgely being her stepfather.

But this time there was no agitation in Kendall's response, just an earnestness he found touching. "I've known David since he was a kid in the first grade, learning how to write his name. He's been a part of my family since he was in the second grade. He's my brother, Spencer, just plain brother. In many ways I'm closer to him than I am to Barry, even though David's so much younger than we are, because we also have a working relationship. He manages my original restaurant, the little drive-through on Main Street. And that reminds me," she said as Spencer acknowledged this information, "I really need your advice about something. You've got so many ideas about business. I have a potential disaster on my hands. . . ."

She explained to him about how the new restaurant in the Sunrise Hotel was almost certain to make her lose the monies generated by the hotel's guests, as well as possibly interfere with her other patrons as well. "How can I fight back? I've got a tremendous mortgage on that building, and I can't afford to lose a dime."

Fortunately for Spencer, Kendall was so concerned about the situation that she failed to notice him biting his lower lip as she spoke. "I understand your being worried, Kendall, but the fact is that restaurants are springing up all over Nile Beach. Your place might not be the first choice for people to go to this time, say, next year."

"I know. But I'll be firmly established by then, while now I'm just getting started. People who eat at Soul Food to Go remember it . . . and nine times out of ten they come back. Like you and Michelle did."

"That's right. But what you're not realizing is that even if people do go to the Sunrise to eat, it's doubtful they won't ever go anywhere else."

Kendall sighed. He had a point, of course, but it wasn't like she expected to have the monopoly on Nile Beach diners. That was being completely unreasonable, but she felt there was good reason to be concerned. "Sure," she said. "They might go to the Japanese restaurant the next day, and the Italian place the day after that, and then go for seafood. That makes sense—they all have different cuisine. But how likely are people to try two soul food restaurants? They usually have a favorite, or they go by word of mouth. From what I've read, the place at the Sunrise sounds like it's going to be the hot spot in town. Where does that leave for Soul Food to Go?"

Spencer hated seeing her look so worried. "Listen," he said, putting an arm around her shoulders, "let me make a suggestion. It's really a lovely night, and the truth is you look too beautiful to make me want to discuss business. Let's enjoy ourselves, and we'll get together another time and talk strategy. When you aren't quite so distracting."

She smiled broadly, not bothering to hide her pleasure at the compliment, but at the same time she didn't want him to forget his promise. "I really could use your help with this, Spencer."

"I promise you'll get it. I know how important this is to you. And I also promise it won't be as bad as you think. Now, do we have a deal?"

"Deal."

"Good. Let's seal it." He had bent his head before she could respond. The kiss only lasted a moment, for both of them knew this was not the place for an ardent display of affection.

Afterward neither of them spoke. Instead, with Kendall's soft hand covered by Spencer's rough one, they silently walked around to the back of the house to rejoin the festivities.

When the sun set, numerous Japanese lanterns and pool lights provided ample illumination for the guests, and the dimmed light served as a type of invisible signal for inhibitions to be tossed aside. The one with the most reserve to lose was Oscar Signeous, who was never at a loss for middle-

aged women to dance with as he practiced his fancy foot-
work, including a step that reminded Spencer of Rufus
Thomas and the Funky Chicken. At one point Oscar was
partner to two women who were dressed in identical pink
dresses and appeared to be twins. The women were about
sixty or so and both were twenty-five or thirty pounds over-
weight. Their dresses fit them a little snugly through the
middle, and Spencer wondered with amusement if they
made it a habit to dress alike.

Oscar's antics aside, Spencer was surprised at Kendall's
display of spirit. When the band launched into the electric
slide song, she joined the group of mostly women on the
floor and soon kicked off her high-heeled mules, apparently finding them too restricting. Spencer watched as she
made a simple series of walking steps—the Electric Slide
was just an updated version of the Bus Stop dance so
popular in the seventies in her hometown of Philadelphia—into a work of erotica. Kendall put more movement
into her upper body than the others. Her hips swayed
tantalizingly and her legs seemed endless when she
extended them in front of her in the side-slit cheongsam
as she turned. He watched, mesmerized, effectively tuning
out the other dancers so that it appeared her seductive
movements were for him alone. He licked his lips, wishing
it was the sweetness of Kendall's mouth he was tasting
instead.

From there the band swung into the reggae-flavored
party classic, "Feelin' Hot Hot Hot." The dancers immediately formed a conga line, Kendall at the helm. Many of
the guests joined in, and those who didn't stood at their
tables and gave in to the call of the infectious Caribbean
rhythm, dancing where they stood.

Kendall's French roll loosened in her frenzied activity,
and by the time she retrieved her shoes and walked toward
him, the entire arrangement had come loose. It looked,
Spencer felt, very becoming, especially since she had nothing to do with the sexy way the black locks cascaded around
her face. He swallowed hard, his Adam's apple bobbing

furiously, and he had to shift positions as his slacks began to tighten around his groin. He wondered if her hair was tousled like that when she woke up in the morning.

Maybe one day he would get to find out.

"I think we can probably call it a night," Kendall said a few minutes before midnight.

"Oh, no, not yet," Spencer replied with a smile. "We have to dance first."

Kendall nodded. The band was following up the rousing previous numbers with a George Benson ballad. The jazz balladeer was Kendall's second favorite recording artist after James Brown, and while the lead singer was no George Benson, he got by.

Spencer wasted no time gathering her in his arms. He was glad when she showed no resistance. After just a few moments she sighed softly and rested the side of her head against his shoulder.

"Tired?" he asked.

"A little. I'm too old for all this wild partying."

"You were wild, all right. But no one's really leaving. Are you sure it'll be okay if we do? After all, you're part of the host family."

"I told my parents I'd probably be making an early exit. Not that it's all that early."

She was right about that, Spencer thought. The party had been going on for more than four hours. The Ridgely's friends were quite a spry bunch . . . not that he expected to find himself wheelchair-bound in twenty years, which was roughly the difference between his age and theirs.

It helped that the hors d'oeuvres trays were still being passed. Chan had opted for these rather than a dinner, which Spencer knew tended to slow down the pace of an evening. All night long he had stuffed himself with tasty morsels like coconut fried shrimp, roast beef pinwheels, catfish fingers, bacon-wrapped scallops and other finger foods. The caterers were excellent. Spencer made a mental note to get their name for future use. The bar was open, too, although now coffee was also being served. None of the guests appeared to be inebriated with the exception of the Ridgely's friend Oscar Signeous, who was talking with another man by the pool. His intoxication was evident by both his louder-than-necessary voice and the wild gestures he was making with his hands. Nearly every other word was accentuated with a movement of either hand or body.

On the dance floor, Spencer's arms tightened around Kendall, as he rubbed the bare skin of her arms, leaving a warm tingly feeling in its wake. "I just want you to know that you really do look lovely," he said softly.

"Thank you." Kendall lifted her face to his. He looked so handsome, she thought. The moonlight softened his sharp, distinct features. "I'm glad we came to the party together, Spencer," she said, her words for his ears alone.

He nodded, not taking his eyes off her beautifully expressive face. At that instant Kendall felt something sweep through her, a nameless premonition that told her she belonged right here, in Spencer's embrace. She had never, ever had that feeling about any man in her whole life. It was as if someone had sprinkled her with a magic potion.

But Spencer felt it, too. Suddenly he knew that Kendall Lucas was the woman he had been waiting for, the special person destined to be his life's partner. But unlike Kendall, he was able to identify the feeling.

He was falling in love with her.

Kendall was still gazing up at him, not even aware of what she was hoping for until Spencer's face was actually moving toward hers. Even then her expression did not change. She felt no fear, no anxiety, just a wonderful feeling from within that this was as it should be. Nothing had ever felt so perfect, so honest and good. Maybe she wasn't so different from other women after all. . . .

Spencer lifted his hands to loosely cup her cheeks. He pressed his lips to hers, and a contented sigh escaped from her throat. Spencer teased her lips by biting them gently, then brushing his tongue over them, which only served to make her hungry for more.

But, of course, this was no place for her to kiss him with the passion pent up inside her. When their lips separated she had to be content by burrowing even closer to him, oblivious to everyone and everything except Spencer, the moon, the stars, and the music.

"Kisses in the moonlight, hmm?"

"And what of it, Zena?" It was just like her sister-in-law to make a sly, knowing comment, even if it was only the title of the song they had just danced to. Zena and Barry would probably never be so demonstrative. That made Kendall curious, for she knew nothing about long-term love affairs—and very little about short-term ones, she thought grimly—and she thoughtfully asked, "Is that what marriage does to people? Kill the romance?"

"No," Zena replied matter-of-factly. "You just learn to be more dignified about it."

Although Spencer had done his share of socializing—throughout the evening he engaged in conversation with Kendall's various family members and friends, as well as the mayor and others present—he managed to do a fair amount of quiet observation as well. Now he watched Kendall make her way across the wide yard as she sought out her mother to make sure Chan had no objections to her leaving. He felt he could never get tired of looking at her. She had a graceful way about her movements—she seemed to be literally floating through the pockets of people who stood talking on the grounds. Her rounded hips against the accommodating silk fabric of her dress seemed to have a life of their own. He was madly anticipating what would transpire between them when he brought her home.

She had almost reached her parents when, just as she detoured around by the edge of the pool to avoid running into Oscar, he suddenly stretched his hands outward to accent something he was saying—and sent Kendall sprawling into the cool water of the pool.

Spencer was up in an instant as a mass, "Ooh!" sounded among the guests at the sudden splashing sound. Kendall sputtered briefly and then, soaking wet, dog paddled a few strokes to the metal ladder to climb out, her mules in her hand. He pushed his way through the crowd that instantly gathered around in time to extend a hand to Kendall as she emerged, tearful and dripping, from the pool. Her dress clung to her figure like a second layer of skin.

Chan, too, had made her way to the forefront. "Quick, in the house," she said to Spencer, then led the way. Spencer, his body directly behind Kendall's, practically ran her to the back door—he didn't like the lustful way the men present were looking at her. For her part, Kendall's free hand was crossed over her breasts, effectively concealing this part of her figure from view.

The caterers were in the kitchen, preparing to bring a large sheet-style cake outside. The staff wore curious expressions but all stepped aside silently to let them pass.

"Oh, God, my dress is ruined," Kendall moaned.

"No, it's not. I'll rinse out the chlorine and then soak it in Woolite," Chan replied in a deliberately cheerful voice.

"Anything I can do?" Spencer asked, not wanting to follow them; they were obviously going to a bedroom so Kendall could dry off and change clothes.

"Not right now, but don't go far; I'm sure Kendall will need you," Chan said over her shoulder just before she and Kendall disappeared around a corner. "Come on, into the bathroom you go," she said to her daughter. "Help yourself to a towel. I'll get you something dry."

Kendall obediently did as she was told.

Paul Ridgely rushed in as Spencer awkwardly waited in the kitchen, his expression a mix of anxiety and concern. "That was Kendall who fell in the pool? What's going on?"

"She's changing. I'm going to take her home as soon

as she's ready. I think she was very embarrassed by the whole thing. But don't worry, sir," Spencer replied confidently, "she'll be fine. I just don't think she wants to face the other guests after what happened."

Paul nodded thoughtfully. "Okay," he said to the catering staff, "let's go on as usual. Serve the cake. The band was about to take a break, but I'll tell them to play something upbeat first."

An exuberant Hugh Masekela number was being performed when Kendall emerged, her towel-dried hair neatly tied back, her makeup washed off, and now wearing a slightly-too-large sheath that apparently belonged to Chan. "Spencer, I want to go home," she said dejectedly.

He was at her side in an instant. "Come on, baby," he said protectively. "We'll go out the front door so nobody will see us."

Kendall nodded. He took her arm and led her through the hall and out the front door. Her movements were stiff, he noticed. "It's all right," he whispered. "I'll have you home soon."

He drove home with only his left hand on the wheel; his right was clasping her lower arm. Finally he could bear the silence no longer. "It could have happened to anyone, Kendall. And I'm sure your dress will be fine. So cheer up, please?"

"Oh, Spencer, it was just so embarrassing," she said fervently. "Everybody there was looking at me. It's the type of thing that makes you wish you were invisible." She sighed loudly. "That Oscar! Why did he have to choose that moment to spread his hands like that? What was he doing, anyway . . . telling the man how big a fish he caught?"

Spencer laughed, and Kendall, already feeling better now that she was away from a hundred pairs of curious eyes, joined in. She felt better already, now that it was just her and Spencer.

They were just about to cross the border that separated Nile Beach from Palmdale when Spencer saw a flashing blue light in the rear view mirror. "Uh-oh, we've got company," he said as he pulled over.

"What does he want?"

"I guess I was going kind of fast. He's probably going to give me a ticket. That's all I need."

He sighed as he waited for the man in blue to get out. He sure was taking his time, but even as he had the thought Spencer knew the officer was running a quick check of his license plate to make sure the Saab was not listed as a stolen vehicle. In the meantime, he got his registration out of the glove compartment and took his license out of his wallet in preparation for the inevitable.

He stayed seated behind the wheel when the policeman finally alighted and approached the driver's side. He was black, Spencer saw, a large brown-skinned man who probably could stand to lose thirty or forty pounds. Immediately he tensed. His experience with black cops was that some tended to be worse than the white ones.

"Good evening. License and registration, please," the officer requested.

Spencer handed them over.

"You're from Georgia," the officer remarked after taking a moment to examine the documents.

"Yes. I just moved to Palmdale a few months ago."

"Well, Mr. Barnes, in Nile Beach the speed limit is thirty-five miles an hour. You were doing forty-eight. We have very strict rules about speeding in our community."

"I'm sorry, officer. I guess I didn't realize how fast I was going. I'm bringing someone home who just had an accident, and I was sort of in a rush."

The officer bent to look in the passenger seat. "You all right, ma'—Kendall!"

Kendall smiled at the sight of an old friend. "Robert. Hi. Fancy meeting you here."

"Are you hurt?"

"Not too bad. I got knocked into the pool at my parents' party by a guest who'd had one too many drinks. I hit my head on the side of the pool when it happened. Spencer wanted to get me home quickly so I can lay down." It was a lie—she had fallen in such a way that she sustained no injury other than to her pride—but she felt if she embellished a bit Spencer might get off without a ticket.

Robert didn't hesitate. "I heard about your father retiring. Gee, it's too bad this had to happen. Tell you what. Everything looks in order. I'll let you go this time." He returned the paperwork to a grateful Spencer. "Where do you live, Kendall?"

Kendall stated her address.

"Okay. I'll give you a police escort. Follow me."

"Oh, Robert, that's so sweet."

"Hey, what are friends for?"

"What are friends for?" Spencer repeated as he pulled out behind the squad car. "Friend of yours, I gather."

"That's certainly a brilliant conclusion," she said with a giggle.

"Old flame?"

"Don't knock it. He saved your butt, didn't he?"

"He doesn't really look like your type."

"He looked a little different when I dated him, about thirty pounds lighter. But they say that's what marriage does to you. His wife is probably a great cook."

"Uh-huh," Spencer replied, thoughtful. Wife. At least that meant Officer Robert wasn't interested in renewing old acquaintances, which was just the way he wanted it.

At her door Spencer hesitated. "I know you're tired," he began.

"But would you come in for just a little while?" Kendall was still feeling downcast in spite of their laughter on the drive home. She would welcome company for a little while. Maybe she could regain the aura of gaiety she had felt earlier.

They sat on the sofa. She put on some music, a classic George Benson tape of mostly instrumental cuts. Spencer removed his jacket—he had placed a quick call to the boys while he was waiting for Kendall to change at her parents', and he knew they were fine—and Kendall retrieved a compact comb from her purse and attempted to run it through her wet, tangled locks.

"That's better. Now I won't have such a mess on my hands when it's completely dry," she remarked. She reached for her mother's wide barrette to put it back in place.

"No," Spencer said. "Leave it loose. I like it."

She smiled at him. "All right." She put the barrette back on the coffee table, then moved in close to where he sat, her head resting against his shoulder.

He stroked her upper arm. "I had a good time, Kendall. Thank you for inviting me."

"Thank you for accepting," she replied. "And I'm sorry about your tux. At least let me have it cleaned for you." Spencer had gotten some of the chlorine-containing pool water on him as he guided her into the house, resulting in some faint green-tinged water spots on his white jacket.

"Absolutely not. I was going to have it cleaned anyway."

"Well, if you're sure . . . I think that party will be the talk of the town," she replied. "Mom and Dad are so happy together, and I'm glad. Both of them went through so much, what with Mom's bad time with her first husband . . ."

There she goes again, he noted.

". . . and Dad's losing David's mother and almost losing David. The poor kid was in a coma for three days, you know. Anyway, it's nice to know that good things sometimes come to those who've had it rough."

"What about you?" he asked.

"I haven't exactly had it rough, Spencer. At least not as an adult."

"No, but . . . can you imagine yourself settling down?"

"I am settled. I even bought this new furniture we're sitting on. Set me back—"

"Seriously, Kendall," he interrupted.

She knew he was serious, but it was a subject she felt uncomfortable discussing because of her lack of success on the romantic front. "I doubt it," she said with a trace of sadness. She had never admitted it to a living soul, but although she had done her fair share of dating over the years, Kendall had never been in love. She was thirty-four years old and feared Spencer would probably think there was something grossly wrong with her. Often she thought there must be something wrong with her. How many women her age could make such an outrageous statement? But the truth was none of the men she knew could empathize with her desire for success. The restaurant business was hard work, involving long days that often stretched into nighttime; and in the days when operating a place of her own was just a dream she was busy putting in as many hours as possible at the various restaurants she worked at and observing every management decision made. The men she met quickly became disillusioned with her devotion to her work. Some even tried to encourage her to give up her dream. Before too long Kendall had learned the danger signs of what was developing into a fruitless situation, and in the end she shed no tears when each relationship petered out almost as quickly as it began, knowing it was the only possible finale.

Even in high school she had not been involved in an end-all first romance, like what her friend Vicky had with Danny Graves. It had been over fifteen years, yet Vicky was so excited at the idea of seeing Danny again she could hardly contain herself. Kendall envied her for that. She supposed some people simply were not meant to have that special spark of love in their lives. But at least she had something to fill her days. Operating her two restaurants was largely like running a household . . . but a restaurant couldn't provide comforting touches for her at night, the way Spencer was doing now. . . .

Both of them grew quiet. Spencer sensed Kendall's wistful mood and thought it best not to question her further. He waited, thinking she might want to say something, but she seemed content to simply sit close to him and enjoy the music. Holding her was certainly fine with him, even if it only served to make him want more. He wasn't about rushing a woman into bed, and Kendall wasn't just any woman. Just because he wanted her so desperately was no excuse for lecherous behavior. And if he did feel his ardor was getting out of control all he had to do was think of the secret he was keeping from her. It would bring him back to reality in hurry.

Just thinking about how worried she had looked when she asked for his help made him uncomfortable. If he had any sense at all he'd get his jacket and leave. How could he possibly pull this off?

"Spencer?"

"Hmm?"

"You all right?" Kendall asked.

"Yes, why?"

"You seemed to tighten up, like you're on guard against something."

He realized she sat close enough to him to be able to sense the sudden constriction of his chest. He relaxed and immediately resumed stroking her arm. "No, I'm fine," he lied. He leaned forward and touched his lips to her hair. It was damp and smelled slightly of chlorine. Kendall's eyes were closed. After a long day and evening she looked completely at ease.

For the next few minutes the only sound in the room was that of George Benson's guitar and the instruments of the back-up musicians. Spencer began to sing along softly to "This Masquerade." He paused as a musical bridge played, then became aware of Kendall's soft and even breathing. She was asleep.

He eased her limp form back into a sitting position. So much for what would happen between them upon their return, he thought wryly. Poor Kendall was exhausted. It was definitely time for him to go. "Kendall," he said softly.

Her response was just a murmured phrase, made unintelligible by sleep. Apparently she was one of those people who skipped the groggy stage and went straight into a deep repose. Then again, the wine she had consumed at the party probably was a contributor as well.

Gently he shook her shoulders, and this time she opened her eyes, but she was frowning, obviously displeased at having her slumber interrupted. Without a word she closed her eyes again and leaned backward until she was completely reclining in the cushions of the sofa.

He chuckled. Clearly she was content where she was. She certainly looked comfortable . . . and very, very sexy. Her damp hair hung loosely around her face, and there appeared to be a slight smile on her lips. He liked to think he had put it there. Was she seeing him as she slept, he wondered.

As Spencer gazed at her, he was reminded of his growing desire for a special woman in his life, one that he would come home to every night, one to share his life with as he watched his sons grow into men, and beyond. He had been aware of that urge for quite some time, long before he'd even begun planning to expand into Nile Beach, but no one had touched him in a special way—no one until Kendall. Everything about her was perfect. It would require some special maneuvering to pull this off, but it could be done. He couldn't back away now—it was too late. It would all work out, somehow.

He smiled, then rose and picked up his jacket. Kendall's front doors, both upstairs and downstairs, locked from the inside. The back door was the one most likely for a burglar to try to use, and he was sure that had been securely locked before they left for the party. Kendall would surely be all right for a few hours without the double latch. He would check on her first thing in the morning.

He took a few more moments to silently watch Kendall as she slept. His gaze lingered on the rise and fall of her chest with each breath she took. Maybe he should look around for a cover for her in case she got cold.

In the linen closet he found a crocheted throw. She didn't stir when he placed it over her. Her only reaction when he kissed her cheek was a slight variation in her breathing.

Spencer took a few steps toward the door, then turned to look at her sleeping form once more before he reluctantly turned and left her.

CHAPTER SEVEN

Kendall's eyelids slowly rose at 7:45 A.M. She frowned, trying to remember what she was doing on the couch.

Then it came back to her. Last night she and Spencer were cozying up on the couch, and after a bit she drifted off. No, she thought, fell out was more like it. Lord, she had been tired.

But how did she get covered up? And who turned out the lights? And where in the world was Spencer?

She swung her legs down and stood up. She was pretty sure he'd left, but it wouldn't hurt to check the bedrooms just in case. Kendall smiled. The idea of finding him in her bed wasn't at all unpleasant.

But he was gone.

Kendall checked the time again, as though expecting it suddenly to be nine o'clock. Only then would she feel appropriate calling Spencer, who now was probably still asleep.

Just then her phone rang. Spencer, she thought.

She rushed to the phone, but out of longtime habit stood and waited for it to ring again before she picked it up. "Hello."

"Kendall, I hope I didn't wake you. It's Eddie."

The night manager at her Nile Beach restaurant. "No, Eddie, I'm fine. Is everything all right?"

"Well . . . yes, but I was hoping I'd be able to talk to you sometime today. That's why I called so early. I didn't know your schedule. I hope I didn't disturb you, but it's kind of important."

She figured as much. Eddie wasn't the type to call her at home unless it was a matter of reasonable urgency. "When would be good for you?" she asked.

"This morning. Why don't we meet for breakfast around nine thirty?"

"Sure. Where?"

Eddie named a popular luncheonette near city hall, frequented by the mayor, court clerks, and Palmdale's legal community. It was less bustling than the larger commercial restaurants, and would be even more so on a Saturday morning. They would be able to talk without distraction.

Kendall's mind raced. This was, after all, her livelihood, and Spencer was pushed to the background as she tried to figure why Eddie wanted to meet. Maybe he had uncovered some kind of illegal activity among the staff. At one place where she had worked during her college years, a theft ring had been operating between one of the shift managers and the assistant manager, who were stealing the meat and selling it to a third party who, in turn, sold it at a roadside stand. All three were arrested. Kendall hated to think of something like that going on at Soul Food to Go. With just a few exceptions, she genuinely liked her staff.

No point in just sitting here, she thought. It would be nine thirty before she knew it. She picked out fresh clothing and, as she was stepping into the shower, realized that Spencer's letting himself out last night meant her door wasn't fully latched. Naked except for a towel, she went downstairs and put the second lock into effect.

She had just gotten under the hot spray of the water when her telephone began to ring, but between the shower and the closed door she didn't hear it.

* * *

"Leaving?" Kendall exclaimed in dismay, so loudly that the few patrons inside the small restaurant turned to glance at her. "Why?"

"Oh, come on, Kendall, it's not that bad."

She looked at him across the table, her gaze unyielding. "Don't pacify me, Eddie. What happened, did someone offer you more money?"

"That's usually the case when you're offered more responsibility. I'm going to be managing a restaurant, Kendall. Full-time manager, not just of the night shift. And it's a nightclub as well as a restaurant. It's all on my shoulders."

Kendall's eyes narrowed in suspicion. "Where are you going to be working?"

The usually confident Eddie flashed a sheepish grin. "At, uh, Clyde Simmons's new place in the Sunrise."

First her customers, now her employees. Clyde Simmons was trying to ruin her. "Did he approach you?" Kendall fired back.

"No," Eddie replied, then added, "not really. My wife and I ran into him at the supermarket. We got to talking about his new restaurant, and he asked if I would be interested in interviewing for the manager position. This was just before the ad started running in the paper. But to tell you the truth, Kendall, I probably would have applied when I saw the ad. It's a great opportunity"—he didn't want to say the restaurant was going to be big; that wouldn't be wise—"and we both know there's not much financial reward in the business unless you're an owner."

"Do you have an interest in it?" she asked, softening a bit. After all, Eddie had a family. Even if he didn't, she couldn't blame him for wanting a better opportunity. Like the old saying went, *a man's gotta do what a man's gotta do.*

"No. Clyde has a piece of it; but most of it is owned by those two guys from Atlanta. The money's good, though. And you never know what it might lead to. I might be an old man, Kendall, but one day I'd like to do what you and

Clyde are doing. Own a piece of Nile Beach entertainment." He didn't tell her he had been moonlighting days to help him acquire the funds needed to reach his dream.

"Humph. Just don't market soul food, and we won't have a problem."

Eddie grinned. "So you're not upset?"

"Well, I wouldn't exactly say that. No employer likes it when one of her best people leaves, especially a management person." Eddie's leaving would definitely create a void in day-to-day management. The night manager was the second most important person at the restaurant, only after Kendall herself. She had a lead line cook and an alternate during the day who received extra pay for supervision duties, but she was usually in attendance during daytime hours to inspect the day's deliveries and handle any major problems that arose, and she wasn't above putting on an apron and helping out on the line in a crunch. Eddie, on the other hand, oversaw the entire operation from 6 P.M. until closing. Under his direction the nightly readings were taken, the night's take dropped into a drive-up night deposit box, and the staff performed a thorough cleaning of the entire building in preparation for the next day. Usually at least one large order of fifteen or twenty meals was called in from employees of the night shift at the hospital in Palmdale before the restaurant's kitchen shut down at 2 A.M.

"I appreciate your being such a good sport about it. I know you were less than enthused about the way Clyde handled it."

"Oh, you mean how he let me read about his plans in the newspaper and then made off with my right hand," Kendall said dryly.

Eddie looked uncomfortable. "There was just one other thing I wanted to ask you . . ." He rushed on when she flashed him a look that suggested he might be trying her patience. "My daughter Tina really enjoys working for David. I hope my leaving won't jeopardize her job."

Kendall's eyes widened in surprise. "You mean you're not bringing her with you?"

"No. She can walk to work, and she has a work schedule she likes that doesn't interfere with her studies. She can come help out if I ever get to open my own place."

"Oh, you'll do it. And you're not exactly an old man, Eddie. What are you, forty-five?"

He nodded, suddenly evasive. "Yeah, somewhere in there."

They spent the rest of the meeting determining that Eddie would remain at Soul Food to Go for another two weeks and discussing possible candidates to fill his position. There were two possibilities, but one was better prepared for the added responsibility than the other. Ideally the more suitable person would accept. Kendall's second choice could serve as assistant manager and take charge when the manager was off, similar to the setup of her day supervisors.

Eddie insisted on paying the check in spite of her objections that it wasn't necessary. Before they parted, Kendall assured him she would make an offer that evening to her first choice of a replacement for him so training could begin as soon as possible.

She knew Eddie was relieved at having broken the news to her, but Kendall knew she would have to switch to working nights at the restaurant during and after the transition, and the idea was less than thrilling. Of course, Eddie would be handling much of the training, but she wanted to see how things were progressing firsthand, especially if it turned out that any of those involved in the shuffle of positions weren't able to handle the responsibility and had to be replaced. Just a few weeks ago working nights wouldn't have bothered her at all, but now that there was Spencer she could think of better ways to spend the nocturnal hours than being at work.

The thought of Spencer automatically made her feel lighthearted. A shiver of excitement ran through her body like an electric current, causing her hips to jump slightly in her seat, at the mere recollection of being in his arms last night. What was going to happen between them next, she wondered, and when?

Spencer hung up the phone, puzzled. It was still early. Could Kendall have gone out already?

He went to the back of his apartment and looked out the window. Kendall's Altima was parked next to his Saab. The two vehicles looked good next to each other, he thought, just like their owners did. He considered going outside and making sure her front and back doors were locked, but she might have gotten up during the night and set the alarm. It would be mighty embarrassing if the police showed up and questioned him. No, he thought, better to wait.

When he looked out the window again her car was gone. Idly he wondered where she had gone so early in the morning, then he silently chastised himself. It was starting already, the proprietary air he feared. She was not only under his skin, she had made her way close to his heart.

Spencer determinedly turned away from the window. He knew what to do. He would go down and check out the progress of his restaurant, the Sundowner. That was the one place where he was sure to be safe from thoughts of Kendall . . . his guilt would not allow it.

Kendall glided gracefully along Palmdale's newly paved sidewalks on her in-line skates. It felt good to relax, and what with having to work nights at Soul Food to Go as well as overseeing the lunch rush, it was a great stress reliever. Already she could feel her adrenaline racing and her heart pumping. There was nothing like outdoor exercise. She was going to make it a point to do it more often, but in the meantime it should tire her out sufficiently that she could sleep well. She wasn't much of a daytime sleeper, but she'd have to learn if she expected to be up half the night.

By the time she reached the park, six blocks from her house, she was out of breath. What a shock—she hadn't realized she was this out of shape. She dropped rather haphazardly onto a bench facing the basketball court. There was a tree directly behind the bench that provided some shade.

Several youngsters were playing ball. The older kids generally waited until the cooler late afternoons and evenings to come out, both the athletes and the girls who liked to watch them play. Just looking at the boys running back and forth over the court, sweat streaming from their bodies, made Kendall feel uncomfortably warm. It was close to ninety degrees outside, and the court was in full range of the sun. She was entertaining the thought of a drive to the beach for a quick dip, or perhaps to her parents' pool.

The game ended and the kids broke up. Several took some practice shots. One of the others stated his intent to sit down. He turned toward where Kendall was sitting. "Hi!" he exclaimed.

"Hello." Kendall thought he looked vaguely familiar, but the neighborhood was full of kids and she couldn't place him.

Apparently her uncertainty showed, for he said, "I'm Brian. I live downstairs from you."

"Oh! Of course, you're Spencer's son." It was easy not to recognize him. There was no family resemblance; she figured he must favor his mother. "How can you play ball in all this heat? I've been skating and I can't wait to get something to drink."

The youngster sat on a neighboring bench and in response raised a tall, plastic drinking container, then took a sip through the straw.

"I should be so smart," Kendall said with a laugh. "Hey, where's your brother?"

Brian pointed with his chin to the boys who were shooting baskets. "Can't get him away from the court. He thinks he's Michael Jordan."

She giggled. "It looks like you two like it here in Palmdale."

"We do, but next week Daddy's taking us to spend part of our vacation with Mom in Atlanta."

"Well, that's good. You need to spend some time with her, too."

Brian made a face. "It'll be nice for a week or so. Then I'll be ready to come back."

Kendall didn't want to pry, but his statement begged for an explanation and she couldn't deny her curiosity. "How come?"

"Our stepbrother and stepsister are real geeks."

"Oh," she replied with a smile. She remembered Spencer saying the kids didn't always get along. "Are they your age?"

"Younger. Nicky's ten and Jeannie's seven." Brian sighed. "I guess it'll be okay. At least Mom'll have her baby while we're there."

"Oh, she's expecting?"

"Yeah. It'll be exciting. I don't want to miss it; she says this will be her last one."

Kendall could well understand why. It would be expensive raising five children, even though it was obvious Spencer contributed to the welfare of Brian and Carlton. But she supposed Spencer's ex-wife wanted a child with her new husband. Such an action was only natural. For most women, she added. The familiar weight of self-doubt began to descend over her like a steel curtain.

She sat up. This was getting depressing, and she was determined not to give in to her long-standing uncertainties about herself. "Well, I guess I'll be on my way. I'm gonna stop at the store and get something to drink. You guys be careful in this hot sun."

"I'm gonna sit here till I cool off. I can't speak for Carlton, though. 'Bye," Brian replied.

Kendall waved as she skated away.

* * *

"Very nice," Spencer commented, obviously pleased with the progress made in the remodeling process. Just about all that remained to be done was the floors. Then they could move in the furniture and open for business.

But first they had to have a complete staff. "The opening is scheduled for two weeks from now," he said to Clyde. "Pete's assistants ought to be completely comfortable preparing all the items by then," he added, referring to the talented young chef he had found in Daytona Beach.

"I know you've got the kitchen staffed, Spencer, but Eddie will be hiring the busboys, waiters, bartenders, and hostess. How's he supposed to hire and train a staff if he's busy working at Soul Food?"

"He works nights. He said he can do four or five hours a day until he goes full time. Besides, I'll be assisting with the training. I want the Sundowner to be known for exemplary service, and one thing I never want to hear is someone saying, 'That's not my job' if they're asked to do something out of the ordinary."

"Sounds good." Clyde chuckled. "You know, hiring Eddie isn't going to go over big with Kendall."

Spencer shrugged. "It can't be helped. Eddie was the best applicant we had, and I wanted the best man for the job. I'm sure Kendall will be able to find someone to take his place without too much difficulty." He spoke with more conviction than he felt, for he suspected Kendall would be absolutely livid when she found out; but he felt he at least needed to put on a good front. While Clyde knew he and Kendall were neighbors in the duplex, he did not know they were seeing each other as well.

"She's already been a little frosty toward me. It's my fault, I guess. I really should have told her about it," Clyde continued.

"How'd she find out?"

"She said she read about it in the paper. That article."

Spencer's mind raced. There had been no mention of

him personally in the newspaper, only the name of the corporation he and Vincent started, Two Brothers, Inc. Kendall couldn't have made a connection. He sighed in relief.

"Anyway," Clyde continued, "Eddie's a good guy. I talked to him this morning. He said he met Kendall for breakfast today and resigned."

So that's where Kendall went so early, Spencer thought. "Did he say how she took it?" he asked casually.

"He said she was real nice about it. It's me she wants to hang, I'm sure." Clyde laughed. "You know, I'm fifty-seven years old, Spencer, but the coldness in that woman's eyes when we had our little confrontation made me want to run for cover. It's a shame. Here I am old enough to be her father."

Spencer didn't even want to think about that frigid gaze being focused on him. "Back to the hiring process," he said to change the subject.

"Oh, yeah. We're putting an ad in Monday's paper. Eddie got it called in before the noon deadline. He hopes to have the hiring complete by the end of the week."

"I'll tell him to get the night staff set first. I want to accentuate the club end to begin with." The liquor license had cost him plenty, and he wanted to start earning back his investment. Besides, dinner was the most expensive meal they would offer. While traditional soul food in itself was pretty basic, Spencer had given the chef creative license to try different menu selections as alternates to the standard menu, as well as with the appetizers that would be offered in addition to entrées. Nightly specials would be offered on individual blackboards that could be changed every night if necessary.

"Sure, Spencer. What about entertainment?"

"I'm working on it. We have George Wallace signed for the opening. It's not a definite yet, but I think we've got the Main Ingredient in the weekend of the college reunion. It's a little harder getting entertainment for the younger crowd. It's more profitable for groups who sell CDs by the millions to play the big concert halls. Our best bet is to go after a comedian." Spencer frowned again. The idea of some foul-mouthed youthful comic performing in his restaurant wasn't too appealing, either. He had sunk a fortune into making the Sundowner a classy, intimate atmosphere, and he didn't want its reputation spoiled by anyone whose humor was in bad taste and offensive to his patrons. He would have to be very, very careful about who was invited to perform here.

"Sounds great," Clyde said. He took in Spencer's thoughtful expression. "You probably want to hang around a while. I'm going back to my office. Stop in if you need me."

"Sure, Clyde. Thanks."

Once Spencer was alone he turned slowly, viewing the restaurant from all angles. The Sundowner was going to be the nicest restaurant and night spot in Nile Beach. The platform was centrally located for easy viewing from all seats, and he had the dance floor put to the side of it rather than directly in front of it. The tables he had ordered were large enough to accommodate either two or four people. They could be arranged to fit larger groups if the need arose. Each table would be covered with a white or an emerald green tablecloth, keeping with the simple color scheme of black, white, and green. His largest single purchase had been a white baby grand piano, which would be set on its own platform on the other side of the dance floor. On nights when there was no name entertainment— which would be most nights while he was getting established—he wanted piano music for the diners' enjoyment. An attractive mosaic pattern of black-and-white tile on the floor, a few mirrors and paintings, as well as large, well-placed plants, would complete the decor. The atmosphere would be airy and pleasant even with dim dinner lighting. For breakfast and lunch, where a less intimate environment was appropriate, all they had to do was adjust the lighting and make the room brighter. It was going to be really lovely.

His mind raced. He would have to take out a full-page ad to announce the opening in the local newspaper that was published especially for vacationers. A few radio spots to get the word out among the locals wouldn't hurt either. They had expanded the size of the original restaurant during the remodeling process, and between it and the bar nearly two hundred people could be accommodated with seats. He wanted every seat, barstool, and standing area occupied, both on opening weekend and afterward.

He reached for his agenda. The box for each day was chock full of notations. As he double checked for reminders about advertising he noticed an entry for the following Friday that said "Brian and Carlton to Arjorie's." He had to go back to Atlanta.

Spencer's brow wrinkled in thought. It really wasn't necessary for him to spend any time in that city, not now. If anything, he wanted to be close at hand here to make sure no problems arose in the brief time left before the opening. In the months since he had relocated, Vincent had pretty much taken over their interests in Atlanta, and even he would put them aside to come to Nile Beach to attend the opening. It seemed silly to take all that time just to drive the boys to their mother's, to say nothing of all the mileage he was racking up on his car. Maybe he'd just put them on a plane.

Or maybe, he thought . . . maybe this was the perfect opportunity to bring everything out in the open with Kendall and put an end to the deceit that was keeping him awake at night.

CHAPTER EIGHT

The more Spencer thought about it, the better the idea seemed. He had to tell her about the Sundowner sooner or later, and the truth was he was tired of skirting the issue. He was in too deep with Kendall Lucas, and it was making him crazy. He was much too old to be carrying on like some love-struck kid. What he needed to do was get everything out in the open as soon as possible. Kendall deserved to know the truth; and he felt he just couldn't lie to her anymore. If learning he was the brains and financial power behind her new competition meant an end to their blossoming relationship, he needed to know as soon as possible. And getting her out of town to give her the news seemed like a pretty good idea, especially if things turned out badly. They could probably reach some kind of truce to make being neighbors easier during the long drive back.

There was a loud whack as Spencer's palm connected to the wall. He didn't want to make a pact for peace with Kendall. He wanted to hold her, kiss her, stroke her hair, and feel her naked body close to his. He wanted to feel her body snug against his as they slept, share her body heat and cup her breasts possessively, like she belonged to him, instead of merely watching the enticing rise and fall of her chest with each respiration she took. What was more, he felt like he wanted to do this every night of his life. Kendall Lucas was in his heart to stay, and he knew it. She had all the attributes of the woman he was looking for in a lifetime partner. What he needed to do was figure out how to hold onto her, not try to cope with a sudden end to their relationship.

He sighed. Business had always been so simple for him. Who would have thought he'd ever find himself in such a fix?

Kendall's car was still gone when he returned, and as he soon learned, the other members of his household were gone as well. Michelle, he knew, was putting in duty at the teen club, making sandwiches for the expected Saturday night crowd before she opened the doors at eight. The boys were probably at the basketball court.

Spencer found the peacefulness refreshing; a powerful relaxant after a busy afternoon. He was going to have to start looking for a house. The apartment was a decent setup for them on a temporary basis—he'd signed a six-month lease—but hardly ideal. There were two bathrooms, but the one in the back was only a powder room and in the old days was probably for the exclusive use of the maid, since it was located in the laundry area behind the kitchen. The full bath, in spite of its large size and being equipped with both a stall shower and claw foot tub—not an uncommon feature in more upscale homes built in the twenties and thirties—wasn't enough for the four of them. And while he and Michelle had private bedrooms, the smaller third bedroom, which with its window-lined walls was actually more of a sunroom, could only be accessed from his bedroom. It served as his home office rather than a room for the boys. Because the kitchen was large enough to accommodate a table with four chairs, Brian and Carlton were relegated to makeshift quarters in the formal dining room, which was not equipped with doors. Spencer knew they were looking forward to the privacy having their own rooms would bring.

The quiet served to bring his tired state to the surface. It had been a long day yesterday, and he had risen early this morning. Exhausted, he decided a nap was in order and retreated to the privacy of his bedroom.

When Spencer awoke several hours later the apartment was buzzing with activity. Music was playing in the boys' room, and Michelle was hollering at them to turn it down. His mouth formed a smile. He enjoyed having his sons live with him, and the arrangement with Michelle was working quite well, despite the less-than-harmonious comments currently going back and forth. It reminded him of his own childhood. There had been eight children in his immediate family, and there was constant infighting about use of the single bathroom in their apartment in a Newark housing project.

"Hey," he joined in as he emerged from behind his previously closed bedroom door, "what's all this racket I hear?"

"They need to turn down that damn music!" Michelle snapped.

"Oh, Michelle, give us a break," Brian replied easily.

"Wait a second," Spencer said in a no-nonsense voice. Joking was fine to a point, but Brian and Carlton were clearly pushing Michelle to a breaking point. True, she was their cousin, but she was also an adult and warranted their respect. "Listen, fellows, when Michelle asks you to do something, I expect both of you to do it without any back talk," he said in a clipped voice.

The boys immediately changed their stance. "Yes, Daddy," they said in close conjunction.

"Is there anything about that you don't understand?" Spencer asked. "If there isn't, you need to clarify it now, because I don't ever expect to have to tell you this again."

"I'm turning it down right now," Carlton said quickly.

Mollified, Michelle disappeared back into her bedroom without further comment. Spencer knew she wanted to rest a bit before she was due at the club. She was finding out just how hard it was to be in the hospitality business. A good portion of her weekend afternoons were spent making submarine sandwiches for the club's patrons, which she then cut into pieces not much larger than bite sized. They weren't exactly canapes, but they weren't much larger, and that was fine. Being small enough to consume in two or three bites would cut down on waste, since it was more likely it would be hastily stuffed into someone's mouth than be put down and forgotten about.

Spencer approached his offspring. "Michelle is working very hard at the club, you know." She was also doing a fair share of partying, often not getting in until the wee hours, which he knew was contributing to her being so cranky. "Keep giving her a hard time and she'll start feeding you bread and water for dinner."

"We didn't mean anything, Daddy," Brian said.

Spencer rubbed the top of his head affectionately. His eldest was already up to his chin. Both Brian and Carlton would probably eclipse him in height, most likely within the next two or three years. "Just remember what I said, both of you."

He leaned against the wall. The boys would be spending the summer with their mother in Atlanta. When they returned he wanted to to be living someplace where they would have their own rooms, even if they had to share. At least then they could play their music without irritating anyone else. Spencer vowed to contact a real estate broker during the coming week. "So how did you guys spend your Saturday?"

"Shooting hoops," Carlton answered. "Then we went to the beach with Kendall."

Spencer blinked. "You did what?"

"Yeah, Daddy, she was out rollerblading and stopped to rest in the park on her way home," Brian offered. "She was talking about how hot it was and that she was going to the beach. Then she asked if we wanted to come with her. Shucks, we can play b-ball anytime, but not go to the beach. We didn't think you'd mind. She's a friend of yours, isn't she?

"Michelle says she's more than a friend," Carlton added, grinning impishly.

"Uh, yes," Spencer said, still digesting news that to him was startling but certainly not unpleasant. He liked the idea of Kendall spending time with his boys. "Yes," he repeated. "And never mind what Michelle says." He could ask his niece a few things himself, like why she didn't get in until daylight when the clubs closed down at two, but he didn't think he would like the answer, which would undoubtedly be that it was none of his business, which technically it wasn't. "So how was the beach?"

"Great! They had real good waves. But Kendall kept telling us not to go out too far. She said she didn't want to have to give you any bad news."

Spencer didn't bother to try to restrain his smile. He was glad the boys enjoyed their time with Kendall.

Then, as the significance of the afternoon's events dawned on him, he suddenly realized there was another potential problem facing them, the last thing he expected to be a source of contention between him and any woman he became involved with. It looked like all his careful planning was blowing up in his face.

At seven thirty Spencer dropped the boys off at a movie theater in Nile Beach. They seemed especially happy tonight, and he was sure it was because of the afternoon spent at the beach with Kendall.

He hadn't had time to call her again, but she was definitely on his mind. He'd call her as soon as he got home. There wasn't exactly freedom of movement—he had to pick up the boys in two hours—but maybe they could spend the time sipping Margaritas on the patio of the King

Street Cafe. Who knows—if things went well, maybe he wouldn't even wait until they got to Atlanta before letting her in on the secret he was keeping from her, and when they went they could concentrate on simply having a good time.

He spotted her getting into her car as he drove down the alley and accelerated, anxious to catch her before she left.

He tooted his horn as he pulled up beside her. The window on the passenger side descended, obviously with assistance from an electronic control panel. "Hi there, mystery man," she greeted.

"Hi. I hated just walking out on you last night, but the truth was I couldn't get you up. You were sleeping like a baby."

She laughed. "I was, wasn't I. I wasn't even sure where I was when I first woke up this morning. Thanks for the cover."

"I didn't want you to be cold."

It was a perfectly ordinary statement, but delivered in a soft, intimate manner that made Kendall's body tremble. Spencer had an uncanny ability to turn an ordinary sentence into a soft-spoken caress.

In a normal voice, he continued, "That was nice of you to take the boys to the beach this afternoon. They had a lot of fun."

"I'm glad it was okay. It wasn't like it was planned or anything. Brian and I just got to talking and one thing led to another."

"They're at the movies now. I've got to pick them up at nine thirty, but I was hoping you and I could kill some time over on King Street. Maybe talk about a plan for Soul Food to Go over drinks."

"Oh, Spencer, I'd love to, but I already made plans."

He hid his disappointment behind a casual shrug. "Well, maybe another time, then."

"Sure. See you later."

She started her engine and backed out, waving to him

as she pulled away. Spencer forced himself to go inside his apartment rather than stand and watch her with what were probably lovesick eyes. But his mind was spinning. Other plans, she had said. What plans? And with whom?

"Oscar said to tell you how sorry he was, Kendall," Chan said.

Kendall bristled. "Sorry enough to lay off the sauce? I doubt it. The next time he's here he'll probably do more damage."

"Try not to be too angry at Oscar, dear. He's a sick man."

"So I'm supposed to feel sorry for him? Tell me, Mom, is that how you feel about my father after everything he did to us?"

Kendall regretted the words the moment they were out, but Chan didn't blink. "As a matter of fact, I do, and he's done much worse to me than push me into a pool at a party. But, of course, I've had twenty years to get over it. You get over everything in time, dear, or at least you should," she added pointedly.

"He's just as pitiful as Oscar," Kendall said disdainfully.

"More so," Chan said calmly.

"What do you mean?"

Chan sighed. "Just that. I had a call a few days ago. Oscar is not well, Kendall, but your father is in the hospital, Kendall. He has end-stage liver disease."

It did not surprise Kendall that she felt nothing. "Humph. I hope he's not sticking you with his funeral costs."

"No. Freda will handle it," Chan answered, referring to her former sister-in-law. "But I'd like you to consider coming to the funeral with me."

"The funeral! You're going all the way back to Philadelphia for that . . . and you expect me to come with you?"

"It all happened a long time ago, Kendall. It's been over and done with for years, and when your father does die—

which will probably be within the next month—the chapter will be completely closed." Chan had another reason as well for wanting Kendall to attend the services, but she didn't feel it was proper to dangle it in front of Kendall's face as an incentive. Kendall should attend the funeral only because she wanted to, not out of obligation.

"Well, that's all well and good, but I don't want to go."

There was an air of finality to Kendall's tone, but Chan refused to back off. "I suppose that's a natural reaction, but just promise me you'll at least think about it."

"All right, Mom. I'll think about it."

"Good. And now, a pleasanter subject. Daddy and I were both quite impressed with Spencer."

Kendall could not control the smile that instantly formed at the sound of his name.

Her reaction was not lost on Chan, who nodded knowingly. "It's nice to see that look on your face, Kendall. It's been much too long."

"Years," Kendall agreed. "And it always faded very fast. But this is different, Mom. It's . . . well, I can't really explain it."

"Uh-huh," Chan said thoughtfully.

"Did you ever meet someone, not even know them all that well, but yet feel like you could trust them completely?" Kendall asked dreamily.

"Yes, but I was usually wrong," was Chan's flat reply.

"Oh, Mom," Kendall said.

Chan patted Kendall's arm. "I don't mean to discourage you, honey. Spencer certainly seems like a decent man. I just don't want you to rush into anything. You might not want to put too many expectations in him until you know him a little better. Remember, it's always wise to take your time in a relationship. If he's worthy of your trust you'll know soon enough. In the meantime, I don't want you to get hurt by moving too quickly."

"Me neither," Kendall answered as the doorbell sounded. "That must be my beloved sister-in-law."

"And my grandson," Chan added. "Listen, you'd better

not let Zena hear you talk that star-struck talk. She'll never let you live it down."

Kendall met her mother's gaze, her eyes sparkling. "Who're you telling?"

For the next few hours the women recounted the events of the previous evening, who was wearing what ("Those twins looked like two ten-pound hunks of boloney crammed into nine-pound bags," Zena cracked,) the latest gossip, Oscar Signeous and, of course, Spencer.

"Did you know that was his own personal tux he was wearing?" Zena asked Chan.

"Oh, Zena, enough with the tux already," Kendall said wearily.

"Hey, that's big news. But if you insist, I'll change the subject. Where's Spencer tonight, anyway?"

Kendall giggled. Zena had changed the subject, but she was still talking about Spencer. "Right about now he's probably bringing his kids home from the movies. He did ask me out, though." She was thinking of the quick look of disappointment that flashed across his face when she told him she had other plans, followed by the undeniable curiosity he was apparently unable to control. It made her glad she had worn a halter romper and put on some lipstick instead of her usual T-shirt and cutoffs. It wouldn't do any harm for him to think she was having dinner or at one of the Nile Beach night spots—anywhere but here, chewing the fat at her mother's kitchen table.

"I guess you'll really freak him out when you take off for Philly," Zena remarked.

Kendall knew her sister-in-law was referring to the expected demise of Kenneth Lucas. "How long have you known about it?" she asked.

"For weeks."

"Weeks?"

Zena looked uncomfortable. "Well, Chan did call this

morning to tell us it wasn't looking good. She said she was going to wait for you to come over to tell you."

Kendall looked at Chan, who straightened her shoulders defiantly. "Well, Mother? Why didn't you tell me?"

"Listen, missy, don't you 'Mother' me. Let's not forget who gave birth to whom," Chan said in the no-nonsense voice Kendall had rarely heard since she had been an adult. "I know how bitter you are toward him—and I can't say I blame you—but that was why I felt there was no need for you to know until his condition became critical. It's not like you would want to rush up there to see him," she added with a touch of sarcasm.

Kendall chose not to acknowledge either the rebuke or the barb. An inner voice reminded her that she should have known better than to tangle with her sharp-tongued mother. "What did Barry say about going?" she asked instead.

"He said he'll come," Chan interrupted. "So if you stay home you'll be the only one not represented."

"I said I'd think about it, Mom."

The tense moment was relieved by the appearance of Paul Ridgely, who held Elgin's hand. "We've been for a walk to see the Good Humor man," he said. "But the little man here said he wanted one of Grandma's popsicles instead."

"Not a bad idea," Zena said. "Here, I'll get them. Anybody else care for one?"

There were no takers. Little Elgin ran to greet his Aunt Kendall, who gave the toddler an affectionate squeeze before letting him join his mother by the freezer.

Paul turned to Kendall. "I thought your young man was very nice, Kendall."

"Dad, he's not my young man. He's just my neighbor, and I thought it would be nice if I had an escort for the party." Kendall pretended not to notice the looks her parents exchanged. It was a lie, of course, but she felt they were making too much fuss over Spencer. She supposed it was standard for parents of eligible daughters to be concerned about their futures, especially once they reached their thirties. Still, her parents knew she had never had a serious relationship, that her future successes would most likely only be business-related. She felt it wasn't fair for them to expect her to settle down and start sprouting out more grandchildren, because hoping for it would only bring them disappointment when it failed to materialize. The only grandchildren they would get would be from Barry and David, even on the off chance she did settle down. Some things just weren't meant to be, she reminded herself firmly before the old feeling of doubt could settle in. While she would love to be involved in a relationship of mutual love, trust, and respect with one special man, the idea of motherhood did absolutely nothing for her and indeed never had. But surely it was unnatural for her not to desire a family of her own, and she had never told a soul how she felt for fear she would be thought odd. Look at her friend Ava Maxwell, who had been told years ago that her chances of conceiving a baby were practically nil. It wasn't fair, Kendall thought. She herself was physically able to have a child—at least as far as she knew— but didn't want one, while Ava would give just about anything to be able to reproduce.

"Well, you seem to have a very nice neighbor," Paul was saying.

When Chan spoke again she talked about George Graves's illness, mentioning she had learned about it from one of the party guests. "The last of the great men of his generation. You know, dear," she said, speaking to Paul, "I wouldn't be surprised if you were asked to give the eulogy."

Good grief, Kendall thought, let the man breathe his last breath already. While she understood why parents wanted to get their children married off, she didn't understand the fascination people her parents' age had with death. Her mother was always talking about how this one was sick and that one was dying. Perhaps in twenty years when she was their age and the names on the obituary

page were her contemporaries and friends rather than
anonymous old people, she would regard death without
the menacing feeling it gave her now, but at this point in
her life she didn't think she could deal with it.

It was ten o'clock when Kendall left her parents' home.
She headed for Soul Food to Go so she could see how
Andrew, her new manager-in-training, was coming along.

She soon learned everything was going smoothly. Kendall fixed herself a frozen yogurt sundae and sat at a rear
corner table. She had only taken a few spoonfuls when
she saw Ava Maxwell come in. Ava didn't see her as she
placed her order, but the clerk who took the order saw
Kendall waving from her seat and alerted Ava, who immediately came over and sat down.

"I didn't expect to see you here," she said after they
exchanged greetings. "I know you're getting your new
night man trained, but I see Eddie's still here."

"Yeah, but I thought I'd check things out myself. It's
not like I expect Eddie to put heart and soul into training
him, if you know what I mean."

Ava chuckled. "I guess. To him it's just a job, and he's
moving on."

"Yeah. I'm glad you're here, I want to ask you something."

"Shoot."

Kendall hesitated. This was so personal, and she knew
the anguish Ava's infertility had caused her. But she
seemed to be doing much better now. The end of her
marriage had happened so long ago. After retreating into
a shell, she had begun to date the last few years. "You're
the only one who can help me with this. It's Spencer, Ava.
I like him a whole lot—"

Ava drew in her breath. "Kendall, that's wonderful! My
goodness, it's been years since I heard you say that about
any man."

"I know. But I'm worried. I know I'm probably getting

way ahead of myself, but I can't help it. In business you have to be prepared for the future, and that mode of thinking is spilling over into my personal life. What if things between us get serious?"

Ava looked puzzled. "I think that would be great. Why, don't you?"

"What if he wants to have more kids?"

"Kendall? What am I missing here? You're not flawed, are you?"

Kendall smiled at the phrasing. Ava always referred to her infertility as her "flaw." "No, at least not in the way you mean. What I am is not interested in having kids. I don't feel that urge. I never have." She saw Ava's incredulous expression and felt foolish. "I guess I must have missed the point when they handed me my first doll baby."

Ava leaned all the way back in her chair. "Wow," she said. "You don't know how much I wish I could feel that way. I've even considered hypnotism to change my feelings, but that idea strikes me as being almost as unnatural as all those artificial methods of conception." She sighed. "I've pretty much learned to accept it—it has been a long time, you know . . . but I think the pain of not being able to have children will be with me, even if only in the back of my mind, until the day I keel over and drop dead." She attempted to chuckle, but it came out as more of a bitter-sounding "harumph."

"You don't know how much this has bothered me. I've never told a soul until now. I think my mother would have a heart attack if she knew. I know she wants me to have a couple of young-uns so she can spoil them the way she does Elgin."

"Oh, Kendall, I wish I'd known. No one should have to suffer alone."

Kendall looked her friend squarely in the eye. "Is that why you practically became a recluse after you got separated?"

"It was a very difficult time for me. Divorce always is, they say, no matter what the circumstances. Besides, it was temporary. Remember how I used to talk your ear off when we were roommates?"

Kendall nodded.

"Number one eighty-seven, your order is ready," one of the clerks said, her voice amplified by a microphone.

"Oh, that's me," Ava said, jumping up with receipt in hand. "I'll be right back."

"Okay."

Moments later Ava returned with a tray holding a grilled chicken salad and a miniature bottle of white wine. "You haven't said hardly anything about Spencer. Does he have kids already?"

"Yes. Two boys. They're eleven and twelve, I think."

"Good. I'll tell you something, Ken. One reason I started going out again was because it occurred to me that men in their thirties had already been married and been, um, fruitful and multiplied, as the Bible says. On the other hand, I try to steer clear of men without kids. I've already gone that route, and it wouldn't be fair to get involved knowing I couldn't—well, every man has a right to have children of his own. But I think it's a good sign that Spencer has them already."

"Maybe. But his ex-wife has remarried. and she's having another one. I'll bet she's hoping for a girl this time. What if Spencer wants the same?"

Ava looked at Kendall for a long moment. "Are you really so much against having children?"

"I know it's not natural. I just don't think I should do it unless I have, well, more enthusiasm about it, otherwise I'm just courting disaster."

"I guess you're right. I wish I knew what to tell you, Kendall. But I will say I don't like that part about it not being natural. Let's clarify that. Wanting to chop people into little pieces is not natural. Not wanting to have kids is more of a personal choice. June Cleaver is no longer the quintessential woman, not in this day and age. And I know how busy you are with this place and the other one, which might not mix too well with raising a child. I do wish you'd consider telling your mother. She might be disappointed, but your mom's cool. She'll probably understand more than you think."

"And what about Spencer?"

"For crying out loud, don't pull the plug on the relationship based on something that might not even happen. Spend time with him. Have fun. And keep your ears open. If he mentions he'd like to have another baby, or if he comes flat out and asks you if you want kids, tell him the truth. Then you two can take it from there. And if it doesn't come up, chances are it doesn't matter to him. He's a businessman, Kendall. I don't think he's going to take anything for granted."

It was after 3 A.M. and Spencer was exhausted. He had been working on the Sundowner's budget in his home office ever since he brought the boys home from the movie hours earlier. There was really no reason for him to stay up half the night poring over figures—he and Vincent had secured a large enough line of credit to keep the restaurant afloat through the crucial make-or-break time— but in his heart he knew the only reason he was doing it was to see when Kendall came in . . . and to see if she was accompanied by anyone.

He was about to call it a night when he heard a car door slam. Feeling foolish, he peered outside at an angle from which he could not be seen. Kendall was getting out of her car. He looked just long enough to make sure she was alone, then discreetly retreated.

He looked at his desk clock. The digital display read 3:45 A.M. Well, Nile Beach was at the height of its season, and all the clubs were staying open later than usual to accommodate the fun-seeking, money-spending vacationers. Restaurants that served breakfast were open around the clock on the weekends, to provide a wind-down for pooped and hungry partyers.

Spencer felt ashamed of his nosy behavior, but in his heart he was glad she was home safe . . . and alone.

It had not been a good night for Kendall. First there was the disturbing news of her father's impending death, which she had initially dismissed but now managed to make its way into her mind no matter how hard she tried to occupy herself with other thoughts.

Then she had taken the total of the receipts for the past two weeks and, thinking of the competition she would soon have, subtracted 15 percent. She was not happy with the results. It would mean serious belt-tightening, and perhaps more emphasis on the Palmdale location, which still stood tall among other restaurants of its type that offered standard fare. She made a list of the employees she would lay off if it became necessary, clipped it to her figures and locked it in her desk drawer.

Although physically drained, she found it difficult to fall asleep, and when she finally did, her slumber was filled with two contrasting images that made her toss and turn— that of her father's face ravaged by illness and of the vacant Soul Food to Go building with a FOR RENT sign across its front.

Over the following week Kendall worked a grueling split shift. She stayed at the restaurant through the closing procedures, offering assistance and guidance but generally trying to stay out of Eddie's way while simultaneously managing to keep a sharp eye on the performances of her employees. She usually arrived home at around 2:30 A.M. She fell into a pattern of sleeping late in the morning, doing her housework and laundry, and then heading back to Soul Food to Go until the lunch crowd diminished. In the afternoons, she indulged herself in some kind of fun activity, usually the beach for an hour or two, before taking a quick nap and returning to the restaurant around seven.

Twice she ran into Brian and Carlton Barnes and invited them to come along, and both times they agreed. Another day they saw her riding her bike and joined her on theirs for a ride through the neighborhood. Spencer had nice kids. They actually were able to talk, and not in that stilted way kids usually reserved for adults, but carry on a normal conversation. Too bad kids couldn't come out of the womb eleven and twelve years old, toilet trained, walking, talking, and eating solid foods, Kendall thought. If that was the case maybe she'd change her stance. Not that it mattered, since she didn't have a partner to raise a child with. She certainly couldn't do it alone, especially with the crazy hours she'd been working.

Even though she got plenty of rest, it was difficult for her system to become acclimated to the change in schedule. By Friday she had had enough. Satisfied that Andrew could handle overseeing the closing with minimal assistance from Eddie, she left after the second rush that traditionally came an hour before the nine-thirty movie started.

CHAPTER NINE

Kendall's apartment never looked cozier than after such a difficult week. She decided some pampering was in order to soothe her tired soul. She filled the bathtub with bubbly water and scented oil, dug up the paperback mystery novel she was reading at her leisure, and after setting up the portable CD player she disrobed and climbed in.

She relaxed for half an hour, then spontaneously decided to wash her hair. Kendall's face contorted as she held her nose, shut her eyes tightly, and then submerged herself beneath the water to saturate her hair. Then she removed the stopper and got into the separate shower to rinse off and lather her tresses.

She was at the final step, rinsing off the conditioner, when she thought she heard the doorbell ringing. It was hard to miss, even with the water running. For one, she had opened the bathroom door once she got into the glass-enclosed shower, and, second, whoever was down there was rather insistent, leaning on the bell for ten-second intervals at a time.

Kendall began to feel anxious. Perhaps something had happened to someone in her family. She had a flash of

Kenneth Lucas in his sickbed but quickly pushed the image away.

She quickly shut off the water, grabbed an oversized fluffy towel and, not bothering to dry her body or hair, ran to the door and hit the landing just in time to see Spencer bounding up the stairs, two at a time.

The towel was securely fastened between her breasts, but instinctively she reached up and held it firm. "Spencer! What in heaven's name is going on?" She sensed that whatever it was it was hardly an emergency, and already her annoyance was growing at the unnecessary panic he'd caused her—not to mention the work of mopping up the trail of water from the bathroom to the front door.

It was too dim in the stairwell for her to see the spark of desire in his eyes as he approached. She was too stunned to move when he suddenly embraced her. Kendall could smell the thoroughly male scent of him stemming from the unbuttoned top of his short-sleeved shirt. She leaned into him, instantly forgiving his indiscretion and simply enjoying his nearness—but still she held tight to the towel with one hand.

"I'm sorry," he whispered, stroking her hair and seemingly not caring that his shirt front was getting wet. "I didn't mean to frighten you. I just had to see you, and right now."

What was it about this man that made her so good-natured? His voice, probably, she decided. With its scratchy quality he could recite the telephone book and make it sound sexy. Besides, there was no denying that it was flattering that he was so desperate to see her. "Come inside, Spencer. I know no one can see us here, but I feel silly standing half naked."

"You shouldn't," he said as he followed her inside, adding to himself, "You look good enough to eat." Here in the light of her living room she looked even more alluring than she had when she first appeared at the top of the stairs. He found himself wishing that towel would just fall off. Not that that was likely; she was holding that towel like it was protecting Fort Knox.

In her brightly lit living room Kendall could see his hungry gaze, and it made her uncomfortable. "Give me a minute to dry off and change," she suggested, knowing she would feel better facing him in less scanty attire and with her saturated hair covered with a makeshift turban.

But Spencer reached out and grabbed her arm firmly. "No . . . wait."

There was an urgent note to his tone, and she halted, her eyes widening as she waited for him to continue.

He pulled her close, his hand stroking her jaw. "I missed not seeing you this week. The boys told me you've been working nights."

"Yes, that's right." His hand was as rough as his voice, but his touch had a sensuous lightness to it, and Kendall felt that if he continued to caress her she would lose control. "My night manager was stolen by Clyde Simmons," she added grimly. "I'm supervising the training of his replacement."

"Oh," he replied softly. He swallowed, his saliva nearly sticking in his Adam's apple but finally going down with what to him sounded like a thud. "So you're having quite a busy week."

She nodded, mesmerized by his handsome face and expressive eyes. She wanted to tell him that she, too, had missed seeing him, that she had thought of him most of the time, even in her dreams. "I'm not used to this schedule. I need to be there during part of the days, too. It's exhausting."

Spencer's hand dropped and captured hers. "I wanted to call you, but I didn't want to disturb you if you were sleeping. I have to go to Atlanta tonight. The boys are going to spend most of the summer with their mother. It's been a week since we were able to spend any real time together, and suddenly I just couldn't stand it anymore." He paused a beat, then said, "I want you to come with me."

"Go with you?" She stared at him incredulously. "You're kidding."

"It's a long drive. The boys will sleep straight through it. You can keep me company."

"That's during the drive, but eventually we're going to get there. And then what happens?"

"We go about our business."

"Your business, Spencer, is delivering your sons to their mother. I know from the boys that she's remarried and expecting a baby, but somehow I can't picture her being pleased to see me." It was almost laughable. Spencer's ex-wife was probably big as the proverbial house at this point in her pregnancy and would thus probably resent any woman with a waistline.

"Whether or not Arjorie is pleased has not been my concern for the past eight years," Spencer replied flatly. "It just so happens I make it a point not to fill her in on my personal life. You can wait at the hotel. It's not like I'm going to stick around at Arjorie's."

"Hotel?" she repeated, an unspoken question in her voice.

"Relax, Kendall. I'm not going to try to seduce you. You'll have your own room, on a different floor if you prefer. I just thought it would be kind of fun for you to come along. I can show you my interests, you can meet my brother, we'll do the town . . ."

"Well, it does sound like fun. But Spencer, I've got so much to do. It's Eddie's last week, and I'll still be working nights."

He put a hand on both of her arms to calm her. "That's the whole point, Kendall. It's Eddie's last week. That means Eddie will still be there to train and supervise." He recaptured her hands again and nuzzled the skin lightly with the pads of his thumbs. "Come on, Kendall. I understand your devotion to Soul Food to Go, but you said yourself you need a rest."

"Well . . . when will you be back?"

"Monday night. You can go right to work if you want."

She broke into a smile. "It sounds like fun. Okay, I'll come. But, Spencer, I've got to dry off!"

"A weekend in Atlanta with Spencer? Mmm. You mean he's going to get to go where few men have gone before?"

Kendall blew out her breath loudly. "Why do I tell you anything, Zena? You can turn the most innocent situation into something . . . unsavory. All I wanted to do was make sure y'all knew where I was going. And if you need to reach me . . ." She named the hotel and location where Spencer told her they would be staying. "Spencer says he always stays there. You can always ask Information for the number."

After speaking with her sister-in-law, Kendall dialed David's apartment. As she expected for a Friday night, he was not at home, so she left a brief explanation on his answering machine. Her last call was to Eddie at the Nile Beach location, who assured her he would handle everything.

She was dressed, packed, and ready to go less than two hours after agreeing to the ride. "I can help drive, you know," she remarked to Spencer as he backed the Saab out of the parking lot, Brian and Carlton in the back seat.

"I appreciate it, Kendall, but that wasn't my intent when I asked you to come along. I wanted your company, not your energy. I make this drive all the time, so often I could probably do it with my eyes closed."

"But do please humor me and keep them open," she responded with a chuckle.

Within half an hour both Brian and Carlton were asleep, sharing a large blanket and each leaning toward their respective windows in the back seat. "See what I go through?" Spencer said good-naturedly. "They leave me to my own devices every time, with no one to talk to."

"I'm sure that's why you brought along all these goodies," Kendall commented, going through the treasure trove of tapes he had in a long plastic case. "If I'd known you had a CD player in here I would have brought my James Brown set. It's a compilation of all his best songs." Unconsciously she launched into a few bars of "Soul Power" as she continued browsing through the tapes. "But you've got plenty of good stuff here. This one here is great driving music," she said as she slipped a classic Johnny "Guitar" Watson into the cassette.

"Yeah, the radio selection is pretty awful until you start approaching Macon. Mostly Country and Western stations. You'd think we were driving through Oklahoma or someplace." He paused and silently took a deep breath to bring up what was for him a delicate subject, but nonetheless one that needed to be discussed, preferably before the truth came out. "About Soul Food to Go, Kendall. Have you thought about putting coupons in that bimonthly booklet that gets mailed to people's homes? A lot of the restaurants do, the major chains as well as the independents."

Kendall wrinkled her nose. "I don't really like the idea of coupons. It's like those rebates the car dealers give. I've always felt they jack up the prices just so they can make it look like they're giving you something when they're not. But I charge a fair price for my product."

"The fact is, Kendall, that a lot of people use coupons, and restaurant coupons are becoming almost as commonplace as those for products. Even the so-called 'nicer' restaurants that serve thirty-dollar entrees are in those entertainment books. Demographics have proven that coupons are instrumental in getting first-time customers to sample your cuisine. And it doesn't have to be a large discount; fifty cents is sufficient. You can even establish a certain amount that has to be spent, say four dollars, to prevent people from using a fifty-cent coupon toward an eighty-nine-cent Coke."

"I'll think about it," Kendall murmured in a tone laced with apprehension.

"Specials is another way of getting business," Spencer continued. "I didn't notice you offering one."

"No, I don't."

"That's another tack you can try. It can be posted in the restaurant itself or on a coupon. You can offer a higher-profit item like whiting sandwiches at a reduced price. Remember, Kendall, what you want to do is get the people *in* your restaurant. Once they try the food, they'll be back. Look at me, Michelle, and the boys. Our first sample was free, and we came in as soon as we could."

He had a point, she thought. That was actually similar to her practice of giving small containers of yogurt, an ounce or two, to children and senior citizens. Both acts were goodwill with a purpose; namely, to please the customer while at the same time assuring their return. And it worked. She recognized many of her elderly patrons from their numerous repeat visits to the restaurant. It was harder to track the children, since so many of them were just vacationing in the area.

"Just watch the timing," Spencer said. "You don't want to offer discounts when there's a big weekend going on and the town is full of hungry people with money to spend. That's why advertising a special on the premises might work better. You can take it down whenever you want."

Kendall thought of the upcoming college reunion week. Several thousand thirty- and fortysomething alumni—it was directed toward graduates of 1985 or earlier—were set to pour into Nile Beach. Every hotel room in town was booked. Spencer was right—money would definitely be made that weekend, which made it no time to be generous with her prices.

"I just wish I knew what Clyde was up to," she said with frustration. "I mean, Eddie tells me he's going to open soon. What I wouldn't do to just get a look at his menu."

Spencer kept his eyes on the road. An inner voice was urging him to tell Kendall about his involvement in the Sundowner. But this wasn't the right time. Not now, while the boys were asleep in the back and he had to concentrate on the road. But soon, he told himself.

Kendall fell asleep after about three hours, shortly after they crossed the Georgia state line. She woke up when she felt the car was no longer moving. "Why have we stopped, Spencer?" she asked sleepily.

"Because we were close to empty."

"Already? But we just stopped a little while ago."

"I hate to tell you this, my dear, but that was over three hours ago. Most of that gas has been burned." He frowned. "I'm racking a lot of mileage on my machine here. I guess I'll have to start using rentals for these trips if I don't want to replace her."

But Kendall's mind was still on his first comment. "Three hours ago . . . Spencer, where are we?"

He chuckled. "A little past Macon. Actually, we don't have a whole lot further to go."

Kendall sighed. "Oh, Spencer, I'm so embarrassed. Here I was supposed to keep you company. And since I've worked the night shift all week I was so sure I'd have no problem staying up."

"No problem. The way I see it, if you're getting some sleep now you'll be awake when we get in. I did want to get out this afternoon."

"But when will you sleep?" she asked incredulously.

"Oh, I'll grab a quick nap after I drop off the boys. It won't take much. A couple of hours and I'll be good as new."

Kendall stayed awake the remainder of the trip. They tuned in to a radio station that apparently specialized in popular tunes from the seventies and eighties, some of which Kendall had not heard in years. If they remembered the words they sang along. *God, I love his voice,* Kendall thought. *The husky quality disappeared when he sang, but* she found it incredibly sexy regardless. Just thinking about his serenading her at her parents' party made her tingle all over. That night had been pure enchantment, or at least it had been, until Oscar knocked her in the pool.

It was light when they reached the suburb where Spencer's former wife resided, but still quite early. Spencer drove to the hotel. He glanced at his sleeping sons in the back seat. "No point in waking them up until it's time to go in. Why don't you come with me as I register?" he suggested to Kendall, who agreed.

"Isn't it kind of early to be checking in to a hotel?" Kendall asked as he held the front door open for her. "I thought they never had rooms ready until the afternoon."

"You can do just about anything the nontraditional way if you're willing to pay for it."

The front desk area was deserted. The clerk, a young man in his twenties, greeted them halfheartedly when he appeared. Kendall wondered if he had been sleeping. "I'd like two rooms, please," Spencer said, "one with two beds. I've got my sons with me, and the other room is for the lady." He and Kendall smiled at each other.

The clerk looked at them both, his expression impassive. "Would you like adjoining rooms, sir?" he asked, directing his query to Spencer.

The implication infuriated Kendall, as well as the clerk acting like she was invisible. She glared at him while Spencer crisply answered, "Not particularly."

Aware he had made an error in judgment, the clerk hastily went into an overview of the hotel's attributes. Kendall's hungry ears grasped on to the part about the breakfast buffet that was served until 10:30 A.M.

They were given keys to rooms on the same floor of the midrise hotel. "That breakfast sounded like a pretty good idea," Kendall said tentatively as they returned to the car.

"Tell you what. I'll square away the boys and we'll go eat."

But as it turned out Brian and Carlton instantly awakened at the thought of food. All four of them went to the buffet, where they hungrily devoured eggs, bacon, sausage, ham, potatoes, and biscuits.

As she stood beside Spencer serving herself seconds from the buffet table, Kendall was reminded of something that she had stuck in the back of her mind. "The cookout you and Michelle had Memorial Day," she began. "Michelle mentioned that everyone brought a dish, but you had real chafing dishes. Restaurant quality, like these."

"Oh, those. I picked them up at a restaurant supply store. They're good to have . . . like a tuxedo," Spencer replied easily. In truth he had simply borrowed them from his restaurant stock. It was disturbing how easily the lie rolled off his tongue. He was just glad the boys weren't within earshot—his behavior shamed him.

Bellies full, they headed toward their respective rooms. "Here, you guys," Spencer said to his sons, holding out a key that was actually a plastic card. "I'll catch up with you."

Both anxious to be the one to unlock the door— although the older, Brian, held the key and consequently the winning edge—the boys raced for the elevator. Spencer, Kendall felt, was deliberately lagging behind. With a touch of nervousness she wondered why.

She hesitated in front of the door to her room. Wordlessly Spencer reached over and took the key from her hand. He opened the door and followed her inside, closing it behind him.

Kendall turned to face him, able to smile once her eyes weren't focused on the enormous king-size bed that dominated the room, which made her a bit ill at ease. "Aren't the boys waiting for you?"

"Let them wait," he said with a touch of roughness. He pulled her into his arms, and she did not resist. This was where she had dreamed of being. It didn't matter to her that it was the morning sun rather than the moon that shone through the window, or that Brian and Carlton were just a few doors away, eagerly waiting to go to their mother's home.

She relaxed against his chest and closed her eyes. His lips found an erogenous zone behind her earlobe, and she felt herself losing control. This, she decided, was simply not right. The place was fine, but the timing was all off, despite the dizzying spin of her stomach and the tingle in her groin that so fervently begged for satisfaction.

"Spencer," she finally managed to say, "if you don't leave now, you won't."

"What's so bad about that?" he murmured against her skin.

Everything, she thought. She was frightened of the unfamiliar feelings she had for Spencer. Moving to the plateau of intimacy terrified her. It would signal a change in their relationship she wasn't sure she could handle. And it wasn't like he was declaring undying love for her; only raw desire. When he was satisfied, what would happen? Lovemaking, while physically fulfilling, had not been sufficient to overcome the conflict in her relationships in the past, and it was foolish to think this time would be any different.

But instinctively she brushed away the thought of being cast aside like the proverbial old shoe. She knew she did not represent a conquest for Spencer; he was well beyond that kind of high school mentality. The only thing Spencer Barnes was trying to conquer was the Nile Beach tourist market. Whatever it was he felt for her, she was sure it was more than mere lust. And she certainly felt more than desire for him . . . but, of course, that was precisely why she was so afraid of being hurt.

Her long silence spoke for her. "All right, all right," Spencer said in a voice heavy with defeat. "I'm going to take the boys over to their mother's. Is it all right if I bring your bag in when I get back?"

"Sure. I won't need it; I'm going to take a nap. Just knock when you get back."

"All right." He kissed her chastely on the cheek. "Get some sleep."

* * *

"So, Spencer, how's Kendall?" Arjorie asked.

"What!"

Arjorie Miller grinned, obviously pleased at catching her normally composed ex-husband off guard. "Brian and Carlton told me about her," she said. "She's made . . . quite an impression on them. That's certainly a change. Most of your girlfriends are merely 'okay' in their opinion."

He shrugged. "That's because Kendall's the only one they get to see independently of me. She lives upstairs from us." It wasn't until after he had spoken that he realized he hadn't disputed Arjorie's characterization of Kendall as his girlfriend.

"Yes, they told me. She's free during the day because she's got some kind of night job."

Spencer smiled. "Some kind of night job" was hardly how he would describe Kendall's occupation, but he didn't bother to correct Arjorie's impression. In the many years since their divorce, he had always made a point to keep his personal life just that—personal. All Arjorie knew was what the boys told her.

"So when do I get to meet her?"

His eyes narrowed in confusion. "What are you talking about, Arjorie?"

She lowered her swollen body into a chair. "From what the boys tell me she's very special. You do remember my introducing you to John before I married him."

"I promise you this, Arjorie, when I consider remarrying I'll be sure to introduce you to my intended, whomever she may be." Things were getting out of hand. First Michelle, now his own offspring. Brian and Carlton were talking out the sides of their mouths. It was as he had said, they had never spent any time with any of the women in his life, and knowing Kendall was interested in them as well and not just romancing their father impressed them to the point where they would go on and on about her.

But discussing Kendall was leading to nonstop thoughts of her, lying alone in that huge king-size bed.

He couldn't stand it anymore. "Arjorie, I'm really tired," he said, rising. "I'll stop in tomorrow to see the boys before I leave."

"That's right, make me get up again," she said as she struggled to get to her feet. Laughing, Spencer extended a hand and pulled her up. "The boys are hoping you'll drop that load quickly," he commented good-naturedly.

"Humph. Nobody's more eager for that to happen than me."

He squeezed her hand affectionately. Spencer harbored no ill will toward his ex-wife, nor did he consider his marriage a mistake. Arjorie was really a fine woman—a woman whose background of childhood poverty had made stability and security of utmost importance to her. Their marriage disintegrated because of her reluctance to accept his desire to give up a lucrative but highly stressful position in the whirlwind of high finance to pursue the uncertain career of an entrepreneur. Although in the end she did back him and even relocated to Atlanta with him, the long period of financial unsteadiness, where most of the burden of their living expenses was on her, coupled with his working from sunup until sundown had proved to be too much for her in the end. She used to complain that she might as well be a single parent, since all the discipline for the boys—who were toddlers at the time and getting into everything—was on her shoulders. They had fought bitterly about parenting and money matters before deciding to part. There was a brief period of awkward relations and mutual resentment during the dissolution of their marriage, but in the years since they had fallen into an easy camaraderie. They both agreed that what mattered most was the happiness of their children, and they knew Brian and Carlton were better for the harmony that existed between them. They each had memories of a good life together, a life both of them knew was firmly entrenched in the past. "See you later," Spencer said in parting.

* * *

"How long has it been since you've been to this area?"
Spencer asked Kendall over lunch.

"Probably five or six years," Kendall replied. "It hasn't
changed much, only that there seem to be a lot more
people here. I didn't think that was possible."

He chuckled. "Traffic is a real problem."

"Actually, a few of my friends from college have settled
here," Kendall remarked. "I figured I could look up one
or two of them. You know, while you're out doing what
you have to do."

"I've already done what I have to do. Now I'm all yours."

She had a sudden vision of the large bed in her hotel
room and swallowed hard.

They spent the afternoon in the city proper, doing typical tourist activities like going through the underground
and touring the King Center and Auburn Avenue. They'd
even gone by the campus of her alma mater, Spelman
College.

"Oh, Spencer, I enjoyed that so much," Kendall said
when they were in the car for the return trip to the hotel.
"I can't remember the last time I've been away from Palmdale, and I think I was due. And," she added shyly, "being
with you is certainly a nice bonus."

"I'm glad you came. But the day's not over. Tonight I
want to take you somewhere."

"Ooh, sounds interesting. Why do I get the impression
you're not going to tell me until we get there?"

"You have excellent intuition, my dear. Dress like you're
going out for the evening, but not too fancy."

"Good, because I left my cocktail dress at home." Kendall felt her excitement growing. She always loved surprises, and she had a feeling the evening was going to be
very special indeed . . . in more ways than one.

* * *

The extension in Kendall's room was ringing when she got out of the shower. "Hello," she greeted breathlessly.

"Kendall, it's Barry."

Kendall, expecting to hear Spencer's voice, was silent for a moment. Her brother was in Palmdale, hours away. "Barry?" she finally repeated.

"Yes. You sound like you're having a good time and I hate to interrupt it, but I promised Mom I'd call you."

Suddenly Kendall understood the reason for the call. "He's dead, isn't he?"

"Yes. This morning. Apparently it happened sooner than the doctors thought. I know you weren't enthused about the idea of going to his funeral, Ken, but it would mean a lot to Mom if all three of us went."

"I told her I'd think about it, Barry."

"Well, think fast. The wake is Tuesday night and the funeral will be Wednesday."

"Tues—for crying out loud, Barry, he's barely had a chance to get cold! How can they have the arrangements made already?"

"I don't know, Ken, maybe it's been a slow week for the undertaker. Just be prepared to leave on Monday morning if you're coming."

"I'm not due back until Monday morning."

"Zena said you'll be in at dawn or before. You'll have time to pack. We won't leave until midmorning. That'll still give us enough time to be there by Tuesday afternoon. You can sleep in the car."

She sighed. "I'll let you know."

The call dampened her spirits. She forced herself to put on a cheery sundress to prepare for her evening out with Spencer. It doesn't matter, she told herself. Nothing in my life has changed now that Kenneth Lucas is dead. For me he died a long time ago.

Somehow she managed to be ready when Spencer knocked on her door. But the sparkle had gone out of her eyes.

She opened the door and matched his broad grin with

a forced smile that failed to reach her eyes. Spencer's expression immediately turned to one of concern. "Kendall? Something's wrong, I can tell."

"I'm fine," she stubbornly insisted.

He closed the door definitively behind him. "You're lying," he accused. "You were fine when I left you a few hours ago. In the interim something's happened to upset you. I want to know what it is."

She turned her back to him, not wanting to look into his stern visage.

Spencer stood watching her. Had she somehow found out . . . ? No, that was impossible. Besides, she was struggling to put up a good front, something he doubted she would do if she had learned about his involvement in the Sundowner.

This had gone far enough, he decided.

She heard him approach from behind before she felt his strong hands on her shoulders, spinning her around. "You realize how ridiculous this is, you standing here looking like you've lost your best friend and refusing to tell me why." Her gaze was fixed on some object behind his shoulder, and with his hand on her chin he gently forced her to look at him instead. "I said talk to me, Kendall. What's bothering you?" His voice was rougher than usual in his impatience.

"Barry called me from Palmdale. Our father died this morning."

Spencer's brow furrowed in puzzlement. Just last week Paul Ridgely had been alive, well, and partying. "Wait . . . you mean your biological father?"

She nodded.

This was deep, Spencer thought. Death had transformed the person she usually referred to as her mother's first husband into her father. "I think I understand. You expected to feel nothing, but your emotions are playing tricks on you," he stated.

"I haven't seen him in nearly twenty years, Spencer. He came to see us just before we left Philadelphia to move to

Nile Beach. Neither Barry nor I was too enthused about his visit. It was the first time we had seen him other than in passing, and most kids don't appreciate being forgotten about, or even worse, ignored. We were downright sullen about the whole thing. Now I wish . . ." her voice trailed off.

Spencer pulled her close and stroked her upper back. "I knew a lot of kids who grew up with absentee fathers. Some of them turned out just fine, and others went down the wrong path. But regardless of how they turned out, I always felt they always had one thing in common—they never got over it."

"You don't get over it," Kendall said softly. "You always feel it was something you did that made him go away and stay away."

"Kendall, from what you've told me your father was an alcoholic. He was that way before you were born. His behavior had nothing to do with you. He simply couldn't handle the burden of a family."

"Yeah," she whispered. Then she faced him. "Can I take a raincheck on tonight? Truthfully, I just don't feel up to being around a lot of people."

"That's fine," he said quickly. As anxious as he was to tell her the truth, he also knew this was not the time to hit her with another shock. Instead he would bring her to brunch in the morning. "Why don't you relax, and I'll see about getting us something to eat?" he suggested.

She stood on tiptoe and kissed his cheek. "You're really a very special man, Spencer Barnes," she said. "I know I've disappointed you—"

"It's no big deal. All that matters is that you get through this. And you will." He cupped her face and, using his bent pinky fingers, arranged the corners of her mouth into a smile. "Now, how's Chinese?"

CHAPTER TEN

Kendall removed her shoes and reclined across the bed, remote control in hand, and prepared to flip channels until she found something interesting. Spencer was so understanding. What a relief it was that she didn't have to go out and pretend everything was fine while she was struggling to understand the conflicting feelings raging inside her.

She would go to the funeral, she decided. If she didn't, she'd regret it always, just like she regretted her lack of warmth the last time she'd seen her father. It was like her mother said. The chapter had been completed a long time ago, but now she needed to close the book once and for all.

In his room, Spencer retrieved the booklet of the restaurant delivery service who catered to area residents and hotel dwellers. Aside from the daily buffet breakfast, their hotel did not have a restaurant and thus no other meal service. Some enterprising individual had compiled menus from various area restaurants and condensed them into a digest-sized booklet. Surely there was a Chinese restaurant included.

It took only a few minutes to decide what to get and place the order. He was informed it would take approximately one hour for delivery. "Delivery to room 314," he instructed, giving them Kendall's room number.

"Ooh, that was quick," Kendall said when she let him in. Her gaze darted to his empty hands. "What happened?" she asked.

"I called in an order. It'll be delivered in about an hour."

"An hour!"

"I know it seems like a long time, but if we had gone out it would have been at least that long, by the time we got there and decided what we wanted."

"Really? And where were we going, Savannah?"

Spencer smiled. "No, merely back into the city."

Kendall nodded. She went back and took her place on the bed. "Make yourself comfortable," she said.

Spencer passed on the opportunity to comment; this was no time for innuendo. Instead he took a seat at the round table at the side of the bed.

"The newest Steven Seagal movie is coming on in a little while," Kendall remarked.

"Great. Dinner will probably be here by then." He paused. "Talk to me. How are you feeling?"

Kendall shrugged. "Confused. I can't make sense of how I feel."

"I can disappear for a while, until the food comes, if you'd prefer," he offered, not really meaning it but not sure what to do.

"No, I'm glad you're here. I think I'd rather talk about something else, though."

"Sure."

They were watching a recap of the day's events on CNN, Kendall only halfheartedly. Her mind was in the past. Suddenly it all become too much, and without warning, a sob caught in her throat. Spencer was at her side in an instant.

He separated her face from the pillow she was using to muffle her cries, substituting his shoulder in its place. "It's all right, honey," he soothed, his palm firm on her shoulder, his fingers massaging her bare flesh. "You let it out. I'm right here."

She cried out the frustration, hurt, and confusion. It seemed like her display of emotion went on forever, but it actually only lasted a few minutes. "I'm acting like a big baby," she assessed, as she wiped her eyes.

"Don't be ridiculous. Your father just died," he said, handing her a handkerchief from the breast pocket of his sports coat.

Kendall patted the damp skin around her eyes and blew her nose. Then she giggled.

"What's so funny?"

"I was just thinking about all those scenes in movies when the man hands the woman a handkerchief, she blows out all her boogers into it and then hands it back to him. Yuck." She loosely folded the cotton square and placed it beside her on the bed. "I'll wash it for you. And thanks."

"I'm feeling very helpless," Spencer said honestly. "It's not a feeling I'm accustomed to. But I don't know what I can do for you, to make you feel better."

"You're helping more than you know just by being here." The last thing she wanted was to be alone. It occurred to her that Spencer had been there to comfort her when Oscar Signeous knocked her into the pool at her parents' party as well. How wonderful it was to have him here so close . . . and how indispensable he was becoming in her life.

She leaned into his chest, and Spencer, overcome by her nearness, lifted her face to his and gently kissed her lips. She needed no coaxing to allow his tongue to enter her willing mouth.

Kendall's spine straightened, and her arms went around his neck as the kiss deepened. She tasted him hungrily, making no secret of her arousal, while his tongue did a slow exploration of her mouth, roaming over every hidden spot.

The knock on the door caused them to break apart, both breathing heavily. "That's probably dinner," Spencer said, disguising the annoyance he felt at the timing. Food was not going to satisfy the hunger in his groin. And now Kendall was averting her eyes, probably out of guilt. Why couldn't she see there was nothing wrong with their wanting each other the way they did?

He answered the door and was immediately greeted by the unmistakable scent of stir-fried meat and vegetables liberally doused with soy sauce. "Thanks. Keep the change," he said, handing the delivery man several bills.

"It smells delicious," Kendall said. She was grateful for the interruption. Heaven only knew what would have happened otherwise. Her behavior was deplorable. She was supposed to be grieving, for heaven's sake.

They ate at the table, feasting on won ton soup, sweet and sour pork, spare ribs, and egg fu yung from paper containers using plastic utensils. Afterward Kendall longed to take a comfortable position on the bed to let her food digest, but she was reluctant to do so. That would be like sending him a signal to join her so they could pick up where they left off . . . and under the circumstances of a death in her family she didn't think that was proper.

Spencer seemed comfortable, leaning back in his chair with his shoeless feet resting on the edge of the bed. His attention was riveted on the action moves of Steven Seagal. Kendall decided it was safe, and she moved to the bed, stretching out on her stomach in front of the television.

The movie was exciting, but the effects of the stress plus the heavy meal were tiring, and she dozed off before it ended. The feel of soft lips on her cheek spurred her awake.

"You all right?" Spencer whispered.

"Ye-es. I guess I must have nodded off. I've been doing that a lot since I've been working nights. I'm not adjusting very well to being a night owl."

"Your body needed the rest." He smoothed a loose strand of her hair. "I'll let you sleep. Tomorrow I'll take you to brunch."

"All right." She pulled herself up into a sitting position, knowing she would have to put the security chain on the door when he left. But before she could get to her feet he leaned over and once more took possession of her mouth. Kendall's head leaned all the way back on her neck to give him the best access possible. Soon they were kissing with abandon, all the pent-up desire each of them had kept inside so long rising to the surface like a Frisbee in the ocean.

Kendall held on to him like a lifeline. She felt like she was floating as they leaned backward into a reclining position, Spencer's hand supporting her back until it met the firm mattress. His upper body covered hers, and when their kiss ended his lips moved to her slender throat, covering it with feathery kisses and tasting her skin with his moist tongue. His hand boldly kneaded her breasts, first one, then the other. She clutched his arm and groaned in delight, loving the breathless way his kisses and touches were making her feel.

"Kendall," he said gruffly, "I'm only human. If I don't leave right now, I won't leave at all," he added, echoing her own words of earlier that afternoon.

Her gaze met and held his. "I don't want you to leave. Not now. I don't know how I'm supposed to be feeling, but God help me, I know I want you."

He put a finger to her lips, determined to erase any feelings of remorse that would almost certainly return to haunt her later. "You have nothing to feel guilty about. Some people feel they should only make love when everything is going well, but the wise indulge because they want to be close to someone, to give the gift of themselves."

"I'm all yours, Spencer," she said simply.

Spencer pulled her back into a sitting position and kissed her again, his fingers impatiently removing the pins that held her bun in place. When it was loose, he ran his hands through the soft masses, then reached behind her neck for the fastening of her halter dress. He ran his tongue lightly over her lips before moving back far enough to be able to pull the fabric down to her waist. Kendall's small, pert breasts jutted out proudly, her nut-brown nipples standing at attention.

"Kendall," he said softly. "I don't think you know how beautiful you are." He leaned forward and planted a kiss on her bare shoulder. Kendall responded by raising her hips an inch or two above the mattress, and Spencer promptly eased the dress over her hips, taking her slip and satin-like panties with it.

Kendall reclined back into the comfort of the big bed. The look of longing in his eyes said it all as he admired her slim form, so perfectly female. For a few moments she merely lay there, enjoying the naked adoration in Spencer's eyes as he assessed her body. Then she was overwhelmed by desire for him to join her on the bed. She sat up on her knees and tugged at his shirt, and he, equally eager, helped undo the buttons. Spencer was wearing a V-necked undershirt underneath, in spite of the heat. He quickly pulled it over his head, exposing a muscular brown chest.

It took him only a moment to undo his belt and pull down his trousers and underwear, and in the same fluid motion he leaned over and removed his socks. It all happened so quickly Kendall didn't get a full view of him until he stood up. What she saw took her breath away. Spencer had a marvelous physique, lean and muscular, with just a smattering of chest hair. It pleased her to know she was responsible for the swollen erection pointing toward her, containing the promise of inconceivable pleasure.

Spencer knelt on the bed and held out a hand to her. She gestured for him to wait a moment and moved to turn off the light. "No," he said, grasping her hand and pulling him toward her. "We're not going to grope in the dark. I want to look at you."

And he proceeded to do just that, as well as explore

her femininity, after positioning her in the center of the massive bed. His hands were big and square—Kendall's small breasts nearly disappeared when he cupped them. She let out an uncontrolled squeal of pleasure when he gently pinched her sensitive nipples, increasing their already enlarged size. Instinctively she reached out and clasped his right wrist, holding him captive to continue his play. Spencer stimulated her tips until they had nearly doubled in size, then took them into his mouth one at a time and rubbed the hard nubs playfully between his teeth. With his free hand he reached between her legs and teased her maddeningly by pulling at the thatch of curly hairs but not venturing any further. Kendall arched her back and swiveled her hips, trying to capture his roaming fingers where she wanted them most . . . inside the growing moistness between her thighs.

Spencer held back as long as he could, enjoying Kendall's frenzied efforts to get him to touch her and wanting to prolong the anticipation. He gasped audibly when his fingers finally made contact with the warm, wet flesh of Kendall's innermost existence. She was clearly ready to mate with him. He glanced up at her face. It was just as he had imagined it would be—her black hair fanned against the stark white pillowcase made for a dramatic contrast. Her eyes were closed, her lips were parted, and she was a splendid sight to behold in her state of heightened sexual excitement.

He ran his palm over her breasts. No way, he thought, would he have let her turn out the light and missed seeing her like this. She was too exquisitely lovely to be a shadow in the night.

Kendall's eyes flew open in confusion when his hand abruptly left her. Nothing could describe the ecstasy she was deriving from his exploring hands. The light grazing he so expertly applied with his coarse-textured fingertips electrified her, and she wanted to know why he had suddenly stopped when she so craved his touch.

He was, she saw, reaching for his slacks. The question

was forming on her lips, but it died when she saw the gleam of the aluminum packet of protection he pulled from his pocket. Her body tingled in eager expectation as she waited for him, but it seemed like he was moving in slow motion. Suddenly she felt that she could stand the wait no more. Reaching out, she firmly took the opened packet from him and gently removed the latex sheath lest she tear it. Forget about being a spectator—she would apply it herself.

Spencer gasped when her hands made contact with his sensitive, swollen organ. Kendall had never put a condom on a man before, but the feel of his long, thick shaft throbbing against her hand with a life all its own gave her the confidence she needed. With one hand she held him steady and with the other she placed the latex ring over the bulbous tip and rolled it all the way down. When she was done she did not remove her hand but squeezed and gently pulled his skin back and forth, rewarded by him swelling in her grasp.

Spencer cried rapturously. He had hardly dared to think of her touching him this way. Kendall was giving him more pleasure than he thought was possible.

But now he wanted to make her cry out in elation. He eased her onto her back and positioned himself between her knees. "I just want to lose myself in you," he whispered raspily as he sensually rubbed the tip of his fully erect manhood against her opening, "and never be found."

There was a swishing sound as Kendall drew in her breath. "Oh, Spencer," she begged. "Don't tease me anymore. I can't stand it."

"All right, sweetheart. No more teasing." With that he slowly slid himself into the haven of her warmth. They both moaned at this, the ultimate of contacts. Kendall's silky legs wrapped around his lower back, while her inner muscles contracted and gripped him tightly. She moaned shamelessly at the sensation, and Spencer took a moment to kiss her hard, wanting to convey to her the immeasurable joy she was giving him. Then he gradually pushed until he was completely immersed within her and began an easy rhythmic movement, to which Kendall moved as well.

Throughout his passion Spencer was careful not to let his body rest too heavily atop Kendall's. In spite of her five-foot, eight-inch height, Kendall had a small frame. He didn't want his weight to make her uncomfortable. A fine sheen of perspiration covered his upper body, a few drops falling from his chest into the hollow between Kendall's breasts.

Spencer balanced himself carefully, then lowered Kendall's right leg. "Hold on, sweetheart," he whispered. They rolled quickly until he was on the bottom, still sheathed inside her softness. He had waited an eternity to be able to touch her body so intimately and would not be put off another moment. It was too difficult for his hands to roam over her while he had to maintain his balance on his knees. Kendall was leaning over him, moving her hips up and down, and he sat up slightly so his mouth could reach her bouncing breasts. Spencer hungrily suckled the round globes, alternately stopping to run his tongue over her desire-stiffened nipples.

It was the strain on Spencer's back from being in a half sitting position that made him reluctantly stop his intimate acquaintance of Kendall's breasts. He laid back and gripped her hips, holding her steady while he rotated his pelvis wildly.

Kendall cried out his name repeatedly. She let out a guttural, unbridled cry as her body began a series of twistings, jerkings, and contractions that she could not control—did not want to control. Spencer pushed inside her for all he was worth before he, too, reached his climax.

He quickly lowered her until she was beside him, then pulled her close. Kendall rested her hand on his chest and felt the racing of his heart, which was in tandem with her own. This was it, she thought. They had crossed the bridge.

It was wonderful.

* * *

They slept like two spoons fitted together, Kendall's back pressed against Spencer's front, his hand intimately resting across her breasts.

Kendall had lain awake for quite some time after they made love, savoring the feel of his naked body so close to hers she could feel his sparse chest hair against her naked back as he breathed. She couldn't remember the last time she had been so happy, had felt so complete. And she wondered if the tingly good feeling she was experiencing was, at long last, love.

Kendall wished the night would last forever, but eventually her eyelids felt heavy, and she fell into a sound asleep. She stirred slightly when she felt warm breath on her cheek, murmured something unintelligible, and shifted position without opening her eyes.

It was morning when her eyes flew open in startled surprise at the feel of movement inside her ear, something warm and wet. Spencer was leaning over her, laughing. He flicked his tongue to silently show her what he had done.

"Oh, you ... stinker," she exclaimed. She reached behind her for a pillow to hit him with, but her movements were still sluggish from sleep, and he quickly moved for the same pillow. She squealed as he struck her on the shoulder with the pillow and scrambled to grab another— the king-size bed was equipped with four. Within seconds they were playfully attacking each other. They went at it until they were breathless and fell back in carefree laughter.

Kendall rolled over on her stomach. "You know, there's something I've been meaning to ask you."

"Really?" Spencer replied. "Fire away. I'll tell you anything you want to know."

"Your name is so unusual. Did your mother name you after Spencer Tracy?"

"She sure did. Lucky for me he was her favorite actor."

"Lucky for you?"

"Her second favorite was Humphrey Bogart. I can't imagine myself named after him. It may have looked impressive on a marquee, but it's hardly an everyday name."

"Even his friends called him Bogie. Just think, everybody would be calling you Barney!"

"God forbid. And what about you? I thought Kendall was a boy's name."

"I'm told they thought I was going to be a boy. My parents were going to name me Kenneth Junior, a notion that apparently didn't occur to them when Barry was born."

"Parents often have names of first children picked out in advance and get less original with other births." Spencer glanced at Kendall, who now looked a little down. "I hope you're not sorry about what we did," he said, putting a reassuring arm around her shoulders.

"No, not at all. I was just wondering how my parents felt when I was born. I'm sure they were still happy together then; that was before everything started to fall apart."

Spencer nodded. It was only natural she would be curious about her parents' lives together now that her father was dead, but he didn't want her to get morose. Though he had hoped to wish her a good morning by making love to her again, he knew the best thing for her would be to get out of this room.

"Tell you what, let's go get some breakfast. Then I want to stop by and see the boys real quick and we can head back for Palmdale. There's no point in sticking around here now, after what's happened. You need to get packed to go to the funeral."

THE RULING CLASS, said the sign over the double doors. Kendall wrinkled her forehead in thought as she tried to remember where she had heard that name before. Deciding it could have been anywhere, she shrugged and resumed her observation of the building. She was impressed by the well-kept looks of the restaurant. It had an aura about it that suggested good food and drink awaited all who entered.

The lighting was light and airy, with high ceilings, floor plants, and a catchy black-and-white tile pattern. Kendall's practiced eye easily determined that all it would take was a subtle reduction in lighting to change the atmosphere from intimate brunch to more intimate dinner. A quartet was performing jazz on a platform against the center wall.

Spencer was greeted by name by the hostess, who offered Kendall a smile of welcome and led them to a rear table. She handed them menus and retrieved the RESERVED sign from the table before disappearing.

A waitress at a nearby table was just finishing taking an order. "Hello, Spencer," she greeted, stopping at their table. "Do you two need more time?"

"Just a little, Connie, thanks," he replied.

"You must come here often," Kendall remarked as Connie moved on. "The whole staff seems to know you. But if you don't mind me saying so, maybe next time they can reserve you a better table."

Spencer didn't tell her he usually sat front and center but today had specifically requested a more discreet location. Instead he said, "It's more than my coming here a lot, Kendall."

"What do you mean? Do you have an interest in the place?"

"As a matter of fact, I do."

"Oh!" she exclaimed, leaning inward with interest at this latest revelation. "You never told me you owned part of a restaurant. It's nice that we have something in common."

Spencer swallowed. Okay, he thought, this is it. "You see, my brother Vincent is a chef. Ten years ago I was a stockbroker commuting to New York every day and on the verge of developing an ulcer. I was looking for something to invest in, and when he came to me about opening his own restaurant we formed a partnership. That's how my little empire got started."

"A partnership? As in fifty-fifty?"

"That's right."

Kendall shook her head. "Well . . . that's wonderful, but I can't imagine why you didn't want me to know. You own a restaurant that's obviously doing quite well, but I knew you were doing well when you showed me what you're doing in Nile Beach. So why did you keep this such a secret?"

Spencer couldn't remember the last time he'd had to do anything so difficult. "Because . . . last year my brother and I made a deal with Clyde Simmons to take over the restaurant in the Sunrise Hotel."

All the moisture in Kendall's mouth evaporated at his words. She swallowed, which was painful because of a sudden lump in her throat. The room began to blur around her, and she unconsciously gripped the edge of the table. How could that be? her mind screamed. Icy fear twisted around her heart as she looked at him across the table, hoping to see something that would tell her it wasn't true. But the look of anxiety on his face gave a very different message.

"You . . ." she whispered, "*you* . . . after everything . . . oh, God, after last night . . ."

She looked so hurt, like a rag doll about to unravel. Spencer reached out to take her hand, but she sprang to life and jerked both her hands into her lap before he could reach her.

"You knew how I felt, how worried I was about the Sunrise, and instead of telling me the truth, there you were, so eager to lend me a sympathetic ear." Her voice, at first a hurt whisper, now dripped with venom. "No doubt you were trying to find out as much as you could about Soul Food to Go in the process. I confided in you and trusted you, Spencer, and you repay me by trying to put me out of business. How could you?" Oh, Lord, her mother

was right. She had trusted too soon, and the resultant pain
was unbearable.

"I'm not trying to put you out of business, Kendall. I
think you know better than that."

"All I know"—she caught the rising volume of her voice
as diners at nearby tables turned to look in their direction
and immediately spoke in a lower tone that was no less
harsh—"is that one day you showed up as my new neighbor, all full of mystery about yourself but wanting to know
all about me. And now after we"—she couldn't bring herself to say "made love"—"after we slept together, you
suddenly decide to be honest. You used me, Spencer."

Spencer was stunned. If anything he thought their lovemaking had cemented their relationship. He had never
felt so close to Kendall, and he thought she felt the same.
He knew she would be upset that he hadn't been straight
with her, but he never expected her to feel he had used
her for sexual purposes. "No, honey, you've got it all
wrong. I've been wanting to tell you from the beginning,
even before we started seeing each other."

Her gaze was unrelenting. "Don't give me that, Spencer.
You had plenty of opportunity, and you know it. All you
wanted to do was get me into bed. I'll never forgive you
for this."

Something about her words inflamed Spencer. Then he
realized that the inability to forgive seemed to be a familiar
facet to Kendall's personality. He knew she was still bitter
toward Oscar Signeous, a harmless old man who enjoyed
his bottle, for accidentally knocking her into the pool at
the party. And then there was the matter of her own birth
father, whom she had only acknowledged after his death.
"Like you never forgave your father?" he countered.

She flinched, then her facial muscles turned to steel.
"You leave my father out of this, Spencer," she said, her
tone low and menacing.

"I just want you to see the impossible restrictions you're
putting on yourself, Kendall. Anyone who rubs you the

wrong way gets written off—permanently. Go through life like that, and at the end you'll have nothing but regrets."

"Don't you dare preach to me—"

"Last night I got the impression that you'd like nothing better than to have an opportunity to go back in time and talk to your father, find out what was on his mind and why he stayed away from you. Now all you can do is attend his funeral in your black dress and sob."

"At least I'll wear black. If it was your funeral, I'd wear a dress the color of sunshine."

They glared at each other. "I think we should leave," Spencer said with a stoic calmness Kendall found infuriating.

Without answering she noisily pushed her chair backward and rose, hastily moving toward the door.

Connie was delivering an order when he passed her on his way out. "Spencer?" she asked in puzzlement.

"We won't be staying," he said crisply.

Kendall stood in the vestibule, struggling to fight back tears. She would not give him the satisfaction of seeing her cry, of knowing how much he had hurt her. She would not falter.

Spencer held the door open for her, irritating her with his cool, aloof manner. She did not speak as they walked to the car or when he seated her. Finally, when he was behind the wheel he turned to her and asked, "Are you going to give me the silent treatment or are we going to talk about this?"

Kendall merely glanced at him with narrowed eyes, then looked straight ahead.

Spencer's voice was cold. "Fine. I think you're behaving like a child, Kendall. This isn't going to solve anything."

"I'd just like to get back to the hotel, please," she replied in a taut voice.

It was a long ride, and Kendall balled her fists so tightly her nails dug into her palms. It was painful, but it helped her keep her resolve. Spencer Barnes was not going to see

her crumble, she thought, forcing herself to look out the
passenger window.

Back at the hotel, Spencer slammed his room door shut
behind him. He had expected Kendall to shout at him,
demand an explanation, call him an expletive, anything
but refuse to speak to him. She hadn't said one word the
entire drive back from town. He was seething at her child-
ish behavior, but he felt she would want to talk out her
feelings eventually. All he could do was wait for her to cool
off. Maybe during the drive back. Seven hours was a long
time to go without talking.

In the meantime, he decided, this was as good a time
as any for him to go say good bye to Brian and Carlton.

Spencer wasn't really concerned when he called her
room a few hours later and got no answer. She had to
know it was him and probably was deliberately refusing to
answer the phone. But when she still wasn't answering by
5 P.M. he felt the first twinges that something wasn't right.
He called the front desk. "This is Spencer Barnes in 322.
I've been trying to reach Ms. Lucas in 314 for several hours
now—"

"Oh, Ms. Lucas checked out early this afternoon."

"What?"

"I wasn't on duty at the time, sir, but I do know she left.
The room's being prepared for the next guests right now."

Spencer mumbled his thanks and hung up. He dashed
into the hall. Sure enough, the ugly metal wheeled contrap-
tion that held the maid's cleaning materials was parked
outside what had been Kendall's room, the room where
they had come together so joyfully just last night.

At the time he thought it was the beginning, but now it
looked like it might have been the end.

CHAPTER ELEVEN

It was a long and lonely drive back to Palmdale for Spencer. All he could think about was that he had blown it by waiting too long to be truthful with Kendall. Now her fury toward him had reached the point where she had taken matters into her own hands and left, probably for the airport to fly standby rather than spend seven hours in strained silence with him.

He expected to see her car when he parked behind the duplex just before 9 A.M., but there was no sign of it. She may have already left for Philadelphia, he thought, even though they supposedly weren't going to begin the drive until a little later. Maybe it was just as well she wasn't around—he didn't know what he would say to her if she were to suddenly appear before him.

The long drive usually wore him out, but today he slept for only a few hours. When he awoke, he knew there was no more going back to sleep.

He had to do something, anything, to get his mind off Kendall. Maybe a drive would help.

Spencer steered the Saab through the neighborhood. He quickly became caught up in the architectural beauty of the buildings. Several houses bore FOR SALE signs. Most were refurbished, but a few were still boarded-up shells. A bell went off in his head. His very first investment had been in real estate up in New Jersey, and maybe it was time he got back into it.

He remembered seeing a realty office on Main Street and headed that way.

To his surprise, Zena Lucas was sitting behind the desk. "Hi, can I help—" she broke off when she recognized him and exclaimed, "Hey there!"

So much for forgetting about Kendall, Spencer thought as the tense feeling he'd tried to escape immediately returned, making his arms and jaw grow rigid. "Hello, Zena. I didn't know you sold real estate."

"Oh, yes. That's my goal, to become Donna Trumpette."

"You didn't go to the funeral?"

She shook her head. "It really didn't make sense for me to go. They'll only be there a few days, and it's an awfully long ride for my son, even though Barry wanted to bring him along. I should be insulted that my husband has no problem being away from me for five days but can't bear to be away from his son, but I'm glad he's such a wonderful daddy. He didn't have a very good role model, but I'm sure Kendall's filled you in about Big Daddy Kenneth."

He nodded, and she smiled at him warmly. "I guess you miss Kendall almost as much as I miss Barry."

Spencer realized she was unaware of what had transpired between he and Kendall in Atlanta. "I miss her very much, but I'm afraid she's rather upset with me at the moment."

"Oh?"

"I told her I own the new restaurant in the Sunrise Hotel."

"You . . . you're Two Brothers, Incorporated?" At his nod Zena shook her head. "Oh, Spencer. This is not good, not good at all."

"Tell me about it," he said glumly.

"I mean, Kendall was just opening up to you. She trusted you. That in itself was pretty remarkable, because my sister-in-law is not easy to get close to. And the girl can hold a grudge longer than anyone I know. Good grief. Look at what it took to get her to her father's funeral. If I know Kendall, she probably feels like you tried to get close to her only because she owns Soul Food to Go. She has this tendency toward paranoia."

"That's not too far off the mark, and I guess I had it coming for not telling her sooner, but in a situation like this there's never a right time. If I had told her in the beginning, she would never have given me a chance to get close to her at all."

"Got that right. I wouldn't have been surprised if she packed up and moved out."

"What I don't understand is how she could have thought I'd bring her all the way to Atlanta just to break her heart. It was a wonderful trip up to that point. It's an awkward situation, and I expected her to be disappointed and even to question my motives—I'd feel the same way if that was me—but I figured once I explained that to her, we would spend the rest of the time working it out, figuring out how we could work together for a common goal of mutual success. The last thing I expected was for her to walk out on me. I don't understand it, Zena. She's a bright girl. Why can't she see that I care about her?"

Zena hedged. "Yes, Kendall's bright. She's got a fabulous business instinct. But it doesn't necessarily extend outside of business."

"Has she always been this way?"

"As long as I've known her."

Spencer smiled. "I've got the feeling there's something you're not telling me."

The way she averted her eyes told him he was right.

"All right, Spencer," she said. "I know you care about Kendall, but the truth is I just don't feel comfortable saying too much about her. I will tell you this—I'd bet money that it all stems from her father's abandonment. Since she's already told you about it I don't feel like I'm crossing any lines by saying that much."

"That makes sense. I'm no shrink, but I do feel that our childhoods have a large effect on our adult lives. Thanks, Zena. When are they expected back?"

"Not until Friday. They left this morning, and they'll start the trip back on Thursday, the day after the funeral."

Suddenly an idea popped into Spencer's head. It was rash, impractical, certainly irresponsible in view of the upcoming opening of the Sundowner and probably just plain dumb on top of that, but he reasoned he had to do something—something to prove to Kendall that he cared, that in him she had someone who wouldn't abandon her. "Zena, where will they be staying?" he asked.

She named the hotel. "I've got the phone number, too, in my purse."

"That's all right." He had more of an up-close-and-personal experience in mind, but he'd have to move quickly if he wanted to pull it off. "Thanks a lot," he said as he approached the door.

"Wait a minute. Aren't you interested in buying a house?"

"I'll get back to you later, I promise."

He tried the airlines first. All their flights were booked, and not even for Kendall could he deal with spending the better part of a twenty-four-hour period on a bus, and besides, bus travel was too slow. But there was one more alternative to driving.

The nearest Amtrak station was in Jacksonville, nearly fifty miles away. And when the train pulled out of the Jacksonville station on schedule that evening, Spencer was a passenger. He would be in Philadelphia the next afternoon. It occurred to him the wake for Kendall's father would be going on by that time and he didn't even know where it was being held, but he ought to be able to get the location from the newspaper, or just by asking around for names of funeral homes that had a mostly black clientele and calling until he found the right one. Kendall needed him, of that he was sure. Even if she didn't realize it, he would be there for her.

He slept through the night, but the train ride still seemed interminable. The stop in Washington, D.C., lasted about an hour, but Spencer was comforted by the knowledge that Philadelphia was only a few hours away.

At the station he took a cab to Kendall's hotel and reserved a room for himself, then arranged for a rental vehicle.

The desk clerk informed him there was no Kendall Lucas registered. On further questioning, he learned rooms were occupied in the names of Barry Lucas and Lily Ridgely. Spencer presumed Kendall was sharing a room with Chan. The desk clerk rang both rooms with no answer. It was six fifteen; apparently they had already left for the wake. Spencer thanked the clerk, grabbed his room key and garment bag, and rushed to his room and the yellow pages. The thought occurred to him that if he were staying at a full-service luxury hotel instead of a mid-level franchise he could simply have had the concierge find out where they were holding Kendall's father's wake.

It was a good thing so many funeral directors included their photographs in their advertising, he thought as he skimmed the listings from the beginning. That, plus the frequent use of family names—Spencer could instantly rule out ethnic places called Holowczak's or Cioppa's—helped him pinpoint the location with only four calls.

He took a hasty shower and dressed in a navy suit and navy-and- white striped shirt. A navy silk tie completed the ensemble. On his way out, he stopped at the front desk for directions to the funeral home.

It was a short drive, as he expected. No doubt its location had affected the Lucases' choice of lodging.

The chapel itself was crowded. It was easy to see from the two organs and the four rows of pews that it could be divided into two separate rooms for less well attended wakes and funerals, but in this case, the entire facility was being used. There was much conversation and laughter

going on. The atmosphere was more suggestive of a cocktail party than of a wake.

The first familiar face Spencer saw was that of Chan
Ridgely. She was talking with someone, or rather, listening.
Judging from her constant nodding—once every five seconds or so—she seemed anxious to get away. Her eyes did
a quick search of the room, another sign of her eagerness
to move on. At first she passed him over but then her
gaze returned, her eyes widening in astonishment. Spencer
watched as she held out a hand to the well-wisher and
quickly excused herself.

"Good heavens, Spencer, is that you?" she asked as she
approached.

"It's me, all right."

Chan took his hand with both of hers. "But what are
you doing here? What's going on? Kendall's been acting
so strangely since you two got back from Atlanta."

You two, he repeated to himself, as in together. So Chan
also did not know Kendall had walked out on him. Apparently Kendall hadn't wanted to discuss his revelation with
anyone, Spencer thought—at least none of her family
members. "Where is she now?" he asked, not answering
Chan's question.

"Up front somewhere, I think. The word must have
gotten out that we were coming. None of us expected this
many people to show up. The kids are seeing friends they
grew up with for the first time in twenty years."

"It's certainly crowded, all right. And Chan, I'm . . . um
. . . never mind. Excuse me." He had initially started to
offer condolences, but after second thought withdrew.
Under the circumstances, it didn't seem appropriate. He
knew Kenneth Lucas had long ceased to be one of Chan's
loved ones. Just the fact that she was here at all spoke
volumes for the type of woman she was. Too bad her
daughter did not possess the same capacity for forgiveness,
Spencer thought with a touch of wistfulness. He hurried
toward the front of the room, suddenly feeling he could
not wait another moment to see Kendall.

Chan stood looking after him. He had ignored her question, but she knew that whatever was going on it was strictly between him and Kendall. He must have gone through quite a bit of effort and expense to get to Philadelphia so quickly. Chan hoped her daughter would not give him the cold shoulder. Certainly none of the men she knew Kendall had been involved with over the years had demonstrated so much devotion. It was obvious that Spencer Barnes cared deeply for Kendall, a fact Chan could only pray her stubborn daughter would recognize.

Spencer easily spotted Kendall in the crowd. She was talking with a woman about her own age—probably one of the former classmates Chan was talking about—and wearing a simple black skirt and long-sleeved, geometric print black-and-white blouse. Her hair was pinned in a sedate bun.

He approached her from behind and abruptly took her hand.

Kendall knew the feel of the hand that covered hers all too well. That coarse texture . . . but it couldn't be.

She whirled around and looked straight into Spencer's serious gaze. Her heartbeat instantly became erratic and her legs felt weak, and for one terrifying moment she thought she was actually going to faint. She would no more have expected to see him here in Philadelphia than she would expect her father to suddenly sit up and talk. "My God . . . Spencer!"

At least she didn't snatch her hand away, Spencer noted. Surely that was a good sign. He nodded to the woman Kendall had been talking with before he approached. "Could you excuse us?" he asked politely.

The woman beamed, obviously delighted to see him at Kendall's side. "Certainly."

Spencer led a dazed Kendall to the corner. "Listen to me, Kendall. I know you're upset with me," he said in a low voice, "but I care for you, and I'm not going to let our business interests come between us. It can be worked out. But we can talk about that later. The main reason I came is because I know you're upset about your father and I wanted to be here with you . . . and for you." He searched her face, looking for a sign of acceptance. The expression of dazed disbelief mixed with confusion was still evident. "Kendall, will you please say something," he pleaded with a touch of impatience.

When she spoke it was in a whisper, and the two words she voiced melted his heart. "Oh, Spencer."

That was all he needed. Instantly he put an arm around her. He wanted to pull her close and keep her there, but he had to be content with discreetly caressing her neck and shoulder . . . for now. Together they walked a few steps and assimilated into the crowd.

The silver casket dominated this part of the room. Spencer glanced at Kendall, who nodded. He let his arm slip back in place at his side as they walked toward it, not wanting to add to the attention he was afraid they had already attracted in this most inappropriate of places.

All things considered, Kenneth Lucas looked remarkably well for a man who died an alcoholic on the threshold of becoming a senior citizen. The damage, Spencer concluded, was probably all internal. Kendall's father only had a smattering of gray hair, and his face was not particularly lined. It was difficult to tell how much of his looks Kendall had inherited, but Spencer suspected it was not much. Both Kendall and Barry strongly favored Chan.

"Does he look the way you remember?" he asked.

Kendall nodded. "He hasn't changed much. A little older, and his face is thinner than I remember. But my aunt tells me that until he went into the hospital a few months ago, he still went to work every day. Or at least most days. He was able to hold quite a bit of alcohol, but sometimes he went on benders and had to sleep it off. It's only because he worked at the plant so many years that they didn't let him go. Of course, after his diagnosis they knew he wouldn't be coming back."

* * *

The wake was scheduled from seven until nine, but Spencer thought it would never end. He caught up with Barry, who was just as surprised as Kendall and Chan to see him here but tactfully refrained from asking questions. Spencer liked Kendall's brother. Barry was unassuming and minded his own business, yet he had a personality firm enough not to be overshadowed by the boisterous nature of Zena, his wife.

During the evening he was introduced to dozens of people, including Kendall's aunt Freda, who had cared for her brother Kenneth during his last days and made his funeral and burial arrangements.

Spencer was talking with Barry and a few other people when he noticed a woman with reddish-brown hair go up to Kendall and envelop her in a bear hug. Kendall's expression of discomfort was nearly identical to the one Chan had worn when he first spotted her. Curious, he watched them interact, wondering why Kendall wanted to get away from this particular mourner. The woman pulled out her wallet and was apparently showing some photographs to Kendall, who nodded politely. Finally Spencer wandered over toward where they were standing, but before he reached them he saw Kendall and the woman share a quick hug and then Kendall was next to him. He placed his arm protectively around her shoulder. The fragrant scent of her shampoo smelled like a field of fresh garden flowers. "You all right?" he asked.

"'Is it time to go yet?"

"Not for nearly another hour. Is something bothering you?"

"I've about had it with all these people, Spencer."

He looked around, puzzled. "But I thought it would make you feel good to see so many people come out for your father."

"If only they had come out for my father."

"I don't get it."

"Some of our close neighbors from the projects are here, and a lot of people from my father's job and people who were tight with my mother and Barry and me. Those folks are all right, but half the people here came out of curiosity and nothing more. My mother and I haven't been back since we left, even though Barry has. They just want to see what we look like after twenty years. And to show off."

"Come on, Kendall, there's no way for you to know what their motives are."

"You can tell if someone's sincere or not by how they behave. If a person says hello to you in one breath and in the next is showing you pictures of their kids or of their house and telling you about their husband's latest promotion, I think it's safe to say their top priority is not to offer condolences. It's like there's this need to let us know they're not living in the projects anymore, like it really makes a difference. Take the one I was just talking to. We weren't even particularly friendly growing up, but she could tell from my father's obituary that I'm not married, so she didn't want to miss an opportunity to tell me all about her husband, her children, her house in the suburbs, her minivan and her damned dog." All the things I would expect to have if I was like any other woman, she thought with a touch of sadness. She knew her own doubts about herself had a lot to do with why she was so angry, but there was no question that this was no occasion to brag about domestic achievements. "If I wanted to see pictures of everyone's kids I would have gone to my fifteenth reunion last year," she concluded.

Spencer shrugged. "I think you're being too hard on everyone, Kendall. You don't have to be best friends with someone to attend the wake of their family member. And I guess it's important to them for you to know they've moved on, too. They probably just don't realize how insincere they sound by mentioning it so quickly."

"Maybe, but that was the fourth time it's happened. My

mother said it was happening to her, too. I'm sick of it, Spencer."

Spencer remembered Chan's uncomfortable expression when he first arrived. She was probably being subjected to a long description of someone's material successes. To Kendall he said, "If it's happened that many times, I can't say I blame you. Just keep being polite, and soon it will be over."

Spencer replayed her words in his head. Kendall was clearly not happy about having to look at pictures of people's children, but that was other people's children. She had given no hints of how she would feel about her own. He wanted to know about her feelings regarding husbands, houses in the suburbs, dogs, and children, especially children.

On the other hand, he was also reluctant to ask . . . because he feared the answer. It was natural for women to want a happy home life, and for most that included children. Look at Arjorie, starting all over with a baby at thirty-seven. Spencer personally thought his former wife was nuts. He was thirty-eight years old and already looking forward to the time when his boys would be adults, which actually wasn't all that far away. The last thing he wanted was to be burdened with a child still in grammar school when he was fifty. He knew Kendall was thirty-four. Her reproductive system was probably just starting the inevitable downward spiral, but she didn't seem concerned about it. Actually, just about the only thing she did seem concerned about was Soul Food to Go. While it was true that most women wanted children, he thought with a smile, it was also true that Kendall wasn't most women.

He considered that he might be getting ahead of himself. All he knew was that he wanted Kendall Lucas to be a permanent part of his life, and the realist in him told him it was best to learn as quickly as possible if they were faced with a possibly insurmountable problem . . . on top of the problem that was already threatening to tear them apart. But her feelings toward domesticity and all it entailed was quite an awkward topic, one that was hard to broach in casual conversation, so as much as he disliked feeling like he was keeping another secret from her, he knew it would have to wait until a more appropriate time.

Finally it was time to go. Only the Lucases, Spencer, and Kenneth's sister Freda and her family remained.

"My, I'm exhausted," Chan remarked. "It'll be all I can do to get a good night's sleep. It'll be ten A.M. and time for the service before we know it."

"Everyone's invited over to our house for lunch afterward," Freda said. "I can't believe all the food our neighbors and Kenny's co-workers brought. Oh . . . and the insurance man will be by tomorrow afternoon as well."

Kendall thought she saw her mother and aunt exchange glances, but neither woman made a comment. She wondered what was up.

"Well, if that's everything, I suggest we go home . . . I mean to the hotel," Chan said.

Outside, no one asked if Kendall would be riding with Spencer. Chan and Barry merely bid them good night and walked toward their own rental vehicle. Kendall suppressed a smile. She knew her mother and brother both were thrilled to see Spencer here in Philadelphia, and she couldn't blame them. She hadn't been the most pleasant person to be around during the long drive north. But learning Spencer had been the financial muscle behind Clyde Simmons's new restaurant had been the biggest shock of her life. No wonder he encouraged her to put coupons in local tourist and resident newspapers, she had angrily thought. It would work to his advantage for her to promote Soul Food to Go as just another fast-food restaurant, while he, in turn, presented the Sundowner as Nile Beach's new, elegant soul food bistro. Then there was her comment to her mother about feeling she could trust Spencer completely, as well as Chan's issue of caution that, of course, she'd failed to heed. Kendall had decided then and there that what had occurred in Atlanta would remain her secret. She felt like enough of a fool, without having everyone know about it.

She ensured her privacy by taking an airport van home from the Daytona Beach airport. Once there she immediately packed her bags and was at her mother's before the sun rose the following morning, lest she run into Spencer when he returned.

There were too many people at the wake for Kendall to have had a chance to think clearly about what Spencer's being here in Philadelphia meant, other than that he cared about her enough to want to be with her at a difficult time in her life. At least that proved his feelings for her were based on more than mere lust, but nothing had really been settled. How could they possibly work out a compromise when their very livelihoods required them to be rivals? They were, first and foremost, friends; also neighbors and now, at least once, lovers. The word "competitor" simply did not belong in that group.

"Where are you staying in town?" she asked when they were in the car.

"Same place you are. I ran into Zena yesterday and she told me where you were staying."

"Do you remember the way back to the hotel?" she asked.

"You'll probably have to help me out a bit. Everything looks different now that it's dark."

Kendall directed him on what turns to take but other than that didn't have much to say. Being alone with him in such close quarters made her a tad uneasy. Part of her was still angry and hurt at his deception, and then there was the other part, the part that wanted to fling herself into his arms and let him comfort her the way she suspected he wanted to, and would if he had just a hint of encouragement on her part. The conflicting emotions churning within her caused a state of confusion that was utterly exhausting. She simply wanted to lie down and give her brain a rest.

Once he brought the car to a stop in a space in the parking garage Spencer rushed to open the passenger door for her, but Kendall had already alighted. "Do you think we could stop in the lounge and talk for a few minutes?" he asked as he took her elbow and guided her toward the hotel entrance.

"If you don't mind, Spencer, I'm really tired. I'd like to just go to my room and get some sleep."

"I understand." She probably was beat. He was disappointed they wouldn't talk tonight, but there'd be plenty of time to clear the air. It was a long drive to Florida.

He walked her to her room, and they decided to be ready to leave for the funeral home by nine fifteen.

She turned to him just before unlocking her room door. "And, Spencer, I do want you to know that I really do appreciate your coming. It means a lot to me. I . . . I guess I was wrong about what I said to you about using me. I'm sorry. I was just so shocked by what you told me, I really didn't know what else to think."

He merely nodded. There was much he wanted to say to her, but a hotel corridor wasn't the place to say it. Instead he said, "It's all right, honey. Good night, and I'll see you in the morning." He bent and kissed her cheek, forcing himself not to touch her in any other way.

"Good night, Spencer."

He waited until she was inside and clicked the lock into place before turning and heading for his own room.

There were considerably fewer people in attendance at Kenneth Lucas's funeral service than there had been at his wake, mostly family and a few close friends and representatives from his job. Only about a quarter of the pews were taken. The management could have put the sliding wall in place and used just half the chapel to make the lack of mourners seem less obvious. Spencer reasoned that the other chapel probably just wasn't needed this morning.

He was at Kendall's side throughout, squeezing her hand

periodically for support. She shed a few tears at the brief
service, but when the funeral director moved to close the
casket for the last time she began crying in earnest, not
sobs, just a quiet torrent of tears streaming down her face,
no doubt thinking of all those lost years. Spencer put an
arm around her shoulders and encouraged her to lean
against him.

She complied, resting her head on his shoulders in spite
of herself. He felt so strong, so secure . . . she never wanted
to move. Thank God for Spencer, she thought. How could
she have gotten through this without him?

At the cemetery Spencer guided her by her elbow lightly,
his touch both urging and protective. He stood behind
her at the brief graveside service for which only eight chairs
had been provided beneath the small shaded tent. Chan
and Barry sat in front, along with Freda and her husband.
Spencer preferred to leave the remaining seats for the
other women present, but no way was he leaving Kendall's
side. His hands rested on her shoulders, employing a subtle
pressure just to let her know he was right behind her if
she needed him. Before he realized what he was doing
he had begun a circular massage, reaching down to her
collarbone and across to the tense muscles surrounding
her neck. Kendall murmured something unintelligible and
put her head back. When he glanced down he saw her
eyes were closed.

This part of the ceremony was even briefer than in the
chapel, but somehow it was easier on Kendall's emotions.
At the conclusion, she rose and laid a single yellow rose
on top of the casket. When she turned to face him her
face was tear-streaked but proud. Spencer offered her his
arm, and she took it and held it securely.

"My aunt is having everyone over to her house," she
remarked as they walked toward the winding road where
everyone had parked.

"Yes, I remember her mentioning it last night." Spencer
stopped suddenly in front of an impressive-looking granite

headstone. The word MURDERED appeared by the date of death.

"Oh, how sad," Kendall exclaimed. "He was only"— she paused to do the quick calculation—"nineteen."

"I suppose his parents wanted everyone to know what happened to him. Most people would be curious about someone who died so young." Spencer stared at the tomb, his mouth set in a hard line.

Instinctively she knew he was thinking of Brian and Carlton. "Murders are rare in Palmdale, you know," she said softly.

"I know. Still, it's every parent's worst nightmare. No child is one hundred percent safe, even in a burg like Sweet Apple, Iowa."

Putting his arm around her waist, he squeezed her affectionately before they resumed walking.

"What time is your flight out?" she asked.

"Actually, I'm driving back. I was hoping you'd ride with me. I think we need some time to sort things through."

Kendall knew her surprise showed in her expression. "How did you get here?"

"The airlines were booked, so I took the train. I've arranged to drop off my rental car at their location in St. Augustine."

"Oh." Kendall's mind was spinning. She wasn't at all sure she could handle being in such close proximity to Spencer for such a long ride . . . a ride that would ultimately require a night on the road. "I don't know what to say, Spencer. I just assumed you had flown up. This comes as a complete surprise."

Spencer suddenly felt that his patience was being tried to the maximum. "I'll get back to Palmdale regardless of whether you come with me or not, Kendall," he stated matter-of-factly. "But it seems like a good opportunity for us to talk things over, don't you think?"

Kendall shrugged. "Sure, why not."

* * *

Freda hadn't been exaggerating when she talked about all the food friends and neighbors had brought. The long rectangular table in her dining room held numerous roast chickens, several hams, a few bowls of fried chicken, fresh vegetables and dip, potato salad, macaroni salad, rolls, and three cakes.

Spencer was going for seconds and Kendall was discarding her paper plate when her aunt approached her. "The insurance man is here, Kendall," Freda said. "He needs to meet with the immediate family."

They went to the basement, which was furnished as a sort of recreation room, with a television, a pool table and a comfortable sofa and chairs upholstered in a nubby plaid fabric. Kendall shook hands with Thomas Graham, a middle-aged, balding man who wore a conservative gray suit and a bow tie. "Isn't it unusual for you to make house calls? My father's job must be paying extra for this type of service."

"Oh, I'm not affiliated with your father's job. He took out a policy with our company about twenty years ago."

"Oh," Kendall replied. She was surprised to learn her father had sought out additional coverage, and at that point in his life, when he was middle-aged and had long since abandoned his family. Twenty years ago . . . then she realized that was right about the time she and Barry had moved to Florida.

"Shall we begin?" Mr. Graham asked. At everyone's nods he cleared his throat. "First of all, my company would like to extend our condolences to you on the passing of Mr. Lucas. I know he was only sixty-two. Sometimes it seems unfair that so many don't get to enjoy retirement after a lifetime of hard work.

"Anyway, many years ago Mr. Lucas came to our office and requested a one-hundred-and-twenty-five-thousand-dollar whole life policy. He never missed a payment in all these years. I don't believe he was even late."

Kendall and Barry exchanged glances.

"He named three beneficiaries, but the divisions were not equal. Two parties will receive fifty thousand dollars, and the third twenty-five thousand." The insurance agent glanced at his audience before continuing. "The two main beneficiaries are Barry Darnell Lucas and Kendall Susan Lucas. The third is Freda Lucas Davis."

Kendall's mouth dropped open. Her father had left her fifty thousand dollars? It was incredible.

It was also terribly unfair. "But what about Mom?" she asked. "She's the one who suffered the most."

"It's all right, dear. I haven't been forgotten," Chan said. "You see, your father never changed his beneficiary from his insurance on the job, even after we were divorced. The policy was adjusted every year for inflation, and it's now worth sixty thousand. I've been well taken care of."

The insurance agent answered their questions before again expressing condolences and leaving. Freda showed him out.

"I want to explain something," Freda said when she returned. "Kenny knew he was not a good father, and he knew he was a miserable failure as a husband. He told me he wanted to do something to help make it up to you. He didn't expect to live as long as he did—he never lifted a finger to take care of his health—and he always said that when he was gone you would both get something to help make your lives a little easier. He never told me the exact amount, just that I would have a little something as well, even after his funeral expenses were paid. Kenny knew Chan would be taken care of as long as he managed to hold on to his job.

"He started giving me a few dollars every week when he got paid—he wanted me to make sure the premiums got paid if he forgot. You know his binges . . . Anyway, I had a feeling from the premium amounts that he had at least six figures worth of coverage. In his own small way he did try"—Freda's voice broke—"to do something to try to make up all the anguish he caused you all."

"Freda, don't cry," Chan said, embracing her former sister-in-law. "You're the best sister anyone could ever hope to have."

"It's such a waste, that's all. My brother's life could have been so different if only he didn't love that bottle so much. But I've gone to sessions for families of alcoholics, and they say the craving for alcohol is a disease."

"Freda, he lived the life he wanted to live. The important thing is that his alcoholism seems to be an isolated case. There's no evidence of it in my children or in yours." Chan hugged Freda again.

"Fifty thousand dollars," Barry said. "I guess now Zena can buy that house she wanted on Deacon Street."

"The blue one with the white trim?" Kendall exclaimed.

"That's the one. This should be enough for a hefty down payment, with plenty left over to invest. We can spend the rest of our lives furnishing it. And it'll probably take that long to do it," he muttered.

"Oh, Barry, I'm so happy for you!"

"What about you? What do you plan to do with your windfall?"

"I don't know," Kendall replied thoughtfully. "There's something I've been wanting to do for a long time . . . maybe this is just the financial backing I need."

"Another Soul Food to Go?"

"No. Two is enough. It was never my intention to start a chain. But something along those lines."

"Don't you ever think about anything else besides business?"

"It's my life," she replied simply.

Barry hugged her. "You really need to do something about that, little sister, or you're going to be a very lonely old lady."

Kendall quickly turned before he could see the tears in her eyes.

CHAPTER TWELVE

Spencer put Kendall's luggage in the trunk of the rented Pontiac. "I guess we'll see you back in Palmdale," he said as he shook Barry's hand.

"Aren't you two stopping at the same place we stayed at on the way up?" Kendall asked.

"Oh, we'll probably stop over the South Carolina border this time," Chan replied innocently.

Kendall stiffened. Somehow she would feel better if she knew her mother and brother were staying at the same motel as she and Spencer. This was her mother's doing; she could tell from that sly smile on Chan's face. She was practically being pushed into Spencer's arms. Not that she minded—but just not so quickly.

She decided not to let them see her uneasiness. "You didn't call ahead and make reservations?" she asked instead.

"No, we'll just stop when we get tired," Chan answered.

"Do you think that's wise, Mom? You know that sometimes the Southern motels aren't too happy to see us."

"We shouldn't have any difficulty if we stick with the major chains. Times are hard, and our money's definitely the right color even if we're not. Besides, we plan to stop for the night long before dark. Stop worrying, Kendall, we'll be fine."

Goodbyes were said all around, and then Kendall was sitting next to Spencer in the front seat. They managed to stay behind Chan's and Barry's rented van until they reached the highway, then the two vehicles quickly blended in with other southbound traffic.

Kendall closed her eyes and thought of the silent truce, the roots of which were in Spencer's offer of comfort to her at the funeral service. He had never been far away from her side after that.

Afterward, they had gone to Freda's, where the atmosphere was mostly jovial since the sad business at hand had been concluded. Freda insisted they all take some food back to the hotel with them so they wouldn't have to go out to eat. Chan had invited Barry and Spencer to come to the room she was sharing with Kendall for supper.

Being in the company of other people all day was fine with Kendall, who knew the trip back to Palmdale would allow plenty of time alone with Spencer. She could wait. She knew he would want to talk about the money her father left her.

She had looked dazed when she emerged from the basement after learning about it, prompting Spencer to rush to her side and ask if anything was wrong. When he questioned her she told him about her unexpected inheritance. She looked at him, still stupefied, and it was at that moment the idea began to form of what to do with at least part of the money. For the rest of the afternoon she could hardly think of anything else. In spite of being deeply affected by Barry's words about the possible consequences of being preoccupied with business, Soul Food to Go was still her priority. On the other hand, she was reluctant to share her plans for the money with Spencer, at least not yet, for fear that he might not approve. Not that she needed his approval—it was, of course, her money—but she wanted to avoid unpleasantness.

When the four of them were eating dinner in the room Kendall shared with her mother, Spencer made an effort to speak with her privately. "Would you care to have a nightcap with me?" he asked when they had a corner of the room to themselves, his husky voice low-pitched and intended for her ears only.

She shook her head. "It's been a big day, Spencer, and we agreed we'd get an early start tomorrow."

He had squeezed her hand in reply.

She opened her eyes. Now it was tomorrow, and she was sitting next to Spencer in the front seat of the Pontiac. It would be just the two of them for the next fifteen hours.

About sixty miles outside the city the local radio signals began to lose strength. "Where're your tapes?" Kendall asked.

"Home, in my car."

She lightly slapped her fingers against her cheek. "Of course. I forgot this is a rental."

They took turns driving throughout the day. Kendall took the wheel just before Washington, D.C., and drove through most of Virginia; and Spencer took them through the North Carolina landscape. They stopped periodically for snacks, drinks, a light lunch, and leg-stretching. There was little conversation between them; the scenery was limited to directional signs, billboards, motels, gas stations, and fast-food establishments at the various exits. The drive was made more tedious by the uninteresting landscape, and both Kendall and Spencer dozed off once out from behind the wheel, leaving the other to drive with only the music from whatever radio station was coming in for company.

It was late afternoon when they reached the motel in the town of Lumberton, North Carolina. Spencer brought the Pontiac to a halt in front of the office, and together they went inside.

"I'm Kendall Lucas," Kendall said to the middle-aged woman behind the desk. "I made a reservation this morning through the eight-hundred service." She pulled a small notebook out of her purse and read a five-digit number.

"Oh, yes," the clerk said after a moment of keying in her computer, "for two rooms."

Kendall didn't dare meet Spencer's eyes. "That's right," she confirmed cheerily.

"Do you prefer upstairs or down?" the clerk asked.

"Upstairs, please."

"That'll be thirty-two sixty-four for each room."

"I'll take care of it," Spencer said automatically as Kendall reached for her wallet.

Kendall looked at him for the first time since the details of the reservations she made became known. There was no anger or stiffness about him that she could discern. It occurred to her that perhaps he hadn't expected them to return to intimacy, at least not so soon. His calm demeanor warmed her heart, and she suddenly was ashamed of her thoughts. "No, Spencer. I couldn't let you do that."

When they were settled Spencer took Kendall to dinner at a local Italian restaurant recommended by the desk clerk. "We need a good meal after eating fast-food all day," he stated firmly before she could beg off.

The bistro's quiet, dim atmosphere was most conducive to conversation, and Kendall knew he had been right to make this suggestion. A few hours of true relaxation was exactly what she needed, not a hurried nap in the cramped front passenger seat of a car. Besides, they did need to talk. There amid candlelit tables, Kendall felt a sudden urge to pour out her heart to him.

"These past few days seem almost like a dream," she remarked. "Was it only last weekend that we were in Atlanta?"

"Seems incredible, doesn't it?" Spencer acknowledged with a nod. "But I don't think we've thoroughly discussed what happened between us while we were there."

Kendall shrugged. We made love and then you betrayed me. She shooed the thought away. She knew she had to hear him out. He'd gone through a lot of trouble to come to Philadelphia. Surely he wouldn't have done that if he didn't have any feelings for her.

Spencer covered her hand with his, completely encompassing it. "I'm not sure how to do this, Kendall. I only know that I've got to make you understand that there was absolutely no malice behind my not telling you about the Sundowner. At first, I kept it secret because I wanted to keep our good neighbor relations intact. You were so nice to us, it seemed downright foolish to say something like, 'Oh, by the way, we're in town to open a restaurant like yours, right next to yours in fact, only nicer' after you were kind enough to bring us dinner our first night in town."

Kendall chuckled despite her heartache. She remembered Michelle's nervousness when she learned Kendall was the proprietor of Soul Food to Go. No doubt about it, it must have been an awkward position for her neighbors.

"Then," Spencer continued, "as time went on, and I started to get to know you, there was an even more important reason for you not to know. The thought of your turning away from me once you learned the truth was unbearable. So the most sensible thing to do seemed to just put off this impossible situation for as long as possible. My backward logic was that in the meantime maybe you might have gotten just as fond of me as I have of you and you'd want to work it out."

Kendall didn't reply—she couldn't. Her throat suddenly constricted and went dry. This was unfamiliar territory, and she felt uncertain and a more than a little frightened. Spencer sounded so sweet, so sincere. Still, there was something she had to know for sure. "Spencer . . . are you trying to close me down?"

"Of course not, baby. That was never my intent, even

before I knew of your association with Soul Food to Go.
Look, Nile Beach has a McDonald's and a Burger King,
and both of them do a thriving business. I expect it'll be the
same for Soul Food to Go and the Sundowner." Spencer
increased the pressure on her hand. "Ground floor, Kendall. I'm in love with you. And I know you feel something
for me; otherwise you wouldn't be torturing yourself now."
His voice became urgent as he intertwined their fingers.
"Let it go, Kendall. Forgive me, and give us a chance."

She was speechless at his declaration. Spencer loved
her—he had just calmly stated as much. She knew it never
would have gotten to this point had he been forthright
about his business interests in Palmdale from the start. It
would have been just as he said; she would have refused
to speak to him, cut all ties, and never forgiven him. Now
she knew how dangerous that was, how much she could
lose by slamming the doors shut and refusing to listen.
Life was too short to hold onto anger—that was a painful
lesson she'd learned as well. Her father was dead, and
nothing could bring him back, not even long enough for
her to talk to him one last time. Her mother always said only
a fool repeats his mistakes, and Kendall had no intention of
being a fool. The hindsight of knowing she might have
missed out on hearing him say those special words to her
was all she needed to know what to do.

She squeezed his hand. "Yes, Spencer, I'll let it go. I
want to give us that chance."

In answer Spencer lifted her hand and pressed it to his
lips.

They sat for several hours, just enjoying the food, the
wine and each other's company. Kendall talked freely
about how her father's death affected her. "Everyone was
right about my going to the funeral. I truly would have
felt awful, just terrible, if I hadn't gone. I had a long talk
with my aunt. He . . . he lived a pretty pitiful life, my father.
It makes what he did for us all the more touching."

"How did Barry react?"

"He was just as surprised as I was. My mother didn't say anything to him."

"Chan knew?"

"My aunt told her. That was why she pressed me to attend the funeral. She could just imagine how low I'd feel if I'd refused and then learned about the money."

"So your mother and aunt stayed in touch all these years."

"Oh, yes, they were always friends. That's how my mother knew my father was sick. I'm actually surprised Aunt Freda didn't tell Barry about the insurance when she saw him."

Spencer knew he was asking a lot of questions, but Kendall was confusing him. "Wait a minute, Kendall. When did Freda see Barry?"

"He saw her a lot during college. He went to Cheyney, so he wasn't too far away." Kendall's fingers tightened around the stem of her wine glass. "Barry told me at the wake that he'd seen our father a couple of times when he was in town. They spent some time together. He told Barry how sorry he was about not being more of a father to us. And Barry said Daddy always wanted to know all about what he was doing, as well as what I was doing at Spelman."

"And Barry never told you about it until the wake?" Spencer asked. As he spoke he wondered if Kendall even realized the radical change Kenneth Lucas had undergone when she spoke of him.

"Actually, he tried to. But I wasn't very forgiving and I always cut him off. I was wrong," she added in a near whisper. "It's just that I've always found it hard to let go of past hurts, and my father's leaving us hurt more than I can tell you."

Spencer smiled. "I know it did. But you know what they say: Admitting your weakness is the first step toward overcoming it. I think developing some kind of understanding of the other fellow is the second."

"Yes," Kendall agreed. "I have to try to understand

Daddy's feelings. He was ashamed of being an alcoholic, but he did care about Barry and me. It just breaks my heart to know that the best thing he felt he could do for us was die. Oh, Spencer! You don't know how much I wish I could go back in time. I would have listened to Barry. I would have called my father and told him I was thinking about him. But I was stubborn and unforgiving, and now it's too late. I'll never do it again." She sighed and wiped the outer corners of her eyes with her napkin. "Good heavens, I'm actually being compassionate. Maybe there's hope for me yet."

"You probably don't realize how far you've come already," Spencer replied softly. "Actually, your father is responsible for it, and this may just be the biggest gift he ever gave you, even more than the insurance policy."

Kendall's mind began to spin the moment they got in the car for the ride back to the motel. It was only a five-minute drive, and soon the time would be at hand for them to either say their good nights or to spend the night together. She didn't know how to handle it. She believed that Spencer was not out to hurt her—she even understood his reasons for secrecy. But everything was so new . . . never before had any man professed to love her. She had been sincere about giving their relationship a chance, but before they could resume their affair she needed time to think about it all, to determine if what she felt for Spencer was love. She knew he had to find her lack of response to his declaration at the very least mildly curious.

"I don't know about you, but I'm beat," Spencer remarked as he brought the Pontiac to a stop near the foot of the stairs. "What do you say we hit the road a little later tomorrow, maybe at nine? It'll give us a chance to get a good night's sleep."

"Sounds good to me," she replied.

They got out of the car and walked up the stairs in

silence. Spencer waited at her room door as she fumbled for her key. "Will you be all right?" he asked.

"Oh, sure." Kendall kept her tone light, but she was female enough to be disappointed that he didn't even try to come in. Instead he merely kissed her cheek and cupped her jaw, locking her gaze with his. There was no mistaking the tenderness in the gesture.

"Get a good night's sleep, and don't hesitate to call me if you feel like talking, no matter what time it is." Or if you want to see me, he added silently. He suspected she was not ready, and for that reason he did not ask.

Kendall nodded. "See you in the morning."

After nearly a full day of driving, Kendall and Spencer arrived back in Palmdale in the late afternoon. "Did you want me to follow you to return the car? You can ride back with me," she offered.

"Nah. I told them I'd bring it back tomorrow. I had a feeling I wasn't going to feel like being bothered with it tonight after this ride. If you're game tomorrow, I'd appreciate it. But there is something I do want to ask you."

"What is it?" she asked, her heartbeat immediately quickening.

"The Sundowner is having its grand opening next Friday. I'd like nothing better than for you to attend with me."

Her reply came without pause, born of an equal mix of desire to accompany him and curiosity about her competition. "I'd love to go with you to opening night."

"Good. I'm going to run by there now to check on it. I'm sure you'll want to check on your place also."

"By phone. I don't think I have enough energy to even drive to Nile Beach. Then I want to make sure Mom and Barry made it in, too."

"All right. I'll see you tomorrow." Spencer kissed her lips lightly; then he was gone.

*   *   *

Kendall unpacked first before stretching out across her bed, phone in hand, to make her calls. Her mother and Barry had arrived hours before, probably, Kendall thought wryly, because they hadn't consumed a heavy meal and a liter of wine the previous evening, and thus had gotten a considerably earlier start in the morning than she and Spencer had.

It was Eddie's last night at Soul Food to Go, and he assured her everything was under control and had been that way throughout her extended absence. Kendall thanked him and told him rather halfheartedly that she might be in later.

The truth was she didn't feel like going to the restaurant. She was exhausted from two days of driving and considerable emotional strain and wanted nothing more than to simply relax and enjoy the comforts of home, but she felt it wouldn't be right not to see Eddie before he left her employ. Besides, she was hungry and didn't feel like cooking. She decided to make the short drive to Nile Beach and get something to eat while she was there. It would only take a minute.

She paused to check her phone messages. "Hey, Kendall, you home yet?" David's voice asked. There were a few seconds of silence and then he said, "I guess not." Kendall laughed out loud as the message continued. "Just wanted to let you know not to worry, everything's cool. I'm going out tonight but I'll check you out tomorrow."

Next was her friend Vicky Sanders. "Ken, I heard about your dad. I'm so sorry, hon. But I do need to talk to you. Please call me as soon as you can."

Kendall smiled. There was no denying the excitement in Vicky's voice. She would bet money it had something to do with Danny Graves. She didn't even know if George Graves had died. She went to the phone to return the call.

It rang before she could pick up the receiver.

* * *

"Mommy, Aunt Kendall is here."

"Okay. Tell her to come in, will you?"

If Vicky's four-year-old, Shay, made a reply, Vicky didn't hear it. But moments later Kendall entered the room with a preceding courtesy knock on the open door. "All right, tell me all about it," she said in her usual forthright manner.

"Oh, Kendall. It's all so wonderful I can't believe it!"

Kendall studied her friend's happy face and felt the corners of her own mouth curve upward, as if some invisible force was pulling them into that position.

"I went over yesterday and brought some food my mom made. Danny answered the door. I didn't even know he was here, I mean, the word had barely gotten out that Mr. Graves had passed. But Danny told me he got in the night before. Apparently the people at the hospital were able to tell his grandfather was failing. He managed to get here in time to see the old man before he died."

Kendall murmured something sympathetic, but in reality she was dreading having to attend another funeral so soon after her father's rites. Fortunately, Vicky was too wrapped up in her excitement to notice.

"The funeral is Tuesday," Vicky continued, "and Danny says he's going to stay the week. I told him to call me if he had some free time so we could catch up. And he did call, Ken. Tonight. He invited me to meet him at Robinson's for a drink."

"And you're going."

"Are you crazy? Of course, I'm going. Help me find something to wear, will you?"

Kendall took in the open closet doors and the garments strewn on the full-size bed. "Take it easy, girl. You're only going to Robinson's."

"I know, but with Danny . . ."

"Whatever happened to keeping your cool about this? I don't want you to get hurt, Vick."

"I know, I know. All right, how's this?" Vicky held up a scoop-necked peach silk chemise that complemented her rich brown complexion.

"Nah, too dressy. You show me a woman who walks into Robinson's with that on and I'll show you a woman who was hoping to go somewhere nicer. Just wear a simple cotton skirt or pair of culottes or something, as long as it looks nice." Kendall stood up. "Listen, I hate to rush, but I told you on the phone I was only going to stay a minute. I want to hurry and get to Soul Food to Go. I need to get some food in me before I get cranky."

"Everything okay at the restaurant?"

"Fine, Eddie tells me. He's wrapping up tonight, and Andrew's all ready to step in and take over." She yawned loudly. "Listen, you have fun tonight. And let me know what happens."

Spencer was pleased with the progress made at the Sundowner during his absence. The floor tiles had been laid, the tables, chairs and barstools were in place, the plants he'd ordered for extra color had been repotted into attractive ceramic containers and the wall ornaments were up, including mirrors and paintings. Everything was ready. Eddie Samuels would be starting full-time training and orientation of the staff on Monday. All that was needed was patrons, and Spencer had no fears about that. The Sundowner was going to be a rousing success, he could feel it. He had gotten the local paper to do an article about the opening that would be published in the entertainment section of the Sunday edition of the local paper, and he had taken out a full-page ad in the free newspaper that was distributed largely to tourists. Finally, the radio blitz would begin Monday. One week from tonight it would all begin.

His brother Vincent and his wife were coming in from Atlanta for the opening. Spencer decided which table had the best location and made a mental note to have it reserved for them. His brother and sister-in-law would share the place of honor with him and Kendall.

All he had to do was think of Kendall to smile. He knew she was stunned and confused when he told her how he felt about her, but he also felt she would come around. What was important was that her anger toward him had dissipated. That was a must before anything more could develop between them. He had longed to feel her firm body under him last night, to be adjoined with her again, but he knew that would be moving too fast. Spencer was determined not to rush her. All in good time, he thought. He'd just have to wait. In the meantime, he'd have to be comforted with the knowledge that once he made love to Kendall again he would make it a priority to keep her close to him.

Satisfied with the appearance of his restaurant, he locked up and left.

Spencer saw a man get out of a car and go down the walkway to the duplex when he was at the stop sign, waiting to cross the avenue and turn into the alley to park. It wasn't anyone he recognized immediately, but then again it was dark out.

Instead of going straight, Spencer turned left and pulled up behind the man's car, anxious to identify the visitor. But to his surprise the man was standing outside Kendall's door. Immediately he tensed. Who was this interloper?

He stayed in the car but lowered the passenger window, which was closest to the curb. He watched in the dark as Kendall's door opened. He heard her squeal of delight and watched as she embraced the stranger. Then the man disappeared inside and the door closed behind him.

In a stiff gesture, Spencer returned the window to the closed position. For a few moments he merely sat there, not sure of what action to take. Kendall had indicated she was tired and wanted to rest, and now she was entertaining a male visitor, someone she was obviously quite happy to see. He didn't want to jump to conclusions, but he had to admit it looked highly suspect.

His thoughts returned to the evening before at that restaurant in Lumberton. Initially he had thought it was a combination of shock and confusion that kept her silent when he told her he loved her, but now he had to consider that perhaps there was another reason.

He turned over the engine and put the car in gear.

No sooner had he gotten to the corner when he realized there was really nowhere he wanted to go. He made a right turn at the first opportunity and circled the block until he reached the alley. He parked the rental car next to his Saab.

He did not alight right away. He sat and pondered a course of action. Briefly he considered knocking on Kendall's door. He could always say he was checking on her. No, he thought, that wouldn't work. Their proximity as neighbors was a sensitive situation, and he didn't want to violate her privacy by starting to show up unannounced. It would be better to ask if she'd gotten rested up when they went to return the rental car tomorrow. He could wait another day. All he'd lose was some sleep.

His apartment was quiet. Michelle was at the teen club. He missed the clamor Brian and Carlton usually created. The duplex was well built, and the only sound drifting down from Kendall's apartment were the faint strains of James Brown and the JBs.

Spencer settled in the living room rather than his bedroom, not admitting to himself the reason for this until he heard voices outside. He had opened the windows to get a good cross breeze, as he often did; but the open window conveniently helped him keep an ear out for activity.

The laughter from outside drifted through the air. Kendall was saying something unintelligible. "Only for you, Danny," she added clearly.

Spencer turned his gaze to the two of them in time to see the unknown man rest his hand on Kendall's shoulder as they walked to the curb. As the man bent to unlock the passenger side of the car for Kendall, she said something to him. From her body language Spencer felt she was asking a question. When the man shook his head in response Spencer knew he had been right.

Just seconds after seating Kendall, the man went around to the driver's side and got in, and they drove off into the night. Spencer's eyes narrowed with anger as he replayed the camaraderie and affection Kendall and her companion displayed. "Only for you," she had said. She'd never said that to him.

"I can't believe I'm getting involved in this," Kendall said.

"You want what's best for Vicky, and what's best for me," Danny answered. "That's what friends are for."

"But don't you think I should take my own car?"

"No. You can borrow Vicky's when you're ready to go. Or mine."

Kendall smiled knowingly. Danny was determined for Vicky to end up either bringing him home or dependent on her to bring him home. Heaven knew the last thing she felt like doing was going out, beat as she was and having already been to Soul Food to Go and to Vicky's. But when Danny asked her to go to Robinson's Bar with him to meet Vicky, she couldn't refuse. He wanted her to help ease the mood so Vicky would be completely relaxed, then slip away unobtrusively, thus allowing him to talk seriously to her friend. Kendall found the whole thing rather amusing. If only Danny knew how Vicky had looked forward to his visit. He certainly wouldn't have to plead with her to work out a way to conduct their rekindled relationship long-distance. She almost wished she could tell him he had nothing to worry about, but that would be a betrayal of Vicky's confidence.

Likewise, she hated the way Vicky's face fell when she got to Robinson's and saw Kendall sitting with Danny. She knew Vicky was thinking it would be just the two of them. Although Kendall had been tempted, she knew to call her friend and tell her of Danny's plan wouldn't be fair to Danny. She hated being in the middle, but she consoled herself with the knowledge that everything would work out.

But the three of them had fun at Robinson's. Danny ordered grilled cheese and bacon sandwiches and a pitcher of beer. Kendall asked Danny how he liked the city of Wilmington, North Carolina, and as he responded, she recalled the desperation in his voice when he told her that with the little time he'd spent with Vicky he was already convinced that they belonged together. "Don't worry, Danny," she told him, "it'll work out. True love always does."

She found her mind wandering. Did she and Spencer have true love? And how would he react to her radio campaign for Soul Food to Go?

From the way Danny was looking at Vicky when he said Wilmington was a nice place to live and raise children, Kendall knew three had become a crowd. "Why don't you guys drop me off; I'm really tired," she suggested.

"You mean you didn't bring your own car?" Vicky asked.

She shrugged. "I've had my fill of driving these past few days. It just made sense to ride with Danny. Why don't you let me take your car, Vick? You can pick it up tomorrow."

Vicky wasted no time handing over the keys. "Wait a minute!" she exclaimed. "What am I doing? You can't drive a stick."

Kendall laughed. "Well, I guess I wouldn't have gotten far." She turned to Danny. "Okay, Bud, give me your car keys."

Kendall parked in front of the duplex. There was a dim light on at Spencer's, she noticed, just enough to put a soft illumination against the curtains. He'd probably left a light on for Michelle.

She swiftly climbed the stairs, not knowing that in his bed Spencer lay awake, torturing himself with thoughts of the woman he loved in the arms of another man.

Spencer slept badly. At dawn he rose, feeling like he had barely shut his eyes. His throat was dry, but even as he swung his feet over the side of the bed his thoughts were of Kendall. He went to his attached office and glanced out the window. Kendall's car was still parked next to his. He didn't even know what he was looking for.

He took a swig of orange juice straight from the plastic jug, a bad habit he'd developed in college but now rarely indulged in. It was highly unsanitary, and if he ever caught either of his sons doing it, he knew he'd raise hell. Barefoot, Spencer wandered out to the living room. The apartment was still, and even outside there were no signs of life.

He walked over to the window and was noting the quiet atmosphere of the street when he thought he saw an outline of the same car that Kendall had gone off in last night. He moved his face closer to the glass, the first twinges of panic rumbling in his gut.

A moment later, as he fully comprehended the significance of the man's car parked outside of Kendall's apartment at 6 A.M., Spencer felt like he'd taken a punch square in the solar plexus. Unable to stay in his apartment a moment longer, he quickly got dressed, got behind the wheel of his car and, fueled on tense energy, drove down the coast until he was exhausted. By that time he was just north of Vero Beach, where he rented a cheap motel room and slept for eleven hours.

CHAPTER
THIRTEEN

"Mom . . . you were about my age when you met Dad. How did you know you were in love?"

It was a difficult question for Kendall to ask, and she had thought long and hard about whom to ask it of. She ruled out her best friends, Vicky and Ava. Vicky was poised for a second chance at happiness with Danny Graves after years of being mistreated by her former husband, and Kendall was reluctant to distract her; while the long-divorced Ava had sworn off love a long time ago.

Kendall considered going to Zena only momentarily. While she felt sure her sister-in-law would realize the seriousness of the situation and refrain from making one of her usual salty remarks or joke about it, Kendall questioned Zena's ability to keep her mouth zipped. She had a disturbing picture of Zena sharing their conversation with Barry or worse—a vision of her sometimes overzealous sister-in-law stopping in at Ava's bridal boutique to look at gowns on her behalf . . . and not being closemouthed about the reason. One innocent remark could travel all over town in a single afternoon, and Kendall was not looking to be embarrassed.

That ruled out everyone but Chan, who had the ability to be completely focused, discreet, and understanding.

Even now Chan did not question Kendall's motives. "Oh, I don't know," she said, a faint smile on her face as she recalled some private memory. "But I thought about him constantly, from the very first time we met. And I always wanted everything to be perfect whenever we saw each other—the way I looked, the way the apartment looked, even the way you all looked. I worried about how you and Barry would get along with David. I wondered if you would object if I remarried. I wondered if Paul would want us to have a child together, even though we were entering middle age." She sighed. "All this within the first two weeks. I guess in my heart I just knew he was the one." She patted Kendall's hand. "I'm afraid I haven't been much help to you, but it's so hard to explain. Paul and I got along so well from the start, and it just grew into this great big fireball that consumed us both."

"It's all right, Mom. You've helped more than you know." The line about being consumed by a fireball made her remember making love with Spencer, and Kendall felt her cheeks grow warm. Sex with him gave her a sweet satisfaction unlike anything else she'd ever experienced. She realized now the reason why. This was no infatuation.

But now her mother had piqued her curiosity about something else. "So how come you didn't have another child?"

"We thought it would be nice, but it just never happened. I was in my late thirties when we married, and even though plenty of women still conceive at that age, I guess I wasn't meant to be one of them."

"Are you sorry?"

"It would have been nice, but I can't complain. No one can have everything. I suppose God knew I needed Paul in my life more than I needed another child, even the child of the man I loved. Sometimes you just have to take life as it comes, accept what you can't change. People who don't only prevent themselves from finding happiness."

"Amen to that," Kendall agreed.

"If it helps at all, Kendall, both Daddy and I think Spencer is a fine man. He's the one you're unsure about, isn't he?"

"Yes. I mean no. I mean, I was unsure, but now I know." Kendall chuckled. It was ironic that she could operate two successful restaurants and yet have so much uncertainty about her personal life. I guess I've just got a real head for business, she thought with a bittersweet smile.

"That's why I don't want you to wait too long," Chan continued. "Your biological clock is going to slow down when you hit thirty-five, you know."

"So?"

"Well, don't you want children, Kendall?"

Kendall took a deep breath. "As a matter of fact, Mom, I don't."

"Really? That's a surprise. Why didn't you tell me this before now?"

She seemed astonished, but at least she didn't seem upset, Kendall thought. "The subject never came up, I guess."

"It's because of your father deserting us, isn't it? All those years in the projects. I knew you hated it there. I hoped you would get it out of your system once we moved down here. Kendall, there's so much more to motherhood than hard times."

Uh-oh. Now she sounded upset. "That's not it, Mom." Kendall shook her head. "I really don't know why I feel this way, just that this is the way I've always felt. Even as a kid I never said to myself that when I had children I was going to do this or that. I guess it was in my subconscious all along."

"It's because you missed your father being with us," Chan repeated stubbornly. "That's why you always said you wanted to go into business. You wanted financial security and didn't want the burden of children. Oh, Kendall, I'm so sorry."

"Don't be sorry, Mom. It's not your fault. Maybe my

childhood does have something to do with it, but the past is the past. I never thought about a connection between going into business for myself and financial security, and I'm not sure if there is one. All I know is that I own two restaurants, and there's no way I could care for even one child and still run Soul Food to Go. I don't believe in that Superwoman stuff." Kendall sighed. "It looks like Soul Food to Go is going to be my only baby. Babies," she corrected.

"Spencer could help you."

"Mom . . . Spencer and I are . . . well, we're in love, but that doesn't mean we're going to walk down the aisle."

"Don't tell me you don't believe in marriage either."

Chan sounded a tad frantic, and Kendall giggled in spite of herself. "No, Mom. I believe in marriage." As she spoke she felt a warm tingly feeling all over, like someone had rubbed massage cream on her skin. "I just figured I'd let you know that having babies is out of the question. Now, I want you to get ready for a shock. Spencer is about to open the restaurant in the Sunrise Hotel."

"He's opening that place? But it's right next to yours! What's going on, Kendall?"

"It's a long story, Mom. We're trying to work it out."

Chan looked dubious. "All right, so you work it out and everything is hunky-dory. Say then you do decide to get married. What if Spencer wants to have another child?"

"I don't know, Mom. I guess that'll have to be worked out, too."

Chan rose and began straightening up the already neat kitchen. "Well, they say love conquers all."

"Mom . . . you aren't upset, are you?"

"Not upset. A little disappointed is all. But it's hardly the end of the world."

Kendall laughed. She got up and kissed Chan's cheek. "I love you, Mom."

* * *

George Graves had been a charter member of the AME church that was Nile Beach's largest, and that was where his funeral would be held.

Kendall arrived a half hour before the service was scheduled to start. She had been to the church before—her parents were also members—and estimated it could seat about five hundred people in its four main sections and two smaller sections on the ends. From the large number of cars present already, it looked like every one of those seats might be taken.

Fortunately, it wasn't difficult for her to spot Ava, who stood near the front door, talking with another mourner. "Vicky's late again, huh?" Kendall said when they were alone. "If I know her, she's agonizing over what to wear."

"No, not exactly."

"So what's the deal?"

"She called to say not to wait for her because she's going with Danny."

"That means she'll be sitting with the family," Kendall said thoughtfully.

"Yes. You know, Vicky's spent just about every waking minute with Danny the last few days. She even called in sick to her job on Saturday night. But he's leaving this weekend, Kendall, and I'm worried for her. I don't see anything good coming from this. There's just too many miles between Florida and North Carolina."

"Oh, I don't know. They can visit. And if push comes to shove, Vicky can always take Shay and go up there."

"As in move?"

"Why not?" Kendall said airily. "There's certainly nothing holding her in Nile Beach. The only reason she's here in the first place is because it made sense for her to come home when her marriage ended. But it's been nearly a year and she's still staying in her parents' house, sharing a room with Shay. She hasn't made any moves to get a place of her own. I have a business, you have a business and now a house as well, but Vicky can pull up stakes and be gone in a week's time."

"I guess her job wouldn't present a problem, either," Ava commented. "R.N.s are pretty much in demand everywhere. Still, I worry about her jumping from the frying pan into the fire and getting burned in the process. This is all moving too fast."

"That's because you've stopped believing that love conquers all, my dear." Kendall unwittingly paraphrased her mother's comment.

Ava shrugged. "That might be true, but since when have *you* started believing love conquers all?"

Kendall shrugged, trying to appear nonchalant, but Ava was not fooled.

"Ah, it must be Spencer who's turned your head. Kendall, I'm so happy for you. It couldn't have happened to a nicer person."

"Oh, I don't know about that," Kendall replied with a laugh. "I happen to think you're a sweetheart yourself. What's happening with you and Leon?"

"Smooth sailing for the moment, but I've since learned that 'his' son is actually his ex-wife's son that he's very close to. I know what's down the road. Eventually he'll start talking about how he looks forward to settling down and having kids of his own, and then it'll be time for me to fade away like an old soldier. If I'd known the whole story from the jump, I wouldn't have let it get this far."

"Ava, don't be so quick to break it off. Give the man a chance."

"A chance to do what? Toss me aside and break my heart? No, thanks."

"You don't know that, Ava."

"Kendall, the man is thirty-five years old and doesn't have any kids. I'm not able to give him any. There's only one possible ending for us, and it's not a happy one."

Her remarks troubled Kendall. Ava had long since convinced herself that happiness was for other people. Her attitude was actually very similar to the way Kendall used to think. But now I know better. Funny. First she had met Spencer, and now the sun was shining on Vicky now that

Danny Graves was back in her life. Surely there was some joy awaiting Ava as well. Kendall wished there was a way to transfer her reproductive system to her friend, whose sometimes dismal outlook on life had been shaped by her inability to conceive. Although Kendall could not sympathize with Ava's fierce desire for children, she did know how it felt to not be able to obtain something you desperately wanted . . . like the unconditional love of a special man.

Kendall took a moment to wonder why she herself had no desire for motherhood. For the hundredth time she silently asked why she felt the way she did. Women were supposed to want children; it was a societal ideal implanted in them in early girlhood. And how would Spencer feel about her wishes? After all, his boys were only a few years away from adulthood. Maybe he wouldn't want to start over with a newborn. Not having children together hadn't hurt her mother and Paul. While Kendall knew nothing was impossible, she seriously doubted she would have a change of heart where this was concerned. Maybe she should try to work it into the conversation, casually letting him know she didn't plan on having a family.

I'm getting way ahead of myself. Just because we love each other doesn't mean we're ready to cut a three-tiered cake. She needed to change her mode of thinking, and to keep quiet about her newfound happiness as well. After all, it wasn't right to tell the world she was in love when she hadn't even told Spencer yet!

To her disappointment, Kendall saw little of Spencer over the following week. She knew how busy he was with the coming opening and overseeing his staff, as well as tending to last-minute details. Kendall's plate was equally full—business was booming at Soul Food to Go—but she gladly would have made time for him if he had asked. Of course, she wasn't in the middle of preparations for opening week, but it seemed that everything was different now that she had identified her feelings for him. It was frightening to think that her feelings for Spencer had eclipsed the ones she had for the business she'd nurtured for so long. After some soul searching, she realized the answer was that Spencer could love her in return, something Soul Food to Go could never do, no matter how successful it became.

The more Kendall thought about Spencer, the more certain she was this was the love that had eluded her all her adult life. And she thought about him often, despite her busy schedule. Andrew, the new night manager, was doing a fine job, but there was a rush around seven each evening, and she liked being there to assist and make sure all the patrons were satisfied. She also made it a point to be present for the lunch rush. One of her biggest problems was her high turnover rate, not unusual in the restaurant business. She constantly had to terminate employees for chronic absenteeism and for not showing up or calling.

When she wasn't behind the counter or working in her office she was at home, experimenting in her kitchen. It was time to make a change to the menu, and Kendall figured it made the most sense to emphasize the healthy side of Soul Food to Go. She'd eaten veggie melt sandwiches at other places, but it never occurred to her to offer them at her own restaurants. Now she was working to put together the right mix of sauteed broccoli and cauliflower florets, onion, green and red pepper strips, mushrooms and eggplant to make the perfect sandwich with melted cheese topping within the three-minute maximum allotment she had laid down for cooking and/or heating customers' orders. Once she had the measurements down pat, she would have to work on the pricing, making sure she allowed for floods, droughts, and other potential nature-related problems that affected the price of produce. Once the ball was rolling, she would assign the night crew the chore of slicing the vegetables and wrapping them in individual packets for easy preparation by the line cooks the following day. Besides, she wanted to include an announcement of the new menu item in her radio ad.

The field she had chosen involved hard work and long hours, but she loved it. She'd always paid close attention to how the restaurants she worked at were operated, because as Eddie had pointed out, the income didn't match the efforts unless you were an owner. She had known it would be years, if ever, before she could afford to open her own place, so she kept working and learning, because when she did attain her goal she wanted it to succeed, and even at the beginning she knew the odds were not favorable for successful new bistros.

Over the years she worked in all kinds of restaurants. In high school she worked at a diner. In college she worked banquets on the weekends. After college she went into supervisory positions, always working at independently owned and operated eateries rather than big chains because they were more personal. She had no interest in becoming a franchisee.

Kendall learned how restaurants offered specials on low-cost items and pushed higher-priced ones. She saw how most menus included at least one considerably lower-priced item to accommodate those whose funds were running low. She asked questions and learned how prices were set based on the ingredients of a menu item, and that a price of nine dollars and ninety-five cents was more pleasing to consumers' eyes than a price of ten dollars. She learned how important measurements were when doling out portions, how to prepare an attractive plate and to limit garnishes, which everyone threw away anyway. She watched managers go into the dining room and speak personally with the customers. Because the restaurant business had such a high failure rate, Kendall knew the service had to be every bit as good as the food if they expected their customers to return.

Finally, she started thinking about what kind of setting she would have and what type of food she would serve if she had her own restaurant. It was the beginning of a dream that had come true.

Now, any spare time she managed was spent preparing

ad copy for her radio campaign, which she was financing with some of the money her father had left her. She wondered if the content was too hard on Spencer and the Sundowner, but then decided business was business. She had to learn to separate the professional from the personal. If she was going to be a softie, she might as well close her doors right now and thus save herself the devastation of failure. She just hoped Spencer wouldn't be angry with her when she read the copy to him.

Didn't anyone take pride in their work anymore? Spencer wondered. He'd already had a repair service in, but the plumbing was still temperamental. The menus had come back from the printer with three errors on them. The furniture delivery was incomplete; they were missing a dozen tables and four times as many chairs. If people weren't incompetent they were slow, like the carpenters, the people installing the flooring, and the artist painting the wall mural that never seemed to be complete.

The staff training was progressing nicely under Eddie's direction, but he nonetheless addressed them on more than one occasion to drive home what he expected of them.

Then there was dealing with the local fire inspector, which was always stressful. Spencer hadn't come across one yet who didn't have a supreme poker face, like they enjoyed making him sweat. He had never failed an inspection, but nevertheless he held his breath until the verdict. This time he had the additional worry about whether the water in the kitchens and bathrooms would cooperate. Fortunately, it did. He framed the certificate and hung it on the wall behind the cashier station in the reception area.

Through it all, he thought of Kendall often. He tried to reach her at home, without success. Her car was never there when he got home, and by the time he went to bed she still wasn't home. When he left in the morning he suspected she was still sleeping, and as much as he wanted to see her, he didn't want to disturb her. It was only a temporary situation. He'd get all the kinks ironed out before Friday's opening, and once Kendall was comfortable with Andrew's management she would limit her night hours at Soul Food to Go. Then they'd be able to see each other more often.

In the meantime, he was ready to tear his hair out, as well as the hair of anyone else who got too close. He was practically subsisting on Excedrins. It was only the thought of being with Kendall that kept him sane.

He had left several messages for her and finally reached her on Wednesday night. "I'm sorry I couldn't get you before now, it's a real madhouse at the Sundowner. I guess I should have gotten the number of Soul Food to Go and called you there."

"I've been there in the afternoons, and I'm going back at dinnertime and staying until after midnight. Andrew's doing well, but with Eddie gone I still want to be around, just in case. How's it going at the Sundowner?"

"Murphy's law reigns supreme, but I'll have everything completed by the opening. Are we still on for Friday?"

"Of course. I'm looking forward to it. Is it formal?"

"No. Casual dressy will do. And Kendall . . ."

"Yes?"

"I miss you."

The day of the opening, Kendall went to the hairdresser to have her new hair growth touched up and her bangs trimmed. She took a leisurely scented bath and dressed in a strapless red taffeta dress with white polka dots. She painted her nails and toenails red and put on low-heeled strappy sandals in red patent leather. The full skirt of the dress ended just above her knees and was flattering to her long legs.

Spencer showed up at her door wearing a loose-fitting suit of raw blue silk, a crisply starched white shirt, and gray t-strap shoes. "You look lovely, as usual," he said softly as he looked at her. Inside his mind was loudly insisting that the exquisite woman standing before him was his and his alone. He felt it in his gut, and his instincts were rarely wrong. She couldn't have spent the night with another man. He didn't feel Kendall was the type to juggle intimacy with more than one man. And even if she was, surely she wouldn't dare be so brazen as to flaunt it in front of his face, especially not after he'd handed her his heart. It was just one of those things that wasn't what it seemed. Just because Kendall's male friend had spent the night at her apartment didn't mean he spent it in her bed. After all, she had plenty of extra room. The guy might have had too much to drink, and maybe Kendall didn't feel like driving him home and let him sleep at her place. It was obvious they'd known each other for years from the way they had interacted with each other. Maybe his curiosity would be satisfied, but maybe it wouldn't. The bottom line was that he loved Kendall and he trusted her . . . even if she had not told him she felt the same.

"Thank you," she said. The sight of him took her breath away. Another sign of how right it was, she told herself giddily, happy to be in love at last . . . with Spencer. It might have come relatively late in life, but she supposed some men were worth waiting for.

"My brother and sister-in-law are here," he remarked as they walked out back to the car.

"Michelle's parents?"

"Yeah. Vincent's my partner, remember. I hope you don't mind if they sit with us."

"Of course not. What about Michelle?"

"She's at Colors."

"The teen club? You mean she can't come to the opening?"

"No. She wasn't too upset about missing it, though. Something's going on with Michelle."

"Oh?"

"New boyfriend, I think. She hardly spends any time at home anymore."

"She's doing all-nighters, eh? How do you feel about that?"

"I'd like to meet the guy. I can't say I think too much of him for never coming around to pick her up or bring her home. She always drives her own car, even if she comes in at dawn. This has been going on for weeks now. I've talked to her about it, but she's assured me it's not like it looks." He sighed. "I know she's of age, but I'm concerned about her. Vincent and Esther kept her pretty sheltered. I'll tell you this, the whole thing makes me glad I have sons."

The three miles of Ocean Avenue glittered at night during the summer season. Those tourists who weren't on King Street were here at the ocean, dining out, doing some late shopping at the numerous surf and souvenir shops that lined the avenue, or heading for an evening of fun at a private party or one of the nightclubs or hotel lounges.

Nile Beach was an entrepreneur's dream, as only two of the major hotel chains had built here, their buildings the newest, largest, and most sparkling among those on the strip. Most of the lodging houses were independently owned, with tropical names like the Dolphin and the Flamingo. For the most part they were small, three or four stories, and less than seventy-five rooms, usually painted in pastel colors like sea green, sky blue, pink, or white.

The Sunrise Hotel was larger, with six stories. Its identifying sign, which was illuminated by strategically placed industrial lightbulbs along its base, bore a colorful logo of a rising sun.

The hotel's parking lot was fuller than Kendall had ever seen it. "Looks like a full house," she commented.

"The word is definitely out." Spencer guided her by the elbow to the front entrance to the Sundowner Restaurant.

"Do you think everything's ready?"

"I know it is. Vincent and I spent most of the afternoon here. I went home only to shower, change, and get you."

Kendall blinked upon entering the club. It was like walking into an oasis, with plentiful lush green plants against a sleek black and white design. One entire wall of the reception area was decorated with a mural of wildlife in the jungles of Africa. A black-vested wait staff, both male and female, briskly moved back and forth between patrons' tables, the kitchen, and the bar, carrying trays laden with drinks, dinner plates, and smaller plates of appetizers.

Just about everyone who happened to be in the Nile Beach area had come out for the opening. Most of the tables were already taken, and the bar area was thick with dateless men and women, chatting easily, heading for the dance floor or just looking around with pleased expressions.

Holding her hand securely, Spencer ushered Kendall to a center table on a low riser. "Like it?" he asked as he pulled out a chair and seated her.

"Spencer, it's gorgeous. Even Cleo's can't compare with this," she replied, referring to Nile Beach's leading night spot, a half-indoor, half-outdoor structure right on the beach.

"Cleo's," Spencer scoffed. "That's a club for twenty-one-year-olds. The Sundowner is for a more mature crowd. You won't find any sawdust on these floors."

"They don't have sawdust, it's sand."

"Whatever. But our patrons are seasoned enough to know to wipe their feet before coming inside."

"I figured you were targeting an older clientele by the music." Instead of the usual heavily hip-hop-flavored recordings that dominated today's R&B charts, the club deejay was currently spinning a Roberta Flack/Donny Hathaway tune that was nearly twenty years old but still inspired folks to move, evidenced by Kendall's own gentle, inadvertent swaying of her upper body and by the patrons on the floor who were obviously enjoying the familiar beat. Minutes later the deejay skillfully blended into another disc, this one a more recent—although not current—Patti LaBelle release, a boisterous number perfectly suited to the

legendary singer's spirited shouts. Apparently the deejay
wanted to make sure the audience knew this was the nineties.

"Vincent's not here yet," Spencer observed.

Kendall quickly scanned the room and took in a number
of familiar faces. She saw Ava dancing with Leon, the same
man who had escorted her to Kendall's father's retirement
party. "Maybe not, but I see a good number of people I
know. Apparently you're getting locals as well as tourists."

"Good. I'll need them when things slow down after
Labor Day. I'll probably open only for special events until
it picks up again at Easter."

"The restaurant, too?"

Spencer shook his head. "Just the club. The restaurant
stays open, even if I have to abduct people from the street
to get them in here."

It was a magic night. The only awkward moment came
when Vincent and his wife Esther arrived. "I've heard quite
a bit about you, Kendall, from both my brother and my
daughter," Vincent said. "We looked forward to meeting
you. I understand you had to leave Atlanta unexpectedly."

Kendall took an instant liking to Spencer's brother and
sister-in-law, but Vincent's remark made her uncomfortable. She shifted nervously in her seat while she tried to
come up with a reply, not knowing how much of her and
Spencer's public spat at The Ruling Class Vincent had
been told about, either by his staff or by Spencer himself.

Spencer jumped into the silence. "Kendall's father died
that weekend."

"Oh, I'm so sorry," Esther said sincerely.

"Thank you. Spencer came to Philadelphia to be with
me at the funeral," Kendall said, beaming at Spencer with
unabashed adoration that she saw reflected in his own
expression. She could hardly wait for them to be alone so
she could tell him just how she felt about him.

With that the moment passed, and the evening progressed in a happy whirl of good conversation, laughter during the live comedy of George Wallace, fancy stepping on the dance floor and Kendall's favorite activity, being held in Spencer's arms as they danced to one of the many slow jams the deejay spun. The generous sprinkling of more laid-back music was another pleasant surprise—recent deejays had all but forgotten about slow tunes. "Who invited all these people, anyway?" she asked dreamily as they did a two-step to Barbara Lewis's classic "Hello Stranger."

"I know it's a big crowd, Ken. Believe me, I'd like it to be just the two of us, too. But just think of the good things this means for us."

"Us? Oh, you mean you and Vincent."

Spencer made a sound that was halfway between a murmur and a grunt. He hoped it sounded sufficiently noncommittal and she wouldn't pursue the matter. The reply slipped out before he realized he shouldn't have said it. Although he already had an idea for his future with Kendall, he didn't think it wise to share it with her yet. It was only daydreaming, and he probably shouldn't even have been doing that. He wasn't really worried about the car parked outside her door last weekend, but at his age he should know better than to be planning a future with a woman who said nothing when he told her he loved her.

At least he felt optimistic. Tonight she was more affectionate toward him than she had ever been before. She was acting almost like he was the center of her universe, and she was obviously eager for the two of them to be alone.

He was looking forward to it himself.

CHAPTER
FOURTEEN

Kendall and Spencer were dancing to a fast number when Kendall thought she saw a familiar face by the door. "Spencer . . . isn't that Robert King over there?"

Spencer didn't bother to turn around. "That's him. He's my bouncer."

"Robert?"

"He stopped in one day and recognized me from the night he was going to give me a ticket. Once he found out this was my restaurant, he asked about doing security. I always like having a policeman on the premises. At least I don't have to worry about him being licensed to carry a firearm."

Kendall lowered her voice to a harsh whisper. "You mean he's got a gun on him?"

"Strapped to his leg. A little awkward if he has to get it out in a hurry, but I don't expect he'll ever need it."

"God forbid."

"His wife is here with a couple of her friends. Eddie reserved a table for them."

"I think it was real sweet of you to hire him."

Spencer shrugged. "He was qualified, that was my main

concern. Besides, I owed him one. A speeding ticket was the last thing I needed on my driving record. It's been years since I've been snagged."

"All because you wanted to get me home and comfortable as quickly as you could."

"Yes, all because I was looking out for you." He smiled at her as he responded to the prompt.

When they decided to return to their table, Kendall and Spencer stopped at Ava and Leon's table. Spencer naturally was concerned with their impressions of the Sundowner and if they were enjoying themselves.

Kendall studied the pair. They made a handsome couple. Ava was showing a fair amount of skin in a textured white patterned silk dress with spaghetti straps. Her burnished bronze hair, just a few shades darker than her skin, was pulled into a classic chignon. Leon, his complexion the color of a Hershey's kiss and just as smooth, wore his head shaved. Not only did they look good, but it was clear they were having a good time. Kendall found herself hoping Ava would change her mind about dumping him. Just about any problem could be worked out. Spencer had taught her that.

Spencer flagged down a waitress and instructed her to bring drinks to their table, courtesy of the house.

"I thought Vicky and Danny would be here," Ava said to Kendall.

"Are you kidding? They've got a lot to work out. He's due to leave Sunday, you know."

Spencer had been exchanging a few friendly words with Leon, but his ears perked up at the name "Danny." That was what Kendall had called her friend.

He decided to join the conversation. "What is this, gossiping again?"

Kendall smiled at him. "No, not really. We were just talking about two friends of ours. They were high school sweethearts twenty years ago. As fate would have it, now they're both available and still have strong feelings for each other, even after all this time; but the situation isn't without complications. They live in different cities, and they're both divorced with children.''

"And you two are trying to push them together?'' Leon asked. Spencer was grateful that Leon asked the question; it made his own motives less obvious.

"This particular path to true love is actually pretty smooth,'' Kendall replied. "My only participation—besides lending a sympathetic ear to both parties—was to allow myself to be dragged over to Robinson's last weekend to help get Vicky to loosen up, then quietly slip away so the two of them could be alone. And I did my slipping away in Danny's car, so wherever he and Vicky ended up that night, they ended up there together,'' she finished with a sly smile.

"You know, I was wondering whose car was parked in front of the house Sunday morning,'' Spencer remarked casually. Relief flooded through him like water through a broken dam.

"Oh, sweetheart. Did you think that maybe I had a secret lover?''

Kendall's tone was playful, and as Spencer laughed he thought, If only you knew. He was right not to doubt her, but he was only human. Only someone devoid of emotion wouldn't be curious about such a set of circumstances.

There was more music and another performance by George Wallace. While Spencer was checking on activity in the kitchen, they were joined by his and Vincent's nephew Todd, whom Kendall had not seen since their first meeting at the barbecue Spencer gave for his Nile Beach relatives. If Todd was surprised to see her as Spencer's date he didn't say so. Instead he took Spencer's chair and fell into easy chatter. Kendall noticed that he did not precede Vincent's and Esther's names with "Aunt'' and "Uncle.''

"Nice place, huh?'' he commented.

"Beautiful,'' they all agreed.

"Are you involved in the operation at all, Todd?'' Kendall asked.

"No, not me. Michelle is the heir apparent to this

empire, and probably Brian and Carlton when they're old enough. They'll have to rename the company Two Brothers and Their Offspring," he joked.

"Todd's too busy becoming a junk tycoon," Vincent countered with a smile.

"Junk tycoon?" Kendall repeated.

"I work over at the recycling plant. I'm supervisor of the aluminum division," Todd said.

Kendall nodded. Much of the money in Nile Beach's coffers came from garbage, but the consensus was that the growth of Kilimanjaro and the surrounding hills of carefully cultivated trash had to be controlled lest the trash situation become overpowering. Recycling had been mandatory in Nile Beach for as long as she had lived there.

The deejay blended into "Movin'," an instrumental recorded by a group called Brass Construction that had long since disappeared after a brief period at the top of the R&B charts. The melody lingered on, however, and it was quite a catchy tune, accentuated by horns and other brass instruments. "I love the music they play here," Esther said. "I can actually relate to it, ancient as I am."

"Much better than all the rap they play at Cleo's," Todd said. He reached for Kendall's hand. "I can tell by the way you're wiggling in your seat that you'd like to dance. Come on."

Kendall shrugged sheepishly at being found out. "Sure."

Vincent turned to Esther. "Let's see if we've still got what it takes."

"You won't have to ask me twice," she replied, laughing as she got to her feet.

Todd was a good dancer, Kendall thought. He had the smooth moves of a man who regularly hit the area night spots. They started out on the edge of the floor but quickly made their way toward the center. The mood of gaiety was infectious among the crowd that was mostly in their late twenties ranging to over fifty. "It's good to hear this again," Kendall heard someone say. She smiled when the person's partner replied, "I never heard it before, but I like it."

That cut turned out to be the apex of the momentum the deejay had been building. Immediately afterward he played an Isley Brothers ballad, inviting the dancers to cool off to the smooth vocals of Ronald Isley.

Kendall smiled at Todd and said, "That was fun." Out of the corner of her eye she could see that Spencer had returned to the table, and she was anxious to rejoin him.

"Wait, where're you going?" he asked, pulling her into his arms but still keeping a respectable distance.

She laughed. "Nowhere, I guess."

"So how'd you wind up here with Spencer?"

Kendall shrugged. "Well, for starters, he invited me."

"I thought you'd want to crown him when he told you he was opening this place. He sure put a sock in my mouth at the barbecue when I almost spilled it. I'll bet he put it off as long as he could."

Kendall didn't like the turn the conversation was taking. Todd was painting Spencer as a treacherous, sneaky person, and it wasn't a fair assessment. "Under the circumstances it was really the only thing to do," she murmured.

"Some guys get all the luck," Todd lamented. "There are those of us who try to be open and forthright, and we end up with nothing. Old Unc instructs all of us to deliberately keep mum about his opening a competing restaurant right in your back yard, and yet he comes to the opening with you on his arm. It doesn't seem fair."

"Bizarre, isn't it," Kendall said tightly.

But Todd didn't notice her tone. Instead he massaged her bare shoulder, immediately causing Kendall to stiffen. "I hate to sound bitter," he said. "It's just that I had ideas about you and me from the first time I saw you. I really wasn't worried about it when Spencer told me you owned Soul Food to Go and he didn't want you to know he was behind your competition. It was clear he wanted to make a move on you himself, but I figured you'd never go for it, and then the field would be open for me."

Kendall had had enough. "It looks like you figured wrong," she said, not bothering to hide her annoyance.

Todd shrugged. "You can't blame a man for trying."

She lowered her eyes and waited for the dance to be over.

The evening passed in a whirl of dancing, conversation, and wine, until finally the deejay played the Sundowner theme, the Quincy Jones instrumental classic "Tomorrow," thanked everyone for coming out, and invited them back for more good times the following evening and also for the Sunday jazz brunch.

"How long will you be in town?" Kendall asked Esther while they were waiting for the crowd to exit.

"For the weekend. We're actually staying right here at the Sunrise. We'll see our daughter tomorrow before we leave. Apparently her boyfriend is going to take us all to dinner."

"That sounds nice." Maybe the fellow Spencer was complaining about wasn't so bad after all, Kendall thought, if he had the good sense to invite her parents to dinner during their visit. "I haven't seen too much of Michelle myself lately. I've been working unusual hours, and I understand she's pretty busy running the teen club."

"Yes, she first got her feet wet working at the club we have in Atlanta. She definitely plans to be a major player in the corporation. Vincent and Spencer thought having her manage the club here would be an ideal next move for her."

"I'm sure you're very proud of her," Kendall replied.

"Absolutely. She's our only child, and I'm afraid we spoiled her a little bit. The responsibility of being in charge, both at the club and at home with Brian and Carlton, is just what she needs."

"I'd love it if you would be my guests tomorrow for lunch. I own Soul Food to Go next door."

"Oh, yes. We saw it when we arrived at the hotel. Spencer mentioned your place was right by the Sundowner. We'd love to have lunch with you, thank you for inviting us."

"Being the owners of two similar restaurants has to require some delicate treading for the two of you," Vincent said. "I'll bet you wanted to kill Spencer when he told you about it."

Kendall laughed. It felt good to be able to look at the sitation with such a lighthearted viewpoint. "That's about the size of it. Tell me, what was Spencer like when he was a kid?"

"He was a tree with arms and legs. All of us were surprised that he stopped growing at fifteen. Still, he's tall for a Barnes. Our family tends to be on the short side.

"He hated being cooped up in the house. Always outside, that kid. And highly competitive. He wanted to be the first at everything. Of course, I'm about a dozen years older than he is, so it's like we weren't close until long after we were grown, probably not until we went into business together. Esther and I moved to Atlanta back in the midseventies. We'd been there about fifteen years when I decided I was tired of working for someone else and set about trying to raise capital to open my own place. Spencer was getting fed up with the goings-on of Wall Street. It all fell into place and worked out pretty good in the end."

"Except when he decided to take a more active part in the business and move to Atlanta," Esther added.

"What happened then?" Kendall asked.

"It affected his marriage. I don't know if he's told you about that or not. Not every woman can stand the commitment involved in restaurant management. Have you ever been married, Kendall?"

"No. And I speak from experience when I say there are men who can't stand that commitment to work either."

"I've got to tell you, Spencer, I'm really impressed. You and Vincent are giving Nile Beach real class," Kendall said.

"Thanks. I'm pleased with the results myself. Everyone I talked to said they were having a great time. We're going to have the club open with earlier hours all week. We'll put out a small complimentary spread and see how many people come back. I'm sure we'll get mostly vacationers, people who don't have to worry about going to work the next morning.''

He brought the Saab to a halt, then got out, and quickly came around to where she sat, gallantly offering her his arm.

They paused as they approached her door. Kendall, reaching for her key, caught her breath when Spencer suddenly drew her into his arms. ''Stay with me tonight, Kendall,'' he said, his voice a tortured whisper. ''Sleep with me. You don't know how hard it is, wanting you the way I do and knowing your bed is right beyond my ceiling.'' He pulled back a little, just enough so they could look at each other. His palm gently caressed her cheek. ''I haven't had enough of you. I don't think I ever can have enough of you.'' It was true, his hunger for Kendall was insatiable. ''Let's make this night ours. I want you so much . . .''

Kendall gazed at him silently, then turned her head to the side and pressed her lips against his palm. ''Yes,'' she said breathily. ''I want to be with you.''

She removed his hand from her jaw and held it in hers. ''Come on, sweetie.'' She gave him a little pull as she began walking the few remaining steps to her front door, then turned to face him quizzically when he remained rooted. ''What is it?''

''It would be better if you stayed at my place.''

Kendall shook her head in protest. ''Are you kidding? And bump square into Michelle when I come out of your bedroom in the morning? Don't get me wrong, Spencer, I'm not ashamed of us, but I do feel we have a right to some privacy.''

''I agree, and that's what I'm thinking of. Look at it this way. Michelle comes home and sees my car out back, but I'm not in the apartment. When I come strolling in tomorrow morning it'll be fairly obvious where I spent the night. On the other hand, my bedroom is near the back door.

It won't be too difficult to get you out the back door without her seeing you."

"Oh. You're right, that does make sense. Your place it is."

Kendall had not been inside Spencer's apartment since the day he arrived in town and Michelle stood amid dozens of boxes, about to tackle the dreaded task of unpacking. Everything was now in order. His living room was comfortably furnished with a velvet-like cocoa-colored Parsons-style sofa and love seat and accent tables in a slightly lighter shade of wood. An attractive wall unit housing the television and stereo dominated the room. "Nice place," she murmured. "I really like your wall unit."

"Thanks. I made it myself."

"You did?"

"Yeah, carpentry used to be a hobby for me. It helped reduce the stress I had at work. I made the boys' beds, too." He gestured toward the room where Brian and Carlton slept.

So that was how his hands had gotten so rough, Kendall thought as she took in the well-made walnut bunk beds.

Spencer watched her silently. She seemed a bit nervous, he thought, now that she was here. He was sure she didn't do this often and decided to make it easier for her.

"You can tell me how much you like my furniture tomorrow," he said. "I've got plans for you now." In a sudden fluid movement, he startled her by lifting her in the air. Kendall was tall, he observed, but she was not a large woman. Plus she was soft and curvy, which made the difference between carrying her and, say, a microwave oven or television that weighed about the same. He easily covered the distance between the living room and the master bedroom with her in his arms.

"Ooh, nice service," she said, her arms automatically wrapping around his neck. Spencer knew she was completely at ease.

He set her down on her feet in front of the bed and proceeded to kiss her thoroughly. Her arms wrapped around her neck, and she melted her body into his as he grasped her rear end and pushed her front against his engorged groin. He felt her grind her hips against him and responded by moaning deep in his throat.

The dress had to go, Spencer thought. Its stiff texture was only serving as a deterrent to the soft, scented skin he craved to feel. He skillfully felt for the back zipper and pulled it down, then pulled back a little to allow the dress to fall to the floor, where its starched skirt held it in an upright position.

She stepped out of it and went to work undoing the buttons of his shirt. "Do you always wear an undershirt?" she asked with a touch of impatience once she had his shirt off.

"I'm old-fashioned. I don't really feel dressed without one. Here, let me." With one fluid movement he pulled the shirt over his head and threw it on the floor.

Kendall immediately went to work on his zipper. "I feel like a sex object," Spencer said with a playful pout.

"I don't know why. I'm the one who's standing here in my underwear."

"Mmm, and looking good enough to eat." Spencer fingered the lace waistband of the shimmering ruby red panties Kendall wore, which on the bikini-cut undergarment was actually well below her waist. She caught her breath. The rarely touched skin of her abdomen was highly sensitive. She had no idea that a mere stroke on that part of her body could be so erotic.

She pushed Spencer's trousers down, bringing his briefs with them. He stepped out of them, and gently lowered her to the king-size bed.

He kissed her lips, then made his way down the length of her body. Kendall still wore her red panties, and he planted feathery kisses around them on both creases of her groin, then right through them at the top of her mound and then lower. The crotch of the panty was wet with the evidence of her desire for him, which was all the encouragement he needed. He pulled them down over her round hips and continued kissing her most intimate zone, now with no barrier between them.

Kendall moaned her delight. In a reflex action, she raised her knees and squeezed her thighs against the sides of his head, making him a willing hostage. Spencer explored her sweetness with his tongue, branding her delicate flesh as belonging to him. Kendall writhed on the bed and reached down to push his head even closer to her musky-scented core. She felt like she was lying on a soft, wispy cloud and reached out wildly to grasp the edges of the mattress to keep from falling off. The large bed was too wide for her hands to reach both edges, so she held on with just one hand.

She heard strange sounds in the room, but it wasn't until Spencer lay atop her and ravished her mouth, silencing her, that she realized the primal whimpers had been coming from her own throat. She kissed him hungrily, new waves of ecstasy spiraling through her.

Spencer's voice was even raspier than usual. "I hate to stop, but this will just take a minute."

She nodded, knowing what he had to do. "Hurry up, please."

His back was to her as he sat on the edge of the bed and reached in the drawer of the bedside table. Kendall waited, her eyes closed dreamily. They opened at the sound of the drawer closing. Now she knew he would be hers.

In an act of raw possession, Spencer pushed her knees apart, gripped her thigh with one hand and with the other guided his swollen erection inside her sex, which was dripping with the liquid fire he had started with his probing tongue. Kendall arched her back and gripped his rear, meeting him thrust for thrust. Her body was aflame with a heat only Spencer could extinguish. She moaned aloud at the feel of his demanding flesh pulsing deep inside her.

Spencer's heart pounded as he kept up their frantic rhythm. His desire for her overrode everything else. He was nearly out of control in his haste to possess her totally. With each forward movement he was rewarded by the feel of her soft breasts bouncing against his chest, as well as the incredible sensation of her inner flesh wrapping so snugly around his manhood. Kendall's body molded to his perfectly. They couldn't have fit together more flawlessly had they been two pieces of a broken coin.

He whispered soft words of love to her as his passion intensified. As Kendall's cries of ecstasy became more urgent, he urged her not to hold back, to let herself go, for he knew his own peak was coming soon.

Her nails imbedded in the hard flesh of his shoulder, she did just that.

Afterward, their breaths came in long, surrendering moans, the only sounds in the otherwise quiet room. "That was fantastic," Spencer said between gasps.

"That it was," Kendall agreed. "I'm thirsty, but I'm afraid my heart couldn't take the shock of a cold drink." She reached for his hand and put it to her chest so he could feel the racing beats of her heart. "Next time let's take it a little slower. We're too old for all this wild lust."

"Yeah, but what a way to go," he said with a smile.

Kendall returned the smile. Then she gently stroked the split in his right eyebrow with the tip of her fourth finger. "What happened to you?"

Spencer chuckled melodiously. "I was about six. My sister Lucy and I were racing to the bathroom—we had two in our apartment, but my parents insisted on having one for themselves, so the eight of us kids had to share the other—and I literally ran right into the doorknob. I saw stars, and there was a lot of blood. My father brought me to the emergency room to get stitched up. At the time it looked pretty unpleasant, but after a couple of years the scar faded."

"I think it gives you character," she said. "Besides, no one should be perfect." She nestled against his warm chest. "Spencer?"

"Hmm?"

"I'm in love."

"Oh? Anybody I know?"

Kendall giggled. "It's you, Spencer, as if you didn't know. I love you. And it's wonderful. I'll never forget you for making me realize there's nothing wrong with me."

"Wait a minute. Who said there was anything wrong with you?"

"No one, actually. But I've never been in love before, not real honest-to-God love. That's why I didn't say anything to you that night in North Carolina. I had to be sure of what I was feeling."

"You've never been in love before?"

"Never."

"Not even with Robert the cop?"

She laughed. "No. Every relationship I was in fizzled out. Every man I knew resented my working so hard; they felt they should be my top priority." A wistful sigh escaped from her lips. "You know what they say. Lovers come and go, but a successful business can be yours forever."

"Oh, is that what they say?" Spencer said with a smile. He supposed restaurateurs were right up there with policemen and doctors in the area of failed relationships, and he supposed for women it was even more difficult. He was male enough to know that most men wanted their mates to drop everything and put their needs first. "There's nothing wrong with you, Kendall," he assured, momentarily tightening their embrace. "And it bothers me the way you say you'll never forget me, almost like you're going away somewhere."

"No," she said softly. "But you have to admit it's odd to be my age and never have experienced love. You made it happen, and I just want you to know you'll always be special to me because of that . . . no matter what happens."

Spencer's arm tightened around her shoulder. The heartfelt honesty of her statement made it all the more touching. Kendall had completely opened up to him— she trusted him with her thoughts and her emotions. It was of the utmost importance that he not violate that trust.

After a few moments he realized the condom was still in place. He released her and leaned forward to remove it. Liquid seeped out from the bottom. "Uh-oh. Looks like it tore."

Kendall sat up with a start, her hand clamped around his forearm. "Tore! Oh, no!"

He cursed his carelessness at letting the words tumble out. The last thing he wanted to do was have her worry so needlessly; he hated seeing that look of distress on her face. Now was the time to confess the final secret he was keeping from her. But he didn't want the marvel of what just occurred between them to be overshadowed by such a somber announcement—especially one that might make her change in her feelings toward him. Just thinking about it was lessening his own euphoric mood. How could he be so selfish to ask Kendall to give up one of the biggest joys and most rewarding experiences life had to offer?

Instead he hugged her with confident arms and assured her it would be all right . . . and he resolved to tell her, and soon, that his days of making babies were over.

CHAPTER FIFTEEN

Kendall waited expectantly while David bit into the sandwich. "Well?"

"It's not bad. I'm just trying to identify what you've got in here. I recognize onion, pepper and broccoli. There's something tasteless that's probably cauliflower." He frowned. "You might want to leave that out. It doesn't add much flavor and it sure doesn't do anything to make it more colorful. I also suspect it's expensive. But there's something in here that tasted like meat."

"That's the eggplant. It's used in a lot of Italian dishes."

"I always thought eggplant would taste like eggs."

Kendall laughed. "No, silly. And don't let anybody know that. It's embarrassing."

"It's pretty good. I'd just suggest you lose the cauliflower. Maybe substitute zucchini. It's cheaper, for one thing. But I'm a little concerned about the eggplant. Your average person in Nile Beach won't be able to identify it right off, and the meaty taste might make them apprehensive about what you've got in here, since it's supposed to be a vegetarian sandwich."

"Well, I know at least one person in Nile Beach who

thinks eggplant has eggs in it," Kendall quipped. "Personally, I think our customers are a lot more sophisticated than you give them credit for, but if they don't recognize the taste, they're sure to ask. Tell you what—I'll whip you up another sample later. Will you be around?"

"Actually, I've made plans. How about tomorrow?"

"That'll work. Hey, you missed a great evening last night. Spencer's place in the Sunrise Hotel. They had a good crowd. Lots of ladies."

"I heard about it. Who'd you go with?"

"Spencer."

David nodded thoughtfully. "So you two have been able to separate love and work?"

"We've gone out a few times, David. Who said anything about love?"

He smiled. "Sometimes you don't have to say anything. It's written all over your face when you say his name. You look like you've figured out why the Mona Lisa was smiling."

"So why was she smiling?"

"Great sex the night before she sat for Leonardo."

Kendall laughed. She couldn't deny this with any conviction . . . even thinking about it made her glow with pleasure.

"I haven't seen Spencer lately," David continued, "but I heard about him going to the funeral. Let me tell you, a man doesn't travel nine hundred miles to be with a woman unless he's got it real bad."

"Oh." Kendall was suddenly eager to change the subject; her newly identified feelings for Spencer were still too fresh to be discussed with anyone. Besides, ever since they made love last night she had been feeling terribly guilty about not telling him about her upcoming radio campaign. She had planned to go over it with him before she turned in the copy, but he was so busy with last-minute preparations before the Sundowner opened that there hadn't been time, and last night she hadn't wanted to spoil the mood by discussing business. But today she would bring it out in the open. There was still time; the ad wasn't scheduled to hit the airwaves until tomorrow. She wanted it to start running at around the same time the Sundowner opened to offset some of the massive publicity Spencer's restaurant was receiving, and the station needed time to record it with background music.

As for him objecting to the content of the copy she'd written . . . well, she'd just have to cross her fingers. But she knew that if the tables were turned and it was him running an ad that built up the Sundowner's virtues while making Soul Food to Go seem like a poor dining choice she certainly wouldn't be happy. Of course, she didn't come out and name the Sundowner, but she did point out that Soul Food to Go's menu had been designed with good health in mind, and that there was no cover charge to dine there. Anyone would see it was the Sundowner, with its traditional fried fare and entertainment, that she was comparing Soul Food to Go with. Well, Spencer said their similar interests could be worked out. It looked like they were about to find out how true that really was.

"Kendall?"

"Oh!" She had become so wrapped up in her thoughts she forgot her brother's presence. "Anyway, the club was a big hit."

"I heard about it, but I had some of the wanderlust in me and drove down to Daytona late last night. Actually, I just got back."

"And who'd you go with, baby brother?" Kendall asked, playfully echoing the question David had asked her just moments before.

"Actually, I was accompanied by a charming young lady I've been seeing lately."

"Sounds promising."

David shrugged. "It was just a little trip out of town, less than twenty-four hours. We didn't leave until midnight because of her schedule."

"Midnight! What is she, a stripper? You'd better watch

out for those one-night stands. Make sure you don't get the cooties."

David laughed heartily. "Not from this one, I promise. See you later, sis." He kissed Kendall's cheek, then bounded down the front stairs.

He had barely turned on the car radio when he heard Kendall's voice over the airwaves. "Hi, I'm Kendall Lucas, owner of Soul Food to Go. Our restaurant was the first to specialize in soul food in Palmdale, and earlier this year we opened a second location in Nile Beach. Unlike other restaurants serving Southern cuisine, Soul Food to Go offers reasonably priced entrees, side dishes, and desserts that are both heart- and hypertension-smart. While the prices of our menu items will be agreeable to your wallet, there's nothing ordinary about our food. From mouth-watering smothered pork chops to crunchy salads to our legendary whiting sandwiches, if it has soul, you'll find it on our menu. Picnic tables are available at the Palmdale location, while Nile Beach has a colorful dining room. Beer and wine are available at the Nile Beach location. Remember, at Soul Food to Go you only pay for your food. No cover charges here—our background music is on the house. And you'll never be rushed to leave before you're ready. Come in today for a satisfying culinary experience." She concluded by giving the exact locations of the two restaurants.

Nice ad, David thought. But he thought Kendall had said it wouldn't start running until tomorrow. He'd have to give her a call when he got in and tell her it was on a day early.

Spencer was tuned to the same radio station. He heard the ad just as he steered the Saab into the alley. Why hadn't Kendall mentioned doing a radio ad, he wondered. He would have helped her write the copy.

Then he heard the part about no cover charges. His hands tightened around the steering wheel; so unrelenting was his grip that had it been a person rather than an inanimate object it would have begged for mercy. It was a direct slur against the Sundowner. In that instant, he knew why Kendall hadn't told him about it.

He quickly realized it wasn't really criticism; he knew it was good business sense to accent the differences between two restaurants serving similar cuisine. What he found hard to accept was, that after all they'd been through, Kendall didn't feel she could approach him with her plans because she was afraid he would object to her unfavorable, if anonymous, comparison of the Sundowner to Soul Food to Go. He thought they would be open with each other after the near-permanent rift his own secrecy had caused between them, but here she was doing the same thing. Didn't she understand he wanted to work with her for their mutual benefit? It didn't have to be a war. Even if their restaurants were on the exact same order, there were still ways to work things out, maybe by promoting Friday nights at one and Saturday nights at the other; Sunday brunch at one and a midnight buffet at the other ... but Kendall just didn't get it. Didn't she realize he'd hear the ad sooner or later? The thought that she could treat their relationship with such a cavalier attitude both infuriated and pained him—he wasn't sure which emotion was stronger.

Kendall's smile quickly turned to a worried frown when she took one look at Spencer's murderous expression. "Spencer! What's wrong?"

"I was just listening to the radio."

She shook her head in confusion. "I don't get it. What about the radio?"

"Your ad, Kendall. The one that suggests that a person would have to be nuts to go to a place that serves over-priced, heavy cholesterol-laden soul food to the accompaniment of exorbitantly priced live entertainment."

Her hand flew to her heart as she simultaneously drew in her breath. "No . . . it wasn't supposed to start until tomorrow!"

"That's cold comfort for me, Kendall," he snapped.

Her heart was thudding in her chest, as her words spilled out. "I don't blame you for being upset, Spencer, but I was going to tell you today. Honest."

"When did you decide to put that ad on the air, Kendall?"

"A few weeks ago, when I was thinking about what to do with my inheritance," she replied truthfully.

"You decided a few weeks ago, but you were going to tell me today. Very considerate of you, don't you think? Very open. Just the kind of relationship we need to have."

She stuffed her hands into the pockets of her cotton shorts and leaned back against the wall. "Spencer, I know it's hard to believe, but I was going to tell you about. I wanted to read it to you and get your opinion, but you know how busy you were at the Sundowner, and what with me still working a partial night shift, it was days before we were even able to catch up with each other. But I was going to tell you today, and that's the truth. I know the ad is a little hard to take—"

"A little hard to take? You just don't get it, do you, Kendall? You don't have the faintest idea of what the problem is here, do you?"

She returned his gaze. "Aren't you upset because I took a few digs at the Sundowner in my ad?"

"No. I would have helped you write the ad if you'd asked. *That's* the problem, Kendall. You didn't ask. You merely assumed I'd be angry, so you chose to keep quiet about the whole thing." His normally husky voice sounded hoarser than usual.

Kendall felt a defense mechanism wash over her like the spray of a cool shower. "Under the circumstances, it seemed like a pretty safe assumption to me, Spencer. Most people don't take kindly when you attack their livelihood."

"It's not about all that!" he yelled.

"Don't shout at me, Spencer," she snapped. "I'm not one of your children."

"I know that," he said in a softer voice that was still louder than normal. "I just figured maybe a little shouting might help you understand, since plain spoken English seems to be over your head. Don't you see that it's keeping secrets like this that nearly did us in in the first place?"

Kendall balled her fists at her side. This was her apartment, where she paid the rent, and she wasn't about to stand here and let him insult her. "You've got a lot of nerve, Spencer. You don't knock down any doors to tell me you're opening the Sundowner even though you had plenty of opportunities, but because our schedules prevented me from telling you what's in my ad you're all over my case. I don't have to take this from you. I want you to leave."

He stared at her with narrowed eyes, then turned and left.

Kendall slammed the door, then leaned against it, eyes shut tightly and trying not to cry. Of all the bad luck for such a thing to happen. She ought to sue that radio station for airing her ad a day early. Just a few more hours and she would have told Spencer about it, along with a heartfelt apology for not telling him sooner.

She didn't know how long she stood there fighting back tears. When she heard someone knocking at her front door she wiped the dampness from the corners of her eyes and went to see who it was.

It was Zena. "Hey, I knew you were in there; I heard somebody shrieking. Either you just had some serious words with somebody or you're playing a Patti LaBelle CD at top volume."

Kendall laughed. Her sister-in-law had a way of always making her smile. "That was me. Spencer and I had a major disagreement."

"Oh." For once Zena didn't try to pump her for information. "Well, it must have been a doozy. But I'm sure it'll be okay once both of you have some time to cool off."

Kendall wasn't so sure about that. Spencer had looked at her like he absolutely despised her. "How'd you get in, anyway?" she asked.

"Your downstairs door wasn't shut all the way."

"Oh. David was here a little while ago; I guess he was in a hurry to see his latest infatuation."

Zena nodded, then stared at Kendall thoughtfully. "Anything I can help you with?" she offered.

"No, not really."

"Want to talk about it?"

"Yeah, I do." She told Zena the whole story. "So what do you think?"

"I think this whole thing's been blown out of proportion."

"Was I so wrong?"

"You were both wrong." Zena glanced at Kendall's pouty expression. "If there's anything I can't stand, it's when a person asks for your opinion and then gets an attitude because they don't like what you say. Do you want to hear this or don't you?"

"All right, go ahead."

"I don't think Spencer was being fair. You told him you were going to read the ad to him before turning it in to the radio people. It's not your fault this was such a bad week for both of you. And, yes, you could have told him you were planning it, but you didn't. So what. Do you have to tell him every time you're thinking about doing something? You're still an independent businesswoman and last time I looked you don't have any partners. I'm sorry, but I don't see what the big deal is. He had his whole place planned out before he said a word to you about it, not that two wrongs make a right. The important thing is that you had every intention of telling him about it and even asking for his input, but circumstances got in the way.

"The biggest problem I see is that he feels you didn't want to confide in him because he wouldn't like what you said about his place. Tell the truth, Kendall. You don't have to tell him every time you have an idea for your business, but isn't the reason you put off telling him about the ad because you were worried about what he might say?"

Kendall crossed her arms in front of her and rubbed her palms over her upper arms, even though it wasn't cold in the room. She stared at the floor for a few moments, then sighed before meeting Zena's gaze. "Yes. We'd gone through so much emotionally . . . I was trying to not rock the boat too soon. Even this morning I was dreading telling him. But I was going to," she insisted.

"I know you were. That's where you're going to have to ask yourself some serious questions. You won't be able to have a relationship with any man if you feel you can't talk to him about anything, even the less pleasant matters; that is, unless he gives you reason not to trust him. I know Spencer wasn't open with you in the beginning, but he really did have good reason not to be, and I think he's done more than enough to redeem himself. I can't blame him for being upset about that. He didn't have to lose his temper, but I'm sure once he calms down he'll apologize."

"And then what will happen?"

"I know you don't really expect me to answer that, Kendall. You know I'm not a fortune teller."

In spite of her pain Kendall chuckled. "Yeah, I know." She hated to think of what her indiscretion meant for their future. "All this is new to me, and I don't seem to be handling it well." Even as she sat still she could feel the old doubts rise within her—the fear that she was different from other women. Who else had so little flair for managing matters of the heart? Just because she could successfully operate a thriving business didn't mean she could handle a love affair.

"I don't get it. What's new for you?" Zena asked.

Kendall stared at the far wall. "Love."

Zena rose. "I think I probably need to let you have some solitude. I didn't really come by for anything special anyway." Actually, she had, but it wasn't anything that wouldn't keep.

"I'm sorry I wasn't more sociable."

"It's all right. You think about what you're going to say to Spencer so you two can kiss and make up."

"I'm afraid it might be too late for that."

"It's never too late for that," Zena said, "even if you're knocking on heaven's door. It's never too late until that door opens and they let you in. Remember that, sweetie." In a rare display of affection, Zena bent and kissed Kendall's cool cheek before leaving.

On Monday, Spencer went to see Zena at the real estate agency. "Good morning."

"Well, hello there! That's right, you did say you were coming back. What was that, maybe two weeks ago?"

Spencer laughed heartily. "I had that coming, didn't I?"

"I was just teasing. Have a seat. What can I do for you?"

"Well, there's this house . . ."

He had spotted the Victorian near the corner of Main Street and even though it was in disrepair, he could visualize it fully restored and beautiful.

"Ah, yes," she said after getting the file. "It has five bedrooms, and it's zoned so it can be used either commercially or residentially." She stated the seller's asking price. "But it's awfully big for a residence, don't you think?"

"Only as a last resort," he said. It was a property crying out for renovation, and it would truly be beautiful once it was repaired. "Thanks for your help, Zena. I'll get back to you. Honest. Just do me a favor . . ."

"This is your business, Spencer. I won't say anything to Kendall."

"Thanks."

He drove past the house again after leaving Zena's office. There were a number of possibilities for its use, but he was having reservations. Nile Beach was a market ripe for development, but Palmdale, despite the resurgence of the historic district, was not a resort. Spencer didn't know if any of his ideas would work in an environment not overrun with tourists with money to spend. He had never failed, and if he was unable to pull this off, it would be costly. Still, the house had been in the back of his mind ever since he'd first spotted it. Whether or not that was an omen he wasn't sure.

One thing was sure, though. If all else failed he and the boys could always live in it. Maybe even Kendall—

Doggone it, couldn't he do anything without thoughts of Kendall sneaking into his head?

Apparently not, he thought dryly, as the minutes ticked by and everything else drifted away except her. Spencer was torn between wanting to shake some sense into her and wanting to pull her into his arms and devour her. Even now, despite his frustration, he had to fight the urge to go up and knock on her door, to try to explain it to her. But he'd already done that. It was really up to her now, but angry as she'd been, he had to face the fact that she might not come around. In the meantime, he needed to do something to keep himself busy.

The one thing he was sure of was that regardless of what happened—or didn't happen—between them, life would go on. It always did.

Kendall stood a foot away from the window at the back stairs and peered out from the shadows, not wanting to be seen in case Spencer was outside. He wasn't, but his car was.

She took a deep breath. She had been miserable since their confrontation, and she wanted more than anything to see him and tell him she had been wrong. She *had* been wrong, and this was no time to be stubborn. She'd already made it clear that she would not tolerate being spoken to like she was a child, but refusing to admit she was wrong when, of course, she had been could carry the hefty price tag of her future happiness. And if Spencer declined to resume their relationship at least she could walk out of his life with her head held high. She had made a serious error in judgment, yes, but at least she was woman enough to acknowledge it. For that she could always be proud, no matter what the outcome.

She heard a car engine just before she opened the door. She cracked the door just in time to see Spencer's Saab take off.

Why do I always come up a day late and a dollar short?

Business was brisk at the Sundowner. Clearly the word had gotten out about Nile Beach's newest night spot. Most of the people in attendance tonight appeared to be tourists, which made sense because most locals had to go to work in the morning. The crowd was nowhere near the size of the previous two evenings, but it was respectable nonetheless. Actually, fewer bodies seemed to increase the air of intimacy. By now many of the visitors to Nile Beach were acquainted with each other, and the air was filled with the sound of chitchat. Spencer stood at the bar, quietly surveying the scene.

"You look awfully serious to be in such a fun place."

Spencer turned to face the speaker, a smiling woman with shoulder-length hair and a complexion that could not be described as either light or dark, but somewhere in the middle. She was quite attractive in spite of an overbite. "Hello. I don't mean to be a party pooper," he said apologetically.

"That's all right. From the look on your face I'd say you're the manager."

"Actually, I'm one of the owners." Although Vincent was on his way back to Atlanta after having dinner with Michelle, Spencer always gave his brother his due.

"Oh, an owner. You must have been thrilled with the crowd that showed up Friday night. I didn't get in until today, but I heard about it." She held out her hand. "I'm Marlis Greene."

"Spencer Barnes." He shook the proffered hand. "What do you think of my little establishment?"

"It's very nice. I understand you're open all week."

"Yes. Are you staying in the hotel?"

"Yes. I've got eight days to enjoy myself. It's my first time to Nile Beach."

Spencer saw no way out of asking the obligatory question. "Where are you from?"

"Greenville, South Carolina."

"Nice city," he said with a nod.

"It's not bad, but I love being right on the ocean like this." Marlis smiled at him warmly.

To her credit she was pleasant without being fawning. Spencer disliked women who fell all over themselves trying to be charming once they learned he was a restaurant owner. He could practically see the dollar signs light up in their eyes. Marlis, on the other hand, only looked friendly. She was attractive enough . . . she just wasn't Kendall, and that alone made her all wrong.

No point in leading her on, he thought. "Will you excuse me? I need to speak with my manager."

"Sure. By the way, I write for a local paper in Greenville, and I thought I'd do a travel piece on Nile Beach, from the angle of the town it was and the town it's become. Would you be interested in being interviewed?"

Spencer brightened. "I never refuse an interview. I'll be here most evenings this week. Give me a call, or just stop in since you're staying upstairs."

"I'll do that. Nice talking to you."

"Likewise. I hope you enjoy your stay in Nile Beach. And do come back to the Sundowner this weekend. From Thursday on we're expecting a big crowd to see the Main Ingredient." He smiled in parting.

He had fibbed about needing to speak to Eddie. Instead he left the club.

Although he didn't feel like working, nor did he really

want to go home. He visualized himself lying in bed staring at the ceiling, tortured by the thought of Kendall sleeping right above his head.

He found himself driving down Ocean Avenue. Cleo's was having a decent night, he surmised from the moderate number of cars in the parking lot of Nile Beach's leading disco. Late-night diners were leaving the numerous restaurants that lined the street. Groups of people were watching the street scene from motel balconies. It was a quiet night in Nile Beach. Spencer figured what action there was would be over by midnight, 1 A.M. at the latest.

He pulled the Saab into the parking lot of the Pancake House and turned around. The shoreline within the city limits of Nile Beach was barely three miles long, and its north end was purely residential. Most of the homes weren't much more than bungalows that had seen little change since the days some fifty years before when luminaries like Joe Louis and Cab Calloway had vacationed in them, but a handful of newer, majestic residences were built, complete with tennis courts and swimming pools on the sides or even out in front, as the community was discovered by those with money. Most of these wealthy owners were white, which had caused considerable concern among the town's longtime black residents, who were afraid that if the racial climate of the area changed too much they would find themselves disenfranchised from a town their descendants had established right after the Civil War. Anyone who could afford to purchase costly oceanfront property was welcome to it, but a silent network existed among the owners of the smaller homes to handle any property sales privately, usually to friends or relatives. It wasn't enough just to be black . . . fourth- or fifth-generation beachites were given preference over second or third, while newcomers without roots in the community ranked dead last. It was very difficult for outsiders who were not wealthy to acquire prime property in Nile Beach.

Spencer turned onto DuBois Street and headed inland. In a matter of minutes he was on Main Street in Palmdale.

Impulsively he pulled into the closest diagonal parking space he could find to Robinson's Bar and went inside.

He sat at the bar and ordered a beer. He had been to Robinson's several times since he had been living in Palmdale, and each time it was comfortably crowded with locals.

The bartender, a short-statured, muscular man with a goatee, set a filled glass beer mug on a napkin in front of him. "What's goin' on, man?" he asked.

"The usual. It's quiet tonight, even out at the beach. But there always seems to be something happening here."

"Yeah, but I don't know for how long."

"What do you mean?"

"Mr. Robinson is ready to close up shop."

"You're kidding! I thought this place was a Palmdale institution."

"It is. It's been open since right after the war. Back then it was the only place black people could go in town if they wanted to relax and have a good time. But Mr. Robinson is tired. It's been over fifty years, and he's in his eighties, and besides, I hear his wife isn't doing too well these days. He's decided to sell out and move in with his son in Tallahassee."

"Maybe somebody will buy him out."

"I hope so. But he says he's not waiting around forever for someone to bite. If he can't sell, he'll just shut it down."

Spencer digested this information. The bar was indeed of legendary proportions in Palmdale. Most likely it turned a tidy profit. But Spencer wasn't really interested in owning a neighborhood bar. It was the loyal clientele that attracted him. He realized that if Mr. Robinson could find no buyers it might well work to his advantage. Somebody had to inherit the bar's customers; it was doubtful they would start staying home all of a sudden. He could promote the Sundowner as a place to relax and watch football and basketball. That might be the key to keeping business booming during the slower winter months. Or better yet . . .

He leaned back in his barstool as he considered his latest idea and took in the surroundings. Robinson's had the no-frills look of an establishment that had been in existence for half a century. Paintings by local artists adorned the walls, with small white signs below each one. Apparently they were for sale. The barstools, chairs, and booths were all upholstered in a worn dark red vinyl, and the navy carpeting was thin, even held down with masking tape in a few spots. Spencer supposed the bar had undergone two or three refurbishings over its fifty years of existence, but it was definitely due for another one. The added expense of redecoration might make any prospective buyers shy away. This, too, would work in his favor. He probably needed to have a talk with Mr. Robinson.

His gaze happened upon a young couple at a back booth, laughing over golden brown grilled cheese and bacon sandwiches, fries, and a half carafe of wine. Spencer's eyes narrowed when he recognized Michelle. Her companion's back was to him, but this was apparently the creep she was running with who let her come home alone in the wee hours of the morning. Well, it looked like the jig was up, he thought to himself as he pushed back his barstool and rose to his feet.

CHAPTER SIXTEEN

There was something familiar about the man who sat opposite Michelle, Spencer thought as he approached. He tried to recall where he had seen the light-complexioned, beefy, bespectacled man before.

They were so involved in each other that neither looked up until he was upon them. "Spencer!" Michelle exclaimed. "What are you doing here?"

Spencer kept his eyes riveted to her companion as he spoke. "I just stopped in to have a quick beer and spotted you." He nodded toward her companion. "Who's your friend?"

"Actually, we've met," the man said, rising to his full height and extending his hand. "David Ridgely."

Spencer recognized the name instantly and knew where he had seen the man before. "Kendall's brother?" he said incredulously as he shook his hand.

"Yeah. We met at my dad's retirement party."

"I remember now." He turned to Michelle. "So this is your mystery man? I don't get it. Why all the secrecy?"

Michelle slid over in the booth. "Sit down, uncle, and I'll explain it to you."

*   *   *

Spencer didn't stay long at Robinson's. He was happy
Michelle and David had found each other, but the truth
was that being around them depressed him. They were
obviously in love, always patting each other's hands and
looking at each other with unabashed adoration. It only
made him long for Kendall's company, to see the look in
her eyes when she smiled at him and to imagine the picture
of the happiness in his own heart whenever he was with
her.

"So where's my sister tonight?" David asked.

Spencer hesitated before answering. "Home, I guess,"
he replied truthfully. "I'm just coming from the Sundowner."

"How's business?"

"It's respectable for a Monday, but not particularly busy.
I was driving past here on the way home and got an urge
to stop in." No need to explain about the disagreement
he and Kendall had. Michelle and David were bound to
find out about it eventually, but after all, they had just told
him that the whole reason they had kept their involvement
secret was to protect their privacy. Spencer knew they
would understand his own reluctance to conduct his relationship with Kendall behind glass walls.

Kendall knew the moment she opened her eyes Tuesday
morning that something was terribly wrong. It took only
a moment for her to recall the argument she'd had with
Spencer.

It was a beautiful day out—the sun was straining to get
in through the blinds, but the way she felt it might as well
have been storming.

She got up and peered out from a slat in the blinds.
Spencer's car was parked next to hers. She thought about
calling him but decided it was too early. Instead she turned

on her James Brown CD and got on with her housework, just like she did every morning.

But the usual bounce that got into her step at the catchy music of Fred Wesley, Maceo Parker, and the other JBs simply wasn't there today.

Spencer slept surprisingly well—once he finally got to sleep—but when he awoke his first thought was that he really needed to see about finding another place to live. It would be unbearable to continue living here, and besides, his family needed more space.

He lay on his back, his head resting on his clasped hands, staring at the ceiling. It was painted a stark white, but a vivid color image of Kendall materialized there. He saw her as she looked the night of Paul Ridgely's party, tall and regal as she made her entrance on his arm and then dancing in barefoot abandon, oblivious to how sexy she looked. Then the image changed to Kendall as she had looked the first time he made love to her, her dark hair fanned out against the pillow and her face contorting in undisguised rapture as his body filled hers.

Recalling Kendall's lithe body thrashing beneath his on this very bed caused a reaction Spencer didn't need. He shut his eyes until her image faded away.

Getting her off his mind was going to be quite a challenge, but Spencer knew he had to do it. He loved a woman who didn't understand how a true partnership worked, and he saw no future in it. At this point in his life he simply couldn't handle the stress. He was pushing forty; life should be getting simpler, not more complicated. This was like the old days with Arjorie, when every other day brought with it a new argument. The nature of the problems might be different, but the concept was the same. He couldn't cope with it. He wanted some peace, a tranquil life with a woman who understood him and whom he understood in return. True, he'd have bet money that Kendall was the one, but he supposed even his highly accurate instincts could be wrong once in a rare while.

Maybe it was all for the best, he thought with false brightness, reminding himself that at least they'd learned of their incompatibility early and spared themselves future heartache.

He shifted into a sitting position. To vent some of his frustration he punched one of the rolled-up pillows. Enough, he thought. His agenda for today was full, and he needed to get an early start.

He was avoiding her, that was all, Kendall thought as she replaced the receiver. Spencer rarely went out this early, but now all of a sudden he was gone at 9 A.M.

All right, she told herself. I can't sit around moping; I've got things to do myself.

Kendall threw herself into her work, spending afternoons and evenings at Soul Food to Go. She studied the fluctuating market prices for produce and set a price for the new veggie melt sandwich, then set up a special training session to introduce the cooks to how it would be prepared. She worked out afternoon specials to help spur business during the slow period between three and six. She delegated her day supervisor to helping out on the line while she took over the expediting of orders for the lunch rush, when usually it was she who joined the cooks. Through it all, she ignored the curious stares of her staff, all of whom were undoubtedly wondering why she was suddenly so hyper.

"Something wrong, Kendall?"

"No. Why do you ask?"

David shrugged. "Well, it just seems strange that you've spent more time here in the past week than you have since you opened up in Nile Beach. You're studying my schedules, going over the receivables and payables, checking the meat deliveries . . . it's definitely unusual. Have I done something wrong?"

"No, of course not. I just feel I should get more involved, at least occasionally. Don't worry, I'll soon be out of your hair." Kendall's intent was to give her Nile Beach employees a break from her presence, which she knew in her present manic state was overbearing, and spend more time here at the Palmdale location.

"Let me make a suggestion," David began. "It's been a while since we were able to get together on a, uh, social basis. Why don't we meet you and Spencer at the Sundowner for dinner Sunday?"

Kendall hesitated. She was reluctant to confess that she had not seen or spoken to Spencer all week. Still, the Sundowner was the one place Spencer was bound to be. Maybe it wasn't such a bad idea, if she ever planned on making good on her plans to apologize. "How about tonight?" she suggested. "I really could use a break. Spencer will be so busy he probably won't have much time to join us," she lied, "but I'd love to meet your mystery lady."

"Mystery lady? But didn't . . . "

"Didn't what?"

"Uh, nothing. How about eight o'clock?"

"Great. I'll call Eddie and get him to reserve a table for us. I have a feeling it's going to be standing room only."

"You know, Kendall, only a true friend drops everything she was doing to come out with you at the last minute because you're too scared to go alone," Ava remarked.

"Come off it, Ava, you know you weren't doing a thing." Kendall smiled as she spoke. She and Ava had been friends since high school. The two of them, along with Vicky, were so tight that Barry had dubbed them Ike, Mike, and Just Alike.

"Are you kidding? It's going to take me years to get that house together."

"Well, you need to take a break from it. You've been to

the Sundowner—you know you'll have a good time. It's not like Spencer and I are going to have an argument in front of everyone." Ava was the only one other than Zena she had confided in about the blowout she and Spencer had. She couldn't stand it anymore. She would speak with Spencer privately as soon as she could get his attention. Before the night was over she'd know whether or not she and Spencer had a future.

"Hello, Spencer."

He only had to think for a moment before he recalled the name of the woman who'd just greeted him. Little things like that were important in the hospitality business; they made people feel more friendly toward him. "Marlis. Glad you could make it."

"I was hoping we could do the interview."

"Ah . . ." Spencer looked around the floor. The staff seemed to have everything under control. Tonight's crowd was respectable, but he knew from the prepaid reservations on the books that tomorrow and Saturday would be the real moneymakers. It was better to let Marlis interview him now than when it was super busy, he decided. "That's fine," he told her. "We can go to my office, where it's quieter."

"Good googly-woogly, it's crowded!" Ava exclaimed when she pulled into the Sunrise Hotel parking lot.

"I'm not surprised. Spencer's had an ad on the radio all week pushing the college reunion weekend."

"Are there going to be a lot of college kids here, God forbid?"

"It's aimed at alumni. They're going to be playing the same type of music as last weekend—pre-rap music." The same music she and Spencer had danced to at the opening. Lord, it seemed like a hundred years ago.

Kendall identified herself to the hostess, who showed

her and Ava to a table near the one they had occupied the night of the opening. She removed the handwritten RESERVED card from the table and told them someone would be there to take their order shortly.

"All right, so where is he?" Ava hissed.

"I don't know. He's here somewhere. I saw his car outside."

"Well, you'd better find him before David gets here. Honestly, Kendall, I can't believe you set up a double date with your brother when you and Spencer aren't even speaking to each other."

"It'll be fine. Oh, here's David now." Kendall's mouth dropped open in unmasked surprise when she recognized the woman David was with. "David! Michelle! Wait . . . you're here together?"

"We sure are," Michelle said, slipping into the chair David pulled out for her.

"But why did you keep it secret?" Kendall asked, remembering David's vagueness about his companion on his brief trip out of town.

"It just seemed better that way. We were afraid of interference if we said anything. We wanted our relationship to develop naturally. And if it blew over, no one would ever have to know."

"But it didn't blow over," Kendall said, looking at David's smiling face.

"No."

Kendall's glance went to Michelle and then back to David. It was serious between them, she realized. "Well, this is wonderful! I don't know why I didn't think of you two together. I would have introduced you myself if I had. Have you been seeing each other long?"

"Not too long. Remember that night you and I talked down at Robinson's?" Michelle asked.

"Oh, yes." How could she forget; the night she learned Spencer's true marital status had changed the course of her life.

"David came in after you left. That's when we met."

Kendall beamed. "Well, I'll be. Is Spencer ever going to be surprised."

Michelle looked puzzled. "But he does know. We ran into him at Robinson's Sunday night. I'm surprised he didn't tell you."

Uh-oh. "Uh . . . no. Actually, I haven't seen too much of him this week. We've both been kind of busy. I guess he figured he'd let me be as surprised as he was." She ignored the kick from under the table that she knew came from Ava's foot and resisted the temptation to kick her friend back. Instead she said, "Cupid must be shooting off a lot of arrows lately. I guess no one's immune." She punctuated her statement with a saccharine sweet smile in Ava's direction. Ava had ended the budding relationship with Leon a few days after the opening of the Sundowner, after he confided in her about his hopes for the future, which included the children she knew she could not give him. Knowing Michelle was happily involved with David only made Kendall more certain that Ava's turn was next.

But Ava refused to take the bait. "Oh, I don't know about that," she said easily. "Love is kind of like the flu. I had that Hong Kong strain when I was six. It just about wiped me out, but I haven't had the flu since." She smiled right back.

Kendall found her gaze wandering as the others conversed, looking for a familiar face. She saw Eddie by the bar and quickly excused herself.

"Hello, Eddie," she said. "Thanks so much for the table. I should have known you'd take good care of us."

"Anything for you, Kendall. You know that."

"Is Spencer here yet?"

"Yeah, he's in the office."

"Thanks."

Kendall practically flew to the office. The door was open, and she froze in her tracks when she heard Spencer's distinctive voice say something and a soft feminine voice reply. Both parties laughed, and as Kendall watched in shocked disbelief from only a few feet away, the door swung to the closed position. She took a few backward steps before realizing she couldn't remain just standing there, so she approached the door once again and this time she knocked. Hard.

The door was opened almost immediately. Spencer just stared at her for a moment, then held out both his hands. "Come in, Kendall."

He introduced her to Marlis. "Marlis is on the staff of a newspaper up in South Carolina. She's doing a piece about the resurgence of Nile Beach and is including the Sundowner in it," he said after they exchanged hellos. "You know, Marlis, Kendall owns Soul Food to Go next door."

"Oh! I've eaten there a couple of times this week. The food is great. I love that veggie melt especially."

"I'm glad you like it."

"I love it. In fact, I've made a note to mention it in my article. I'd take your picture, too, but photographs detract from the text."

"That's wonderful. I appreciate the mention. Is there any way I can get a copy?"

"You can get it from me," Spencer said. "Marlis has promised to send me one so I can see how my picture came out."

For the first time she noticed the camera that rested on a free surface. "You took pictures? In here with all this clutter?"

Marlis laughed. "Spencer had to stand against the door. It was the only space available." She picked up her camera and held out her hand to Spencer. "I'd better get upstairs. I don't want to miss the show. Thank you so much for your time, Spencer. I'll try to do right by the hotel and the restaurant."

"I'm sure you will, Marlis. Thank you," he said as he shook her hand.

"Nice meeting you, Kendall," Marlis said, and then she was gone.

"Same here."

For a few moments Kendall and Spencer stood staring at each other, neither one speaking. Finally Kendall found her voice. "I'm so sorry, Spencer. I was wrong. I handled the situation very badly." She wanted to tell him that she understood everything now and to ask him to forgive her, but the words simply wouldn't come. Why was it so easy to hold a grudge against someone who'd done you wrong but so difficult to apologize when the tables were turned?

He reached out and touched her cheek with his fingertips. "Come here, baby."

Just two steps forward and Kendall was in his arms. They held each other there in the doorway, her head resting on his shoulder. "I've been waiting for you," Spencer said.

"Waiting for me?"

"Michelle told me she was looking forward to coming in tonight. She mentioned you and David had set it up when I told her I didn't know what she was talking about."

"Oh." Poor Michelle, she must be thinking they'd both lost their minds. First Michelle acknowledged a date that Spencer knew nothing about; and then there was her own remark about how surprised Spencer would be to find out Michelle and David were seeing each other. Kendall hoped Spencer's niece had swallowed the explanation about their busy schedules preventing all but minimal communication between them. After all, she was in the business and knew how frantic it could be. Kendall did not feel her whole circle needed to know that she and Spencer had quarreled—it was no one else's business.

"I've been looking for you all week," she said, "but you weren't ever in."

"I've been keeping myself occupied all my waking hours. Anything to keep myself from banging on your door and begging you to forgive me."

Kendall smiled. "That's sweet of you, but I know I should have talked to you about the ad. Instead I was procrastinating because I didn't want a confrontation." She looked up at him. "Do you think I'll ever get the hang of what it takes to be in love?"

"How about if I promise never to be too far away to help you out if you need it? And that you'll forgive me if I should mess up."

She squeezed his waist. "You've got a deal. That's easy— you're the one who taught me how to forgive."

It was quiet at the beach. Kendall and Spencer walked hand in hand, the only other hints of activity coming from the occasional patrolling police car that cautiously drove across the damp sand.

"That was something about Michelle and David, wasn't it?" he said.

"I have a confession to make," Kendall announced.

"And what is that?"

"When you first moved in, I thought Michelle was your wife."

"Wife!" Spencer exclaimed incredulously. "Are you kidding? How could you think something like that?

"It was actually pretty easy. I mean, when I knocked on the door there she was, unpacking like the proverbial happy housewife. What would you have thought if there was a man living in my household, plus two children? Not that I thought Michelle was the boys' mother; I could tell she was only in her twenties. Then at the barbecue you guys had, there were all your aunts saying how you needed to hang onto her. How was I to know they were her aunts, too?" She laughed. "And then I was getting these vibes from you like you were interested in me. I wanted to strangle you for being such a cad."

Spencer laughed. "This is just too funny. You know, Kendall, you're absolutely right. No wonder you seemed so uncomfortable with me. It just never occurred to me that you could have made a mistake like that. I always figured Michelle told you why she was staying with me." He scratched his head. "I guess she, in turn, figured *I'd* mentioned it to you." He put an arm around her. "Look at what we almost lost out on because of a silly lack of communication. It all goes to show how important it is for us to talk to each other.''

She squeezed his hand. "No more secrets. I promise. I've learned my lesson.''

Spencer suddenly stopped moving. "But there is something you and I do need to talk about, Kendall.''

She tensed—he sounded so serious. "What is that?''

He took her hand and rubbed his thumb against the back of her palm. "I know I should have told you before now. I guess I've been afraid it would change how you felt about me.''

"Something like your reasons for not telling me about owning the Sundowner." Kendall's voice was steady, but she was becoming more frantic by the second. What could Spencer possibly have to say that might affect her opinion of him?

"That's right. Kendall, after I was divorced I naturally started seeing women again. Many of the ones I dated were divorced also, and most of them had at least one child. I always expected to remarry one day, and I realized that when I did it would be to a woman who already had a family, so . . . well, I decided to do my part toward population control and, uh, got a vasectomy. That way I wouldn't have to worry about having any accidents." His eyes searched her face, which looked rather confused. "I can always try to have it reversed, but the way it is right now, I can't give you any children, Kendall.''

She made a choking sound, and he looked at her in alarm. But in an instant he realized the strange sound was actually suppressed laughter, which she soon let out full force. She laughed so hard her entire body shook and slow tears spilled out from the far corners of her eyes. Finally she developed a coughing spasm from all her mirth and collapsed onto the sand.

"Good, God, Kendall, will you tell me what's so funny?'' Spencer demanded as he bent to pat her on the back. This was the last reaction he had expected.

Slowly she caught her breath as her coughing ceased.

"Spencer ... oh, I'm sorry to laugh like that. I can only imagine what you must be thinking. It's just that I've never felt any maternal urges, nor have I demonstrated any talent in that direction. Zena won't even let me baby-sit for my nephew anymore. The last time I had him, I accidentally fed him Jamaican beef patties that were much too spicy. It didn't occur to me he wouldn't be able to digest them. I just didn't know any better. Poor thing, he was sick for two days."

"But what if you change your mind? Women have been known to do that, you know," Spencer said ruefully.

"I seriously doubt it. I'm thirty-four years old, Spencer, and I'm busier than I've ever been with Soul Food to Go. It would be very, very difficult to run my restaurants and still be able to devote the necessary time to a child. The child would be the one shortchanged in the long run, especially with both of us putting in twelve hours at a stretch and at all hours. The way I see it, what's the point of having kids if you have to hire somebody to raise them?" She sighed. "Actually, I'm glad it's out in the open. I always felt something was wrong with me for not feeling maternal urges, just like it seemed unnatural for me not to ever have been in love ... before you, of course."

He sat in the sand beside her and gathered her in his arms. "Oh, Kendall," he murmured against her hair. "I'm crazy about you, you know that?"

"I know. I have a hunch you're feeling tremendous relief right now, too."

"You don't know the half of it."

"No wonder you were so sure I wouldn't get pregnant the night of the opening! Well, so much for practicing safe sex. Now you can throw away all your condoms for good, since we don't have to worry about birth control and we know we don't have any cooties."

Spencer laughed. "I was afraid you'd want to leave me for someone who had ... activated sperm. Someone like Todd."

Kendall scoffed. "Todd! Puh-leese. Don't take this per-

sonally, Spencer, but I think your nephew is full of himself."

"I'm not at all insulted. I think so, too. And if he so
much as looks at you sideways, I'm going to kick his butt
right out into the street. If he puts his hands on you, he's
dead meat. I already talked to him once about forgetting
any ideas he was having about getting next to you, but I
had to remind him about it after I saw him dancing with
you at the opening. My kids'll be the first to tell you, I
don't like to repeat myself."

"Ooh, I love it when you stick up for me."

"Always. You're a special woman, Kendall Lucas, and
I'm glad you're my woman." He leaned in close, and even
in the moonlight Kendall saw the seriousness in his gaze.
"That was the last barrier between us, Kendall. No more
secrets, I promise. Now I know you're the one. I love you.
I think we're perfect for each other, and I want you with
me always." He kissed her soft lips. "Marry me, Kendall,"
he whispered. "Soon. I don't ever want to be without you
again, not even for a single day."

"Spencer," she breathed. She wanted to say how unexpected his proposal was, but uttering something like, "This
is so sudden" seemed so cliched. The truth was that she
really was floored. "I never expected . . ."

Spencer stiffened. Perhaps she had never pictured herself as a wife, either. Well, if she did feel that way, he'd
have to work to get her change her mind. No way was he
going to take no for an answer.

Kendall realized her lack of response could be miscon-
strued as apprehension. "This is truly the most wonderful
thing that's ever happened to me. You"—she pressed her
fingertips alongside his mouth—"were a long time coming, but you were worth the wait." She paused. "But would
you mind terribly if I asked you something first?"

"What do you want to know?"

"What went wrong in your first marriage? You never
mentioned it, and, well, I kind of think I should know.
How do I know it won't be a problem with us as well?"

She remembered what Vincent and Esther had told her, but she wanted to hear it from him.

Spencer threw back his head and laughed. "It won't, sweetheart. I'll tell you all about it, but it won't. I can promise you that."

CHAPTER SEVENTEEN

"So how's Mom?" Spencer asked Brian.

"She's okay. She looks different, though."

"She's gained a lot of weight," Carlton added, speaking on an extension phone.

"That's only natural. She just had a baby."

"I thought she'd look like she used to once the baby was out."

"Well, it is baby fat, but it'll take a little while for it to come off. It's natural for people to get heavier as they get older."

"You haven't," Carlton pointed out.

"I haven't had any babies, either," Spencer said with a smile. "Okay, fellas. We need to talk about something important. It's about Kendall and me. You like her, don't you?"

They spoke at the same time. "Yeah!"

"How would you feel if I married her?"

"All right, Daddy!" Brian said.

"I think that's great," Carlton agreed. "Kendall's all right. Some of those ladies you took out were really phony."

"They were trying too hard to get us to like them or something," Brian added. "But Kendall's real."

"Do you think she'll say yes, Daddy?"

"I've got a confession to make. I've already asked her, and she already said yes. I had always planned I'd talk to you guys first, but the urge hit me kind of suddenly and I asked her. One day you'll know what I mean."

"So when's the wedding?"

"Nothing's firm yet, but Kendall likes the spring. It'll probably be in May or June of next year, before you guys go back up there for the summer."

"That's great, Daddy," Brian repeated.

"Both of you are sure it's okay?"

They assured him it was.

"All right. I miss you guys, but I want you to have fun. Enjoy your new sister. Kendall and I are going to drive up to get you in a couple of weeks. Let me talk to Mom, now, okay? I'm going to make good on a promise I made her last time I was there."

"Are you sure I can't help you, Kendall?" Chan asked.

"Positive. Spencer's cooking the meat, and the salads and bread are all ready. Come on, let's go sit down."

"I'm in love with your furniture," Chan said when they were seated in the living room.

"Thanks. Oh, that must be either Barry or David," she said when the doorbell rang.

It was Zena. "I left Barry and Elgin downstairs with Paul and Spencer," she said after the three of them exchanged greetings. "David and Michelle are down there, too. They're completely shameless, standing around talking and watching poor Spencer work the grill."

"Oh, Spencer doesn't mind," Kendall said. "He loves being a host."

"Well, I had to come upstairs. I couldn't stand that smoke—" Zena broke off and put her hand over her mouth. A gagging sound escaped from her throat.

"Are you all right, Zena?" Chan asked.

"You look like you're going to be sick," Kendall said.

Zena tried to say something, then ran into the bathroom and closed the door. Kendall and Chan were staring at her with concern when she emerged.

"Relax. It's just morning sickness—in the afternoon," she said.

Kendall and her mother shrieked with joy. "That's wonderful, Zena!"

"Yeah, yeah. Just don't try to hug me. I won't be responsible for the consequences." Zena gingerly lowered herself into a chair. "This has been going on for days now, and all day."

"You weren't this sick with Elgin, were you?" Kendall asked.

"No."

"Maybe this one's a girl," Chan said.

The others came upstairs then, Spencer holding a tray of grilled steaks and whole mushrooms. Chan hugged Barry, and as news of Zena's pregnancy spread to Paul and Spencer hearty congratulations were given.

"Oh, I can't think of anything that would make me happier," Chan said in a teary voice.

Spencer and Kendall exchanged glances. "Well, Mom, I know this isn't a contest . . ." Kendall began.

"Kendall! Are you pregnant, too?"

Her mother spoke with such obvious hope that Kendall's heart wrenched. "No, Mom," she said.

"Good, because I'm too old to go running after Spencer with a shotgun," Paul joked.

"No shotgun needed, Paul," Spencer said. "I'm going to marry her anyway."

There were more shouts, hugs, and kisses.

"Oh, my baby girl," Chan said, now openly crying. "We'll have to start planning the wedding right away."

"Mom . . . can we eat dinner first?"

CHAPTER EIGHTEEN

Spencer brought the car to a halt in front of a large house near the corner of Main Street.

Kendall looked at him, puzzled. "What's this?" she asked.

"My wedding gift to you."

"This house? But it's ... it's lovely, Spencer, but it's huge. That's probably why it was on the market so long. It's also right smack dab in the middle of downtown Palmdale. When we talked we decided to get something in Nile Beach close to the ocean, so I don't understand."

He leaned over the armrest and spoke softly. "It's not for us to live in, Kendall."

"Then what will we do with it?"

"This will be the new location of Robinson's. Mr. Robinson is moving to Tallahassee. Haven't you heard?"

"Well, of course I heard, but I didn't know you were interested in buying him out."

"Come on, I'll show you the inside."

The house was in need of a complete renovation, but showed great promise. "Spencer, it's so big!" Kendall exclaimed. "What will you do with all this space?"

He turned her to face him and gripped her shoulders. "Not what will *I* do, but what will *we* do. This is ours, remember? I want us to form our own corporation." No point in telling her that Vincent had balked at the idea of restructuring Two Brothers, Inc., to include Kendall when he suggested it. That was all right, though. He and Kendall would start from scratch. He already had a name for it. He would take their first and middle names—Kendall Susan and Spencer Ivan—mix them up a bit and call their company KISS, Inc.

"All right, so what are we going to do with all this space?"

"Knock down the walls and make it into one large room, except for an office, a storage room, restrooms, and the kitchen, which we'll need to expand."

"I don't know why. How much room does it take to prepare grilled cheese sandwiches and French fries?"

"You're thinking small, Kendall. We'll need more room to provide dinner and breakfast for the overnight guests."

"Oh . . . for our what?"

"Overnight guests. There's going to be lodging upstairs. All our guests will receive a cooked-to-order dinner and breakfast. It'll be ideal for people celebrating anniversaries or who have just gotten married. Or for people who get bitten by a sudden romantic bug."

"Spencer! You want us to operate a bordello?"

"You think that people only have trysts at cheap motels? Why do you think hotels have bars and restaurants? So people can meet, get acquainted—or reacquainted—and then adjourn to a more private setting. That kind of thing goes on at the Plaza and the Four Seasons all the time."

"All right, now that you've made it sound respectable. Come on, show me."

They climbed the stairs. "This is great!" Kendall exclaimed. "These rooms are all large enough to accommodate a king-size bed, a table for two, and a love seat."

"Now you're talking. I thought it would be a little silly to put a writing desk in an atmosphere designed for romance."

"No, I'm thinking more like draping around the beds, chaise lounges wide enough for two, sexy stuff like that. We'll have to reserve space for a little chest of drawers, though, so if people are staying for a weekend, they won't have to live out of their suitcases." She disappeared temporarily into the door on the side of the room. "That's right, a bath. One in every room, right?"

"Right. The claw foot tubs should go over big, since they're large enough for two."

"They sure will. Of course, they'll have to be sanded and painted. And, Spencer, the private balconies. We can put a table and chairs out there in case people want to take their meals outside by candlelight. I'm going to have a fabulous time decorating these rooms!"

The master suite would be the grandest of all. It would be the honeymoon suite, and Spencer told Kendall that anyone who rented it would automatically receive a complimentary bottle of champagne each night and the finest of meals: eggs Benedict . . . seafood salad . . . filet mignon . . . lobster . . . baked Alaska.

"It's wonderful," Kendall proclaimed. "I just wish it could be ready in time for us to spend the night of our wedding here."

"Well, if that's a hint to postpone the ceremony, no dice. But we can take a room whenever we need to take a break from the boys."

"It's going to be wonderful, Spencer."

"The nicest part is that we have built-in clientele for the bar. The lodge will probably take longer to catch on, but it's low maintenance. We'll need a cook and someone to stick around at night in case the guests need anything, that's all." He squeezed her arm affectionately. "Happy wedding present, Kendall."

She turned to him and wrapped her arms around his neck. "Thank you, Spencer," she whispered before pressing her lips to his.

He chuckled. "I have to hand it to Zena. She handled

the deal, and I was afraid she would spill the beans, even though she promised she wouldn't.''

"Oh, she can keep her lips zipped when she wants to, especially if there's a commission involved. Besides, she's all caught up in the wedding plans. You'd think she was the bride.''

"You're going to be one beautiful bride, Kendall.''

"I plan to be. Just wait until tomorrow.''

They descended the stairs. "Do you forgive me for keeping all this secret from you?'' he asked.

"Haven't you heard I've given up holding grudges? Life's too short, and there are much more important things to do.''

"Such as?''

"Such as,'' she said, pressing her body provocatively into his, "sowing our wild oats before we stand up in front of the minister tomorrow.''

Spencer, lost in the magic of her kiss, could only murmur his affirmative response.

EPILOGUE

"So how's married life, Kendall?"

Kendall groaned. "I can't tell you how often I've heard that question over the past six months. If I hear it again I'm going to scream. But," she added hastily, realizing she risked antagonizing the well-wisher, "we're very happy, thank you."

She joined Vicky and Michelle at their table in the newly relocated Robinson's Bar, where they were having a get-together. Vicky had relocated to North Carolina, where Danny lived, and they had returned to town to be married.

"So why isn't Ava here?" Vicky asked.

"Oh, something came up."

"Everything all right?" Michelle asked.

"Everything's just peachy. As in a male peach," Kendall added with a chuckle.

"Oh, I hope so," Vicky said. "She deserves to have somebody special. There hasn't been anyone since she broke up with Leon, has there? Did she say who this one is?"

Kendall shook her head. "I did meet him for a second

when I went by her shop. I've never seen him before, but I'll tell you this, the man is drop-dead handsome."

"Sounds interesting," Vicky mused. "I wonder who he is."

"Lots of luck trying to find that out. You know how private Ava is. She can clamp up tighter than a nun's—"

"Ken-dall!" Michelle exclaimed.

"Sor-ree. What, you went to parochial school or something?"

Vicky giggled. "As long as she makes it Friday. I'm going to need both my maid and matron of honor there with me if I'm going to carry this off without falling on my face."

"C'mon, Vick, you know she wouldn't let you down like that. But are you really sure you want to do this?"

Vicky cast a sidelong glance at Kendall. "What do you mean, am I sure?"

"Well, ever since Spencer and I got married everybody keeps asking me how married life is. I don't think I can take much more of this."

"Just grin and bear it. It's all you'll hear right up to your first anniversary," Vicky said with a smile.

"Next thing you know they'll be asking if I have a bun in the oven," Kendall lamented.

"You can always tell them you don't intend to bake," Michelle quipped.

Kendall rolled her eyes in Michelle's direction while Vicky smiled dreamily. "Just think, after tomorrow night I'll be hearing that question again myself. I'm rather looking forward to it."

"A Friday night ceremony. Doesn't anybody in this town have traditional weddings anymore?" Michelle asked.

"Sure they do," Vicky replied. "But, Michelle, this is a second marriage for both Danny and me, and we want to keep it small, especially with it being so close to Christmas. Besides, I'd think you'd be glad we're having it at your club."

"Oh, I am, believe me. I'm looking forward to hosting

adults for a change instead of all those pain in the butt kids. All I meant was that when I get married I want a big wedding with a church ceremony, a long white dress, a bunch of bridesmaids, a huge cake ... the whole nine yards," Michelle said. "Nothing against your wedding, Kendall," she added hastily.

"You mean you don't want to get married outside in a nightgown that matches the color of your groom's T-shirt," Vicky said.

Kendall laughed. As far as she was concerned, she and Spencer had had the perfect wedding. Chan organized a repeat of Paul's retirement party last June, exactly one year later. Kendall, wearing a simple scoop-necked ice-blue chiffon dress with spaghetti straps, a flared hem that flowed just above her knees and a matching scarf draped around her neck, and Spencer, in a blue suit of raw silk and light blue T-shirt, took their vows poolside, with Brian and Carlton serving as best men and a radiant Zena, fully recovered from a difficult pregnancy that had ended with the birth of a healthy baby girl three months before, as matron of honor. Immediately after they were pronounced husband and wife, David played a specially mixed version of James Brown's "I Feel Good," with a series of the singer's famous squeals preceding the music. David's lighthearted gesture came as a pleasant surprise to everyone, the bride and groom included.

After the receiving line had passed, Spencer and Kendall, who had decided with Spencer's full approval not to change her last name, were introduced to their guests by a beaming Paul Ridgely as "Ms. Kendall Lucas and Mr. Spencer Barnes, but as we all know, folks, they're married," took to the floor for the first dance, George Benson's "Lady Blue." It was a private salute to Kendall's blue silk cheongsam outfit the night of the retirement party. That had been their first date, and the memories of the magic and promise of that night were still so sweet for them that in addition to being married on its anniversary they decided to both wear that color to take their vows.

"My wedding was . . . well, comfortable," Kendall said.

"I'm only teasing, Kendall," Vicky replied. "I really did enjoy it. I know everybody who was there had a good time."

"Especially that old guy, what was his name, Oscar?" Michelle asked.

"Especially Oscar," Kendall agreed. "That man single-handedly keeps the cab company in business. I don't even know why he bothers to drive anywhere; he knows he'll need a ride home. But he's all right . . . as long as he doesn't get too close to the pool. Oh, here are our drinks." She removed the champagne glasses from the tray the waitress held. "Thanks," she said brightly, and the girl nodded with a smile.

"Champagne! Oh, Kendall, you shouldn't have," Vicky said.

"What the heck. You only get married once—I mean twice. Here's to you and Danny." Kendall raised her glass in a toast, and the others joined in.

Vicky giggled. "I still can't believe how beautifully everything worked out for us. Our kids get along, I have a job at the hospital up there . . . things couldn't be better."

"I think it's so romantic, you two getting together again after all those years," Michelle said with a sigh.

"Sounds like somebody else is having thoughts about matrimony," Kendall said, poking Vicky in the arm. "What's wrong, Michelle, doesn't that brother of mine want to move off his duff?"

"Oh, I'm sure he'll get around to asking me one of these days. I'd say yes in a heartbeat. I'm crazy about the man. Besides, I'm getting old. I want to have my first baby before I'm thirty, and I'll be twenty-seven next month."

Kendall and Vicky both laughed, and Kendall realized this was the first time someone referred to having babies without her feeling those pangs of doubt and shame that had plagued her for so many years. She now knew it was okay for a woman not to want children of her own. She was an authoritative figure to her stepsons Brian and Carlton, and a pal as well . . . and she never felt guilty about not being around to serve dinner promptly at six. Instead she kept the freezer filled up with frozen hamburger patties and microwave meals and snacks.

Vicky patted Michelle's hand. "Well, don't you worry. Maybe tomorrow night he'll get a hint."

"Who'll get a hint about what?"

The three of them turned at the sound of Spencer's distinctive voice. "Hi, honey," Kendall said. "We're just indulging in some girl talk."

"Pre-wedding-night jitters, Vicky?" Spencer teased.

"Not a chance. You just see that our suite is ready for us tomorrow night."

"It will be. You know, we really appreciate your using our club for your wedding and our inn for the first night of your honeymoon, Vicky."

She winked at them. "I guess somebody has to help you get that new beach house built. Kendall said the cost of the land alone was equal to the rest of her inheritance, and I hate to think of you guys sleeping in the sand."

Spencer joined Kendall when Vicky and Michelle left. "You look happy," he said.

"Why shouldn't I be? I have everything I ever wanted, and then some."

"And what's that?"

Kendall counted her blessings off on her fingers. "A successful restaurant, ownership in an established bar that will be profitable until doomsday, an inn that's getting off the ground nicely . . ."

"Go on."

Kendall knew what he was waiting to hear, but nonetheless continued her list. "A dream house being built on the beach, two handsome stepsons who are big enough to do their own laundry and fix their own dinner . . ."

"Anything else?"

"And the most wonderful husband in the world," she

concluded, putting her hands down. "I love you, Spencer Barnes."

"I love you, too, Kendall Lucas. And I have a question for you."

"What's that?"

"How does it feel to be a bridesmaid for a change?"

She beamed. "It feels good, but nothing compares to being a bride. I think we should reserve the honeymoon suite, so we can pretend it's starting all over again."

"How about Saturday night?"

"Hey, you're on."

About the Author

Bettye Griffin had two dozen romantic short stories published before trying her hand at writing novels. She is a medical transcriptionist by profession and works out of a home office. Originally from Yonkers, New York, she now makes her home in Jacksonville, Florida, with her husband and teenage stepson.

Dear Reader,

I hope you enjoyed *At Long Last Love*. It's important to note that while there are a number of black-founded towns and communities in the state of Florida (Eatontown, American Beach, the Lincolnville settlement in St. Augustine, and the ill-fated Rosewood), Nile Beach is not one of them. This town stems purely from my imagination.

Thank you for your support. Happy reading!

Bettye Griffin
BUnderw170@aol.com

COMING IN FEBRUARY ...

ONE OF A KIND   (1-58314-000-X, $4.99/$6.50)
by Bette Ford

Legal secretary Anthia Jenkins and Dexter Washington, director of a Detroit community center, were good friends. But Anthia wanted more than friendship. Once unjustly convicted of his wife's suicide, Dexter didn't want to love again. But he couldn't control the passion between them and now he needs to convince Anthia to believe in him and in love.

TRUE BLUE   (1-58314-001-8, $4.99/$6.50)
by Robyn Amos

When her sister announces they've won the lottery, Toni Rivers is off to the Florida coast and a new life. Blue Cooper is ready to sweep Toni off her feet when she walks into his nightclub. But the powerful feelings between them frighten Toni. She holds back more so when a dangerous past surfaces. Now he must find a way to prove that his love is true.

PICTURE PERFECT   (1-58314-002-6, $4.99/$6.50)
by Shirley Harrison

Davina Spenser found out that her father was actually the brilliant painter Maceo James, who had gone into hiding for a murder he didn't commit. She was determined to clear his name and take his paintings from Hardy Enterprises. But the handsome new CEO Justin Hardy was a tempting obstacle that could bring her delicious disaster or perfect love.

AND OUR VALENTINE'S DAY COLLECTION ...

WINE AND ROSES   (1-58314-003-4, $4.99/$6.50)
by Carmen Green, Geri Guillaume, Kayla Perrin

February is for Valentine's Day, but it can also be a time of sweet surprises for those who aren't even looking for love. Delight in the joys of unexpected romance with reignited passion in Carmen Green's "Sweet Sensation," with the eternal gift of love in Geri Guillaume's "Cupid's Day Off" and renewed hope in Kayla Perrin's "A Perfect Fantasy."

Available wherever paperbacks are sold, or order direct from the Publisher. Send cover price plus 50¢ per copy for mailing and handling to Kensington Publishing Corp., Consumer Orders, or call (toll free) 888-345-BOOK, to place your order using Mastercard or Visa. Residents of New York and Tennessee must include sales tax. DO NOT SEND CASH.

SPICE UP YOUR LIFE
WITH ARABESQUE ROMANCES